ASSASSIN WITCH

THE BONEGATES SERIES

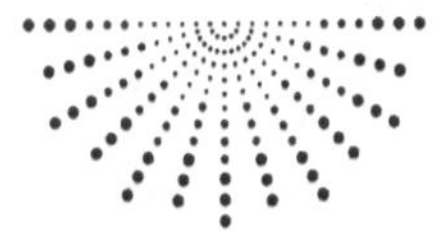

ASHLEY MCLEO

MERAKI PRESS

CONTENTS

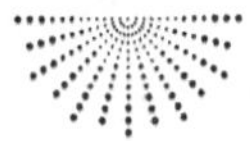

My heart threatened to fling itself out of my chest as the door to my father's private chambers cracked open. I peered into the room.

No one was there.

"He knows I'm coming, right?" I twisted to ask Garret. "He said we'd meet a couple of hours after the Pinning Ceremony. We're not too early?"

I thought back to the ceremony where my new rank had been announced to the fae of Lyonesse. I was sure that's what my father had said, but had he changed his mind? Dread swirled in my stomach.

An amused grin lined my guard's handsome face. "From what I hear, the king likes a bit of drama. I bet he's trying to make an entrance. If he didn't want you in his chambers, the door wouldn't have opened."

He nudged me forward. "You shouldn't loiter.

You've been waiting years for this. I'll stay here and escort you to your room afterward."

Garret wasn't exaggerating. This moment had been my dream since I was small. Although I had fulfilled my dream of meeting my father two weeks ago, we hadn't had time to get to know one another— or even talk—until now.

Inhaling deeply, I placed my hand on the door inlaid with an intricate gold feather, and gave the portal a firm push.

My eyes took a moment to adjust to the darkness. When they did, the first thing I saw was a fire burning in the center of the room. It was contained in a metal firepit the size of a four-person dining table, and the flames rose to the height of a full-grown man. Even meters away, my skin tingled from its heat, although the scent of smoke was strangely absent.

I walked deeper into the room and my steps took on a different resonance when they hit the ground. As if the floors of the king's chambers were hollow, rather than solid marble typical of Castle Phoenix.

When I reached the fire, my mouth fell open. Swirls and runes covered the black metal pit. Some glowed, a sign that they were working magic. But it was what flickered inside the flames that truly startled me.

An entire town lived in the fire. Fae walked the streets, spoke to one another, and went about their business as if they were not trapped inside an inferno. What was this thing?

A grinding of stone on stone echoed throughout the chamber. I jumped away from the fire and twisted toward the sound, my heart hammering.

"It is something, is it not?" my father, King Oberon of Lyonesse, asked as he rose out of a circular hole in the ground.

I loosed an exhale. That explained why the floor sounded hollow. I walked above a hidden chamber.

"My firlon acts similarly to a scrying bowl," my father continued. "Although it uses fire and shows the present, not the future. I've heard witches in the Old Land still use scrying bowls. Are you familiar with them?"

"I've never used one. Those who do are usually diviners," I replied, my eyes never leaving his. "Some-times psychics too."

He didn't respond and silence fell between us as we examined each other. My eyes, a strange vibrant gold since arriving in Faerie, were twins of his. As was my fair complexion. But perhaps the most pronounced similarity between the pair of us was how we took each other in curiously, wondering how this new relationship would work.

Finally, my father nodded, breaking our mutual spell. He pointed to the firlon. "This is Lyonesse. I observe it the most, although I can glimpse into other kingdoms." He turned and motioned for me to follow.

"This," my father stopped before a long, sturdy table near the back of the room, "is where we will take our private meetings. Those will occur at least once a week, more often if my schedule permits. There will also be a weekly gathering where we assemble with the Feathered Fae and Prince Casimir."

I nodded but said nothing. It was odd being near him, my dreams coming true. I didn't trust myself not to say something dumb yet. I only wanted to soak it all in.

"Please take a seat." He gestured to the table. Once we settled in, he continued. "Casimir assured me you would be among the top contenders. For once, my firstborn was right."

I blinked. Aside from my first day in Faerie when my father told the story about Casimir being weak as a young child, he'd always spoken highly of his firstborn son and heir. My mouth opened and then closed again quickly—unsure of what to say.

"Forgive me," my father backtracked, taking in my discomfort. "That was out of line."

He rubbed his temples. "It's just, as of late, Casimir has been more opinionated than usual. I sense he feels threatened by having so many talented new siblings around. Especially siblings who are to go on missions for Lyonesse."

"A bit of adventure is exciting," I said. Even for someone like me, a person who loved a quiet walk in the woods and a good book more than anything, I could see the appeal. Felt it even.

My father leaned closer and tented his moon-white fingers beneath his pointed chin. "Casimir has always wanted to be of greater use to his kingdom. I suspect that marrying you was part of his plan."

I stiffened, but my father had glanced away, perhaps hearing something in the flames, so he didn't notice. By the time his gaze met mine again, I'd regained my composure.

"Honestly, it *was* a decent idea," he said. "Unifying two lightworkers would be powerful, indeed. Although, now that you've won the Successional, Casimir's marriage would be even more useful to Lyonesse if it were diplomatic. I believe he's coming to terms with that scheme falling through."

I let out a sigh. My brother *had* insinuated that a marriage between lightworkers would make our father happy. While siblings marrying siblings was not unheard of in Faerie, I wanted *nothing* to do with it. Thankfully, as I was second in line for the throne, it wouldn't make sense for us to wed, anyway. Now I no longer had to risk pissing off my extremely powerful and moody brother.

"I doubt Casimir has anything to worry about and will recognize that soon," I said truthfully.

As far as I knew, none of my siblings desired the crowned prince's position. To be a royal had been more than enough for those of us from the human world.

My father nodded. "I agree wholeheartedly. Now, tell me a bit about yourself, Lana."

I bit my lip. Where to start? Did he want me to tell him about my childhood? Or begin with the moment I touched the bonekey and was transported through a portal into Faerie? Surely he didn't want to hear the day-to-day stuff. That would bore a king to tears.

"How did you come across your hawk? Naela, I believe you call her?"

My lips turned up and my nerves eased. This was a story I enjoyed telling, so I launched into the tale of when Finn and I had found our hawks as eyas.

My father listened, his smile growing ever wider as I flowed from my first few months with Naela to other anecdotes. I left out the bad bits of my life, like how before coming here, Finn had been my only friend. After all, there was no need to tarnish our first bonding experience with sadness.

Instead, I focused on how I had attended Trinity College with Finn, and the good times we had there. I also told him about my adventures with Gran, and the time Naela and I won a hawking competition. For someone who shied away from revealing too much to people I barely knew, it felt amazing and strangely *right* to let him in on my life.

"Astounding," my father beamed when I'd finished. "I'm glad you found your way home."

Home.

It hit me that I hadn't thought about the Old Land in days. Of course, I thought of Mam all the time. I missed *her* and, when I looked out the castle windows, the green scenery I'd grown up surrounded by. Everything else? I could take it or leave it.

"Actually, speaking of home, I was wondering . . . would it be possible for my mother to visit? I promise it won't be awkward between you two."

Mam would be frustrated to learn that my father had lied to her about his identity, but I'd convince her to keep her cool. If it meant visiting me and spending time in freaking Faerie, I was sure she'd get over it —eventually.

His face fell slightly. "Unfortunately, I cannot accommodate that request. Only those with fae blood can enter Faerie. While I courted your mother, I did not sense even the slightest hint of fae blood in her veins."

My stomach hardened. It must have shown on my face, because my father leaned close.

"However, I promise that you can return to the Old Land to visit as you wish. If things work out as planned, it should be easier than ever."

I cocked my head to the side, wondering what plans he was referring to, and my father smiled.

"All in good time, Daughter. You will learn all you need to know, I promise, but not at once. In fact, I imagine you have so many questions for me it would be impossible to answer them all. But let's try, shall we? We'll start at the beginning. Why did I remain out of your life all these years?"

My eyes widened. He had already explained why he'd stayed away—to keep the knowledge of my siblings and me from Queen Pari of Buyan. After learning that fae parents in Faerie were different from those in the Old Land—more hands-off—I'd figured we wouldn't get any more from him. In this case, I was happy to be wrong.

I leaned back in my chair and the wood creaked beneath me. "I'd like that."

He stood and moved toward an alcove that housed a cabinet. The doors snicked open and my father pulled out a half-full decanter of wine and two goblets.

"What I told you upon your arrival in Lyonesse was true, but of course there's more." He set a glass before me. I was startled to see his eyes were filled with tears. "However, I want to reiterate that I truly regret not knowing you and your siblings all these years. Hearing your story and knowing there are many more like it, some of which I'll never get to hear, upsets me greatly."

I couldn't help but mirror his sorrow as images of Kate and Kumar, my healer sister and naga brother who had perished in the Successional, flitted through my mind. Although we'd only known each other for two weeks, I missed them so much it hurt. Hell, I even felt a small degree of remorse for Nigel, their murderer. A part of me wondered if this was because Nigel and I were related, and blood would always grieve blood. Or perhaps I was confusing sadness with guilt. I'd been the one to kill Nigel during the tournament.

Once my goblet was full of ruby wine that smelled of violets and cherries, my father filled his, and sat once again. I laid my fingers on the glass, feeling awkward in my stillness.

"Staying away from my children was the hardest thing I've ever done. But it was *absolutely* necessary. Queen Pari of Buyan is cunning and dangerous. Had she realized that I'd sired children in the Old Land—" My father gripped his glass, and his fingers whitened as he shook his head. "You would not be here today."

From what I'd learned while in Faerie, I couldn't deny that he was right. Queen Pari's thievery of my father's bonegate had left everyone in Lyonesse at a loss.

Children born here were often magically weak compared to those born in other Faerie realms. Or worse, the babies didn't even survive their first year. Her cruelty knew no bounds. She affected all races, neighborhoods and classes of fae.

Including the royal house.

Prince Casimir's mother had lost many children before the prince quickened in her womb. When she finally carried Prince Casimir to term, his birth cost the queen her life. Rumor had it that my father changed after his wife's death.

Depression gripped him, and he became obsessed with ensuring the survival of his line. So he had ventured to the Old Land in secret to produce strong spare heirs. Only my father's desperate desire for more children made it possible for me to be here—alive—today.

While I didn't agree with his actions, the past was the past. What else could I do but forgive? Demand to go home? Just the idea made me cringe. I loved Mam, and sometimes missed Ireland, but I didn't belong in the Old Land. I never fit in there and was done trying.

"We get it—or at least, most of us do," I assured him and took a sip of wine. Berries and tannins danced across my tongue in a way that no wine from the Old Land could ever mimic. "Being here, seeing the differences between the Old Land and Lyonesse, helps."

"How could it not, with the state of my land being what it is?" My father released his grip on his goblet, rose, and beckoned for me to follow.

We approached a dark alcove near the firlon that I hadn't noticed before. A tapestry hung there, illuminated by dim lanterns. The tapestry depicted a regal elf standing on a massive white rock in the middle of a great plain, an azure sea pouring down upon him from another world above—the Old Land, I assumed.

"This," he pointed to the elf, "is my great-grandfather, one of the Sinkers of Faerie."

My eyes bulged. This was one of the fae who'd given their lives to create a safe haven for all races of fae. Quickly, I did the math.

"So, because all the Sinkers died, you're only the third ruler of Lyonesse?" I tried to hide my incredulity. The fae had created Faerie centuries ago. I'd known fae were long-lived, but *damn*.

He tore his eyes from the tapestry to meet mine. "Actually, I'm the second ruler of Lyonesse. My grandfather was the first. My father died in battle before he could wear the crown. Fae lifespans are long compared to those of humans, but we are not immortal."

"Oh . . . I'm sorry," I mumbled uncomfortably.

"There's no need to apologize. I came to terms with his death long ago."

His slim digit touched the depiction of the white rock beneath the Sinker's feet. "I wanted to show you this tapestry not for the history, but for the symbolism. This rock represents a bonegate. They are *everything* in this land. The Old Land provides us with a stream of magic, and bonegates are the point where it flows through. They're also access points to the Old Land, and an escape route, should fae need them." He turned his gaze upon me. "On a personal level, the Lyonesse bonegate is my inheritance *and* yours. After the Great Sinking took each Sinker's life, their bones were harvested. My great-grandfather's bones were enchanted and buried to create the bonegate that Queen Pari stole."

My father's face fell. "For half a century, my kingdom, *your inheritance*, has been in decline. Now we are nothing but a joke among the fae."

My heart broke, and I opened my mouth to say something comforting, when my father turned and approached the firlon. He waved his hand before the flames and mumbled a few undecipherable words.

Suddenly, a woman I recognized from a painting I'd stumbled upon appeared in the fire. She sat at a desk, reading a letter, her jaw tight.

"This is Queen Pari of Buyan. She is the enemy of our kingdom. Pari is the reason my subjects rely on food rations. Why my lands are dead. Once you and your siblings are fully trained, your primary mission will be to assassinate her."

My mouth fell open. The ask wasn't *entirely* unexpected. But the way my father said it—as if assassination was an everyday occurrence—struck me.

He tilted his head and took me in thoughtfully. "You find my language unappealing?"

Unsure of what he'd consider the right answer, but also unwilling to lie, I nodded.

He gave me a grim smile. "In truth, I do too. But when you're a king, you learn that setting clear expectations is important. My armies have attempted many assaults on Queen Pari, even upon our own bonegate, over the years. Every attack has failed. The queen is well-prepared for anything that I may throw at her." He quirked a white eyebrow. "Anything, except for my children from the Old Land. The city of Buyan and its surroundings are heavily warded, but only against fae."

"But we're all part fae," I commented.

"Of course. However, I have reason to suspect that your power will not register. As you're an illuminator, not a wardmaker, I expect that you have little experience with wards?"

"Only in training."

He nodded. "Let me assure you, wards are tricky bits of magic. They're most effective when they are very specific. Which means Pari's wardmaker would do well to target her boundaries to certain fae species, especially since there are no other types of magical creatures living in this dimension. Each of you, even those who inherited fae blood from their mother, also possess human blood. We believe your human blood will protect you."

"But how?"

"We've tested our theory with creatures who are not full fae. Those who have tried to infiltrate our lands and now . . . reside here."

I shuddered as I pictured supernaturals from the Old Land being kept in the castle dungeons, alongside the giantess, naga, spriggans, and chimera from the Successional. If my father had imprisoned those who broke into Faerie, I was sure he had a good reason. And yet, despite my belief in his righteousness, my fears regarding the invasion of Buyan were not dispelled.

"But what happens if our human blood doesn't hide us? Will the ward zap us to death?"

Gold eyes widened almost comically. "Not at all, Daughter! A ward of that nature can only be produced on a small scale. It takes far too much energy to maintain, especially around an entire kingdom. Pari has one extremely powerful wardmaker, but not even she could accomplish such a feat."

He smiled, which calmed me a little. "Please don't worry. I'll not throw you to the wolves. We'll send more prisoners to test my theory while you prepare. Not to mention that, before this mission, you will need to prove that you are ready by completing other, smaller missions. If you fail at those, I may have to reconsider my plan. However, after getting to know you better, I believe that will not be the case."

My father swiped his hand over the firlon, and Queen Pari disappeared. "This attack against the Queen of Buyan will change the course of history. I'd be lying if I said I didn't want my line involved in bringing glory back to our kingdom and safety to its people."

When he put it that way, it felt more like a rescue

mission than an assassination. I realized this was much more important than *anything* I ever could have accomplished in the Old Land.

Here, I had the chance to better the lives of thousands—including the families of those who I thought of as friends. Not only that, but succeeding would make my father proud. After years of not knowing him and desperately wanting to, I couldn't deny this was a huge draw too.

I exhaled slowly. "I don't relish the thought of shedding more blood, but I think I can do it. Especially if it means the lives of others will be saved and bettered." I hoped he didn't hear the waver in my voice.

He placed a hand on my shoulder.

My muscles eased slightly, and I chanced a smile up at him.

"I'm thankful to hear that, daughter. It's the kind of selfless attitude we, as rulers, need to have."

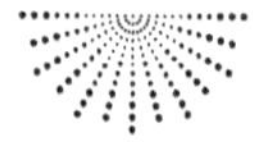

I floated out of my father's chambers with an ear-to-ear grin on my face. For the first time ever, my father and I had shared stories. He wanted to know me. He'd told me I helped to change thousands of lives. We'd bonded in a way I truly never thought would happen, but had dreamed about for years.

"Lana!" I jumped as Garret appeared at my side, his eyes disbelieving. "You walked right by me when you left King Oberon's sanctum. How'd it go? You were in there for quite a long time."

I laughed. In my haze of happiness, I *had* walked right by him.

"Sorry," I grinned. "It was great! A little intimidating at first, but then we got to talking, and things just . . . clicked. He showed me this tapestry that had my great-great-grandfather, the Sinker, on it, and some fire thing that reveals people and places."

"A firlon," Garret supplied with a nod. "They're common in royal households. I've never seen King Oberon's, but I've heard it's impressive."

"It is!" My grin grew. I wanted to grab Garret's hand and dance around the hall, but refrained. My guard wasn't exactly the dancing type. He was a serious soldier type.

"Would you like to share a celebratory drink with me at dinner?" I asked. "After all, I couldn't have done any of this without your help and guidance before the Successional."

"I can't tonight." His shoulders fell slightly. "Perhaps another time?"

"Why? After I get cleaned up and changed, I'm heading to the great hall for the feast, and I want you to come with me. Don't tell me you have something better to do?"

I slapped my hands over my mouth. Had that sass just come out of *me*? While I was no stranger to teasing people I was close to, Garret and I had only known each other a short time. Perhaps my lapse in courtesy was a side effect of the stress of the Successional colliding with the excitement of meeting my father?

"I see you're slipping into your princess role rather well." Garret's lips quirked up, telling me he wasn't offended.

"So what are you doing tonight?" I asked, trying to move on quickly.

"Now that the Successional is over and you're officially ranked, I'm no longer your personal guard. I was assigned a rotation on night duty this morning."

I didn't know how I felt about that. I'd grown used to seeing Garret often. "Who assigned you to your new rotation?"

"Meegra."

I frowned, and annoyance coiled in my gut. The Master Feathered Fae wasn't my biggest fan, and she knew that Garret and I got along well. She'd probably assigned Garret to night duty just to be difficult. Unfortunately for her, I now held sway that I didn't have before. And I was damn well going to use it.

"I don't like that we won't see each other. I'll talk to her, make sure you're assigned during the day with me—Ryker, Sai, and Ebba, too."

"I'd appreciate it." A dimple popped in Garret's left cheek when he grinned, and my stomach flipped.

What the hell was wrong with me?

Glancing away to calm myself, I noticed that I'd nearly walked right past the hall that led to Half-Elf Tower, where my siblings and I were staying. I made a sudden right turn, but was stopped when Garret grabbed my shoulder.

"Where are you going?"

"Umm . . . to my room," I replied, trying to ignore the tingles shooting down my arm.

"I see His Majesty didn't tell you that you've all been relocated. Your new suites are larger and grander, in accordance with your rank. The rest of your siblings were shown to their appropriate accommodations while you met with the king. I was told to escort you to yours after your meeting. It's down this way." He turned left.

I blinked. Rooms in accordance with our rank? What did that even mean?

Garret led the way. We took a couple more twists and turns, landing us in a part of the castle I'd never ventured into before. He pointed out a door. "I saw Crystal's guard show her to that room. Don't worry, yours isn't close by."

"Thank fecking goodness," I muttered, and Garret chuckled.

We walked the entire length of the hallway and then stopped. I shot Garret an excited glance. "Does this corridor end in a tower room like the common area of Half-Elf Tower?"

A room at the end of a hallway meant more privacy and space, both of which I coveted.

"Let's find out." Garret's gray eyes twinkled as he pushed the door open.

"No way," I breathed.

A smile bloomed on Garret's face. "It's something else, isn't it?"

Plush rugs laid atop white marble that flowed seamlessly from floor to ceiling. While white marble was the standard for Castle Phoenix, the marble in *my* suite was enhanced. It was veined with gold, brass, and silver, creating a rich mix of metals that resembled glittering rivers, waterfalls, and constellations. Vast windows at least three meters tall lined the curved walls.

Before the Successional, my bedroom had looked out on a dying forest, but from here, I could see over the castle gate. The entire city of Lyonesse sprawled out before me. I could even make out individual tiny figures in the distance going about their daily work. Not only was it a more pleasant view, but it would be a great motivator to see those who I'd be helping.

I inhaled contentedly and smiled. It even smelled posh in my room, like the perfect blend of sage and citrus.

"Naela is going to love this," I said, and then glanced around for my hawk's cage. "Where is she, by the way?"

"Out flying. She's already been by to see your new accommodations. Her area is through there." Garret gestured to one of three other doors in the room.

Behind it, I found a luxury mew, with numerous knobby perches designed for a hawk of Naela's size and a little ceramic bathtub that she could use. The window in this space was smaller and had a latch, making it easy to open and close. It would allow Naela to come and go as she pleased, as long as I left it open. The setup was far superior to the cage she'd been confined to in the corner of my old bedroom.

"King Oberon uses the same design for Xerxes'

space, which is just off his private chambers. He requested you inform him if things need to be altered to fit Naela's preference."

"Are you kidding me? This makes Naela's mew in Ireland look like a bloody prison. Which, for the record, it absolutely was not!" I clapped excitedly. "I love that I can keep her window open but close the door to my space. Keeps the cold out."

As I moved through the chamber, I delighted in all the luxurious touches—like my enormous canopy bed topped with feathered comforters in a gleaming gold hue, and the two high-backed crimson reading chairs next to a lit fireplace.

There was even a small library behind one of the three side doors, featuring floor-to-ceiling shelves lined with books. Some of them were from Faerie, while others clearly originated from the Old Land.

"How are these here?" I asked, pointing to the latest bestseller I'd seen in the hands of every Trinners student before I'd been sucked into Faerie.

Garret cocked his head. "I haven't read that one yet. The Feathered Fae make a habit of bringing back books from their voyages to the Old Land."

"Why?"

"Otherwise, we would be stuck reading the same boring tomes from the past decades. Everyone in the castle signs up to read them when they arrive. I suppose someone thought to put some of them in your room to make you feel more at home."

That was interesting. If you'd asked me two weeks ago if I thought human or fae stories would be more entertaining, I definitely would have said fae.

"Why haven't the fae written many books in the recent past?"

"I should amend that statement," Garret said. "The fae of Lyonesse haven't written many books. Since we lost our bonegate to Queen Pari, most occupations in Lyonesse have tended toward utilitarian, rather than creative."

"I see." I frowned and backed out of the library. I'd always loved reading and couldn't imagine a world with limited stories.

Behind the third door, I found the largest bathroom I'd ever stepped foot in, complete with a clawfoot tub and a glittering chandelier. There was steaming hot water in the tub.

"You've been assigned a good maid," Garret commented, looking pleased. "She's already drawn you a bath, should you want to clean up before dinner."

A maid had drawn me a bath? What life was this?

A faint knock sounded from the main door to the apartment. I went to answer, wondering which of my siblings was paying me a visit. Instead, when I opened the door, a tiny, thin, brown fae with huge lips stood before me. Her hands were shaking, and her eyes locked on the ground.

"Good afternoon, Princess Lana. My name is

Tess. I'm your maid. I'm here to assist you in preparing for the feast."

Garret's heavy boots echoed throughout the cavernous room. "That's my cue to be moving on. My watch begins shortly anyhow. Enjoy your new rooms, Lana. I hope to be at your side again soon." He winked, which caught me off guard and filled my stomach with butterflies.

"Absolutely. See you later." My hand jerked side to side in a wave before I dropped it to my side. My cheeks warmed. Why did I have to be so awkward?

Once he left, my focus returned to Tess. "Sorry about that. I didn't mean to ignore you."

"A maid's greatest achievement is to not interfere with her mistress' life. We strive to assist unseen." Tess spoke the words as though they were memorized lines.

I frowned. "Why don't you come in and tell me a bit about yourself?"

Her head shot up, and shock rushed across Tess' face, breaking my heart. I knew how she felt. Whenever anyone other than Finn had invited me out back in Ireland, I'd reacted in almost exactly the same way.

I'd been such a recluse that it always came as a surprise when someone reached out. To be honest, it still felt a little odd, but after spending two weeks around my new siblings, I'd become more used to being included, and had even found a few more friends.

Tess might not have any real friends. Briefly, I debated if it would be inappropriate for me to pursue a deeper relationship with her. Then I decided I'd gone long enough without close ties to care. I'd just lost two of the best mates I'd made in years to the Successional.

The time I'd spent getting to know Kate and Kumar had reminded me I'd been missing out in life. It was time I stopped isolating myself, one person at a time.

I ambled over to the fireplace and sat in one of the armchairs. "Please, Tess. Will you sit with me?"

Tess remained frozen in the doorway for an uncomfortable length of time before following me. She stopped shy of sitting on the chair that I offered her and merely grazed the soft fabric with her hand.

"My lady should not feel pressured to be kind. I realize you're new here, but it is not customary for ladies and maids to socialize." Her eyes fell to the floor once again.

"*Please*, have a seat," I said, my tone more commanding than questioning this time.

She eased herself into the chair, and my eyes ran over her. I guessed she was three years younger than me, perhaps seventeen or eighteen. Not old enough for her fae aging process to slow and make her age impossible to deduce.

"You'll have to let me know if I ask something out of line. Since I arrived here, I've primarily been around others from the Old Land and guardians. I don't expect those interactions are commonplace among the other fae of Lyonesse."

Tess' full lips quirked up, though her eyes remained downcast. "Whatever you say will not be out of line, Princess Lana."

I had sincere doubts, but no one could say I didn't warn her. "All right, then. I'm curious. What type of fae are you?"

Tess' thin body stiffened. Apparently, I'd already veered into inappropriate waters. "A mixed goblin, Princess Lana. But please do not take it as a slight. I was quite good at managing my previous mistress' affairs."

"Why would I take it as a slight that you're a goblin?"

A look of profound discomfort flitted across Tess' face. "Many of elven descent believe goblins of all types belong in the Free Realm. But my family has been here since the time the Fullfeathers sank Faerie, serving your royal house. We have no intention of leaving."

There was a hint of grit in her voice. Maybe she wasn't so meek after all.

"Your lineage doesn't matter to me," I assured her. "I asked because I know magic and skills vary among the fae. I was hoping to identify the various races here better by asking."

"Oh. Okay, princess." Some tension left her face.

I smiled. "Between us, I only want to know that I can trust you. And perhaps, we can even become friends."

Tess stiffened. Her light blue eyes nearly bugged out of their sockets. "*Friends*?"

"If you'll have me. I'll admit, historically, I'm pretty slow at making friends." I gave her a reassuring smile, and she returned a wobbly one of her own. "You said you have no intent to leave Sinkers Realm. Is it because Sinkers Realm is much better than the Free Realm?"

"It is not that, princess. I only meant we would rather face the prejudice of the nobles here than leave."

"Oh . . . but why?"

"Because my family loves His Majesty and all that the Fullfeathers have done to create Faerie. Few families have been able to rise above their common station to become royalty. We see your lineage as an inspiration. You give us faith that, although we are still lowly, perhaps one day we may rise as well."

"Is that why you chose to work here? To achieve greater status?"

"I did not choose to work here, Princess Lana. My parents sold me to His Majesty once I was old enough. They needed food rations. I didn't garner as much as I would have if I had the skill to become even the lowest ranked soldier, but still—it is something."

My eyes widened. "Your parents sold you! How could they?! And how could my father buy you? That's—"

"You misunderstand!" Tess cried, and her hands flew to her mouth when she realized she'd cut me off.

"I apologize. But truthfully, I'm pleased to be here. My parents and siblings are no longer starving. I have work and a home. It was a situation where everyone benefited."

Tess wrung out her hands. "Please do not think badly of my family, and especially not of His Majesty. He has saved us all by accepting me into his house-hold. The king had enough servants already—he didn't need to take me in. It was a blessing to be chosen."

My mouth snapped shut. Her family had been starving, and she'd saved them. Suddenly, my discussion with my father came rushing back in a different light. Would Tess' family be better off if Lyonesse still possessed a bonegate and hence more magic? If they were more powerful, would they be able to rely on themselves more rather than his assistance? Was I looking at another victim of Queen Pari's cruelty? It certainly seemed that way.

I sighed. I still had so much to learn.

A bell tolled outside, signaling that dinner would

begin in an hour. I'd heard it many times before, but eventually tuned it out because I didn't need to pay attention to it.

While I'd been training for the Successional, either Garret or Sai had always escorted me to dinner. However, now that I was ranked, there was no such need for an escort. I'd have to listen for the bells like everyone else and get myself to meals on time—which was just as well, because I was starving.

"Thank you for chatting with me, Tess. It was enlightening, but I think I should probably prepare for dinner now."

"I'm ready to assist, Princess Lana." Tess leapt to her feet.

My brows furrowed.

"I shall help you undress. Wash you, if you please?" Tess explained.

I coughed, and my cheeks warmed uncomfortably. Right, royalty can't do anything for themselves. "Actually, I think I have all that handled."

Tess opened her mouth to dissuade me, but I stopped her.

"But what I *would* love is a hot drink. Maybe one of those fae apple tisanes? I'll be fine bathing on my own, but would you mind running to the kitchen to get me a pot? I'm so thirsty, I could kill for a cup right now."

Tess let out a strange squeak, and her body trembled as she bowed before scampering out of my room.

Only once I'd sunk into the deep tub did I realize I would probably have to eliminate the phrase "I'd kill for" from my vocabulary.

After the Successional, many could be apt to take me seriously.

The next morning was a novel one in Faerie. It was one of the few times Garret had not woken me by pounding on the door and yelling that I was late for training. That was because for once, there was *no* training. I had nothing to do and planned on savoring every second of free time.

A rustle of feathers informed me that Naela had returned from her morning flight. I set aside the murder mystery book I had plucked from my library after waking and rose to meet her.

"Morning, Boss," I said, entering her mew to find Naela splashing about her small bath. She paused in her merriment, tilted her head, and blinked her golden eyes. "Pretty swanky new rooms, right?"

Naela let out a low keen, her way of saying she was happy with our circumstances, and I chuckled as I stroked the top of her head.

"Me too, Boss. You know, I think I'm going to follow your lead. A soak sounds brilliant."

I made my way to the bath, turned on the faucet, and poured a copious amount of violet-colored salts into the tub. After the stress of the Successional, the days of grieving for Kate and Kumar, and the previous night's celebration to glorify the Pinning ceremony, I was more than ready to relax. The aroma of lavender filled the room as the salts dissolved, and I sank into the hot water with a sigh.

This is the life, I thought, trailing my fingers over the silky water and listening to the faint sounds of Lyonesse outside. The city was bustling despite the early winter chill. I wondered what I'd do that day. Finn had mentioned flying our hawks, which sounded fun, but so did uninterrupted hours to myself.

When the water grew cold, I reluctantly got out and wrapped myself in a soft robe. Making my way back into the main room, I noticed the fire had been lit and someone, probably Tess, had delivered a steaming hot plate of breakfast.

I could get used to this.

Cozied up next to the fire, I inhaled the eggs—pheasant, I was told—and fresh-baked bread. Feeling satiated, I meandered into the library and perused the books again.

There had to be nearly five hundred titles in my personal collection. Many were popular fiction, which had probably been easy for the Feathered Fae to find.

Although, as I inspected the titles more closely, I noticed that some were illegible, written in a language I could not translate. Elvish, perhaps?

I cracked open a velvet-bound book with gilded lettering on the spine. The luxurious material tickled my fingertips as I flipped through a few pages before abandoning the text and returning to my murder mystery.

Hours passed. Naela swooped in and out of her mew, and Tess delivered lunch before I finally shut the book. I went to the window and gazed out upon the village. Fae buzzed about, working hard to make a living. I wondered what they thought of those living in the castle. Did they all view the king and my family as Tess did? As veritable saints?

A blur of gray caught my eye, and I looked down the castle wall. Directly below my window was a small herd of unicorns. It was one of the few times I'd actually seen the herd that lived at Castle Phoenix. I watched as one of the unicorns shook her mane and galloped around the corner, out of my sight.

There was no doubt the herd was sick. When I was studying before the Successional, I'd seen pictures in the library of glorious gleaming white and gold unicorns, but so far, I had not seen any like that in real life.

Suddenly a lump formed in my throat. My life here was so easy and plentiful, but it wasn't the same for everyone—or even the majority in this kingdom, including the animals. Destruction, disease, hardships, and broken families surrounded me.

My father is right, I thought. We have to do *something*. We have to take back the bonegate and return magic to Lyonesse. Creatures should not be dying. Little girls should never be sold to a king so their family could feed themselves. How could Queen Pari be so cruel?

Initially, I'd come to Faerie to get to know my father, learn what parts of him I'd inherited, and hopefully, heal myself. I still wanted those things, but I needed more. During the pre-Successional parade, I'd discovered my passion for helping the fae, and my talk with my father had truly driven that desire home.

Was this why I could never figure out what I wanted to be in the Old Land? Why nothing held my interest? Because I wasn't supposed to be there, but helping in Faerie instead?

At the very least, the thought of helping Lyonesse lit a fire within me. That was so much better than slaving away at a job that I cared nothing about.

I whirled away from the window, suddenly determined to get started. I needed to talk to Finn. He was infinitely more charismatic and natural with people. He'd know where to begin. Plus, I'd missed him these last two weeks and wanted to spend time with him.

I dressed simply in loose pants and a T-shirt, ran a brush through my hair, and was ready.

"See you, Naela. Finn and I might fly Kane later,

so don't venture too far if you want to join, all right?" I called out as I slipped into the corridors.

The castle hallways were strangely empty. This made the search for my best friend more difficult. Unfortunately, except for Crystal, I had no idea where anyone's quarters were located—and I wasn't about to seek her out for help. Maybe everyone else was content to hang out in their rooms and rest today? We'd certainly earned a day off.

It was a good thing that I was in no major hurry, because at one point, I found myself lost. I was wandering down a previously unexplored wing when a plaque hanging above the threshold to another corridor caught my eye. I rushed up to it, hoping it was something I could use as a landmark, or better yet, a map.

This must be one of the guards' wings, I thought, taking in the shape of a shield bearing my father's crest, a black phoenix with two swords crossed in front. I wondered if Garret's room was down this hall-way. He would know where Finn was, but then again, even if this was where Garret lived, he'd been on duty all night. I shouldn't bug him.

Just keep looking, I told myself. He has to pop up at some point.

After a few more twists and turns deeper into the labyrinth of Castle Phoenix, I found a second plaque, this one starker than the first. It bore a large black feather surrounded by ten others on a field of white. It didn't take a genius to deduce that this was where the Feathered Fae lived.

I peered down the corridor, curious.

The hallway leading to their rooms was strangely different from those found elsewhere in the castle, enhancing the Feathered Fae's air of superiority. The marble was still mostly white, but with an ominous gray undertone, perhaps meant to echo the long black cloaks the Feathered Fae wore. Not a single sound came from behind the doors, no evidence of life.

They must all be out on missions or in a meeting.

A yearning to discover how my father's elite forces lived trickled through me, and my eyes locked on the door at the end. If this wing was like where I lived, the terminal room would be the highest-ranked person's room—Meegra's. I wondered what her personal quarters were like. As grand as mine?

There was only one way to find out.

I took one step forward toward insanity, when suddenly the resonance of stone grinding upon stone shot through me. I leapt back and whipped around just in time to see a wild-haired person stumbling out of a doorway that I hadn't noticed before.

My eyes narrowed, taking in the exact area where the person had appeared from. It reminded me of the secret door in the floor that my father had in his chambers. Was this some sort of private area too?

I moved toward the person who had yet to spot me. I was just close enough to tell that the door opened onto a staircase leading down, when the person whirled about, let out a moan, and began shuffling toward me.

I froze in place, taking in the man more closely. He was tall, probably well over six-feet, and looked much like a regular human, hinting at his elven blood. Despite appearing to be muscular, every step seemed to pain him. His hair hung in long limp curtains around his sallow face, and his skin clung weakly to his bones. Most chilling of all were his eyes, which were ringed in black, the irises a lifeless brown.

Although we were still a fair distance from each other, I could tell that something was wrong with this fae. Even the weakest person I'd seen in Lyonesse appeared healthier than this guy.

He shambled my way, moaning and groaning with every step, until suddenly, he stopped about ten meters away. I quirked my head to the side, trying to figure out what he was doing, when a voice cut through me, making me jump.

"I apologize, Princess Lana! Did he lay a hand on you?" A creature even smaller than Tess, but who looked strikingly similar, with light brown skin and watery blue eyes, poked his head out from behind the man. The goblin's extended arm shook, a tell. He was working magic against the poor guy to hold him in place.

"No. He didn't get close to me, although he star-tled me a bit. What's wrong with him?"

The goblin glanced up at the person as if checking that he was truly under his control and then back at me. "He's quite ill."

"Obviously. But with what?"

"We aren't sure," the goblin said, his tone shaky. "All we know is that it's dangerous. Hence why I asked if he'd touched you."

So they didn't know what this guy had, but they suspected it was contagious. Then, realizing where we were, my eyebrows furrowed. "But aren't the healers' wards on the third floor?"

I didn't know exactly where I was at the moment, but I'd been to the healers' wing after my Achilles had been sliced in half during training. At the very least, I knew that I'd ascended two sets of stairs to get there, but this guy had seemed to appear from the floor below. And now that I thought about it, all the patients in the healers' wing had been put in white gowns and slippers, but this fae was barefoot and wore thin beige pants and a matching top.

"Why is he dressed so differently from other patients?"

"The healers' wards are on the third level," the goblin agreed.

"But this man is a danger to all who deal with him —he's already caused three others to fall ill." He gulped, clearly nervous by the prospect of a violent contagion getting loose. "He is being kept quarantined, and is dressed differently so that if he escapes, others know to be wary."

My stomach twisted. There wasn't much worse than being ill, but being sick and unable to be around others? That was torture.

"I see," I said, realizing that the goblin was waiting for me to respond. "Well, I'm glad you found him before he could infect others. He doesn't seem to realize what he's doing is wrong."

"Not in the slightest," the goblin commiserated. "If that is all, Princess Lana, may we go?"

I nodded and watched as the goblin twirled his hand through the air, and the ill fae turned on his heel in response. The pair made their way back toward the hidden doorway, the goblin coaxing the poor guy with hand gestures and magic every step of the way.

Tears pricked in my eyes as they disappeared and the door closed to reveal a flush wall of white marble. No one knew what was wrong with that guy, but whatever it was, I suspected it had something to do with Queen Pari and the imbalance of magic in Lyonesse.

Suddenly, a roar pierced my thoughts, and my spine straightened.

Was that a lion? Why would Dak be in lion aspect?

I scurried toward the sound and was at the intersection of two main thoroughfares when a second roar echoed from somewhere, sending shivers up my spine. Then I caught the tinny resonance of something else.

I paused. Is that . . . metal clanging? Sword fighting?

I followed the sound, curious who was sparring. Perhaps it was a session for the guards or Feathered Fae. They hadn't been able to train often for the last two weeks, as my siblings and I had taken up most of the castle resources to prepare for the Successional.

Landmarks I recognized began popping up, and the sounds grew louder the closer I got to the training hall. I must have approached it from a different direction.

As if in affirmation, another bout of metal crashing against metal vibrated down the hallway, crescendoing into a wolfish howl.

Wikolia?

I froze, and my heartbeat picked up as dread washed over me.

Oh shite . . .

Forcing myself to confirm my fears, I tiptoed the rest of the way to the entrance of the training hall. Recognizable voices were exchanging tips and critiques on how to improve their form. I waited until the sound of sparring begun before peeking around the heavy wooden door.

All my siblings were there, alongside Meegra. My

stomach plummeted as I took them in, everyone drenched in sweat from training.

I inched away from the door, grateful no one had noticed me. Keeping my steps light, I retraced the path to my room, my heart pounding hard the entire way.

Why didn't anyone tell me we had practice today? Was I just supposed to know? Who had called for the training session? Was that my job, or someone else's responsibility?

I pushed open my door, questions whirring through my mind.

Naela's wings beat furiously as I entered my apartment suite, and a loud screech of excitement ripped from her beak. I bit my lip, feeling like an arse for what I was about to say when she was clearly anticipating the flying session I'd promised.

"Sorry, Boss. I have to push back our stroll a bit."

I ran to change, pulling on a pair of leggings and a tight tunic Tess had laid out for me that morning— the outfit I'd ignored when I'd opted for comfy, loose-fitting pants and a T-shirt.

No wonder Tess had looked at me strangely when she dropped off my lunch. Clearly, I was meant to be training, not lounging. Who had informed her that the new princess general was being lazy and would need room service?

"We'll go out after dinner, all right?" I said,

catching Naela's indignant glare. "I promise it'll happen. I just have to go do something now."

Naela screeched, accusing me of breaking my promise as I rushed out the door.

CHAPTER FOUR

I jogged back to the training room, the pit in my gut growing deeper with each step. There was no way I was actually going to admit I hadn't known we were supposed to be training. When had the others found out? Certainly not at the feast. Finn had been with me all night, blathering on about flying our hawks, and definitely would have mentioned training.

Come to think of it, why didn't Finn tell me when he found out? Anger flashed through me for the briefest of seconds until I realized that if I didn't know where his room was, then he probably had no idea where I slept either. Plus, once someone told him, Finn probably would have assumed that I'd been informed. Why wouldn't he? The question I really should have been musing was why *I* hadn't asked what would constitute a normal day after the Successional.

An exasperated sigh burst from my lips. I'm a

freaking *general*; I can't be making bloody stupid mistakes. I shook my head, then rounded the corner to the training hall and slammed to a stop as someone nearly mowed me down. Hands prevented me from toppling and righted me.

"Lana? Where have you been?"

I looked up to find Garret. My brows knit together. "What are you doing up? Weren't you on duty all night?" I asked, sidestepping the question while I worked out what to say.

"I couldn't sleep. My body hasn't adjusted yet, so I stopped in on the training session. Meegra said you hadn't shown up yet today. I was coming to check on you."

My eyes met his and found not anger, or even disappointment there, only worry. I winced. It was my first twenty-four hours without someone watching over me, and I'd already screwed up. There was no way I could tell Garret that I'd merely been stupid and didn't realize that generals and princesses didn't take days off.

"I've been in meetings with my father all morning," I invented wildly.

"Oh." His shoulders loosened. "Meegra won't like hearing that. She was convinced you were just lounging about your rooms eating sweets. Not to mention she hates not being included in King Oberon's plans. But then again, she's not the top dog any longer, is she?" He winked.

I groaned internally. Not only was I going to have to traipse into training late and lie to Master Meegra, but I also had to make good on my word and demand that Garret be pulled off night duty. Meegra would be *so* pissed.

"Nope, not anymore," I said, false cheer in my voice. "I guess I should probably go set her straight. I'll let you know about your new station at dinner."

He saluted me jokingly before retreating towards the guards' wing.

After Garret left, it took a solid five minutes to gather my courage and enter the training room as if I hadn't screwed up royally. My steps were so soft that I was halfway to where the group had congregated before anyone noticed my arrival.

"There she is!" Crystal stepped out of the circle in which Meegra was demonstrating a fancy tactic with a broadsword.

My nemesis' ginger eyebrows were raised, and her mouth was open in mock surprise. Although her face was smeared with blood, she presented an impressive figure—not at all cowed by the false bravado I was trying to project.

"So our fearless leader *finally* showed up today," Crystal pressed. "What kept you, General Lana?"

My face grew hot as everyone turned to stare. I tried to focus on Finn's expression of concern, but I couldn't help but notice Meegra's sneer, Victoria's haughty chin raise, and Crystal's ever-growing smirk.

I took a deep breath, trying to quell my anxiety, but the scent of sweat and metal filled my nostrils, and my palms dampened.

Being the center of attention had never been my thing, but I'd have to get used to it—and a million other things. Like dealing with people who wanted to bring me down.

Bloody hell, I was so done with that.

"Not that it's any of your business, Major *Second Order*," I spat out. Crystal's lips turned down at the reminder of her rank, and the anxious shaking of my arms lessened. "But if you must know, I was in a meeting with the king."

Meegra's lips flattened. I'd hit a nerve. "King Oberon didn't inform me of a conclave."

I shrugged. "That's not my concern. Nor yours, I suppose. If the king wants to speak with a superior officer, he will."

A few gasps sounded. Himari and Maria, my wind weaver and earth rumbler witch sisters respectively, averted their faces to hide the fact that they were trying not to laugh.

But Master Meegra was not easily unnerved.

She stepped closer, closing the distance between us until I could extend my arm and touch her. Then she sniffed. "It is funny, though. I thought His Majesty was meeting with the Sinker Divine, who I welcomed into the castle this very morning."

Sinker Divine? What in the hell of all hells was

that? My heart rate hit max speed. Why was I still so ignorant?

Meegra stood there like the cat who ate the canary, and suddenly I realized she'd probably been the one to call the training and neglect to inform me. What a bloody arse.

Anger bubbled within me, and I tilted my chin to the ceiling. Even if I didn't know what the hell she was talking about, I was done letting Meegra intimidate me.

Despite my outward defiance, Meegra's smile widened. "Truth be told, I'm happy for my error. I'd hate to think our new general spent the entire morning lounging around her rooms and bathing in lavender while we trained tirelessly."

My mouth gaped slightly. Shite. Why was lavender such a bloody strong scent?!

Meegra smirked and shook her head almost imperceptibly.

My lips pressed firmly together. I wouldn't let her have this win. Meegra had already had her day. She'd spent the last two weeks bullying me, but today was *mine*. I might have felt like a nervous, pissed-off wreck on the inside, but "fake it until you make it" had just become my new motto. And I knew just how to turn the tables.

"I'd hate to think so too," I replied, my voice coming out far more confident than I felt. "Almost as much as I'd hate to consider a guard being put on the night watch when his talents are better served assisting *my* army. I'm calling Garret back to help train the Fullfeather line. There's no task more important, and I want only the best by my side."

Meegra's jaw tightened. "You have no right—"

My hand flew up, palm out, and the Master Feathered Fae jerked back, her green eyes an equal mixture of wary and furious.

"Let's get this straight," I said, my tone firm, in control. "*I* am the general of King Oberon's army and a princess of Lyonesse. I have every right to station guards where I want them. You may control the Feathered Fae, but everyone else, save my father and Prince Casimir, is under my command. Don't forget that."

Meegra's mouth dropped open, and the tingles rushing through my veins intensified. Victory blossoming within me, I turned to my siblings and cocked my head.

"Now, what are we all standing around for? Shouldn't we be training?"

That session was the longest one of my life.

Every time I turned around, I found Meegra staring daggers at me. With my first show of power, I had tempted a true beast.

Crystal wasn't much better, tossing verbal jabs in

my direction whenever she thought she could get away with it. I pretended I didn't hear them. They were merely her typical mind games, and relatively harmless. At the very least, I thought it was fair to give Crystal a few more days to cool down from losing the Successional before I told her to shut it. And if I was being honest, I simply didn't have the energy to deal with her. My nerves were completely shot from confronting Meegra.

A servant inched into the training room, and I called for everyone to cease what they were doing as I gestured for her to approach. The dryad—or at least, I was pretty sure that's what she was, with her bark-like skin and leaf-green eyes—trembled as she approached. She stopped a couple meters away from me.

"I have been sent to inform all of King Oberon's heirs that dinner will be served earlier than normal in the great hall. His Majesty is well aware that some heirs take longer than others to prepare." Her gaze ran over Victoria and Maria, both of whom took hours to do their hair.

"If you wish to clean up beforehand, His Majesty suggests you do so now." The dryad bowed and then rose, but instead of scuttling back out of the room, she remained before me, her eyes wide and searching.

I cocked my head to the side, wondering if there was something else. Then I noticed all the guards' eyes were on me, and it clicked. *I* was now the person responsible for dismissing the troops and determining how long our sessions would last. Everyone was waiting for my cue to leave.

Add that to my list of things to get used to.

"Thank you for informing me," I said. "You may go."

The servant scampered away.

I turned to face the crowd behind me. "Good work today, everyone. Meet here at the same time tomorrow."

I made a mental note to ask Finn when that was and to push it back an hour if it was too early. "You're free."

"All except the Feathered Fae. You will remain here," Meegra growled.

Ellette, the Feathered Fae who'd arrived in Ireland to tell me about my father, slumped. Her blonde hair was damp from exertion, and her chest heaved.

I bit my lip. Meegra, desperate to maintain her power, had pulled the five Feathered Fae present away from the rest of the group and worked them separately.

While those I commanded took snack and water breaks and observed demonstrations put on by other guards, the Feathered Fae had sparred nonstop for hours. I hoped Meegra wouldn't keep them at it all night, working them to the bone just to prove that she was still their leader.

I exited the training hall, and quick footsteps

followed me. I turned around to find Finn, his blond curls bouncing wildly as he ran after me.

"Wow. Where did all that gusto come from, Lana? You were like a bloody real general in there!"

I sighed, not really in the mood to revel in my victory over Meegra. Though exhilarating at the time, keeping up the act of being in control and knowing what the hell I was doing had been exhausting.

I leaned closer to Finn so that only he could hear me. "I was just tired of her being mean and bossing me about. Wherever that flash of inspiration came from, I don't feel like much of a real general right now."

"I wouldn't have known it from watching you," Finn said, wrapping his arm around my shoulder a bit awkwardly.

Unbeknownst to me, Finn had loved me quietly for years, only to find out that I was his half-sister. Not only that, but when we'd arrived in Faerie, he'd learned he was a supernatural—a demon born witch. They were the rarest type of witch and a sect that, to my utter mortification, I'd often spoken poorly about.

Discoveries of such magnitudes were bound to change a relationship, even if the parties involved took them in stride—which I had not. Still, we'd recently made up, and I hoped we could get over this awkward patch quickly. I wanted things to return to the way they once were. I wanted us to be the Lana and Finn who could talk, laugh, and share life together the way only best friends could.

"Thanks." I gave him a weak smile. "I just wish I felt my new role more in my bones. Being a general does *not* come naturally."

Finn's free hand flew to his mouth in mock surprise.

I rolled my eyes. "Shocking, I know. But seriously, I'm having mega imposter syndrome right now."

"Don't be so hard on yourself, Lan." He mussed my short, brown hair. "You're not the only one who has to learn an entirely new skill set."

I fixed the wayward tresses. "Of course not," I said, embarrassed by my self-centeredness. "How are you and your mam taking it?"

Finn shrugged. "I wrote letters to Mam when we weren't speaking and told her I'll be staying here for a while. I know I won't have access to our father the way you do, but I can't go back—not now. After years of coveting your magic, I finally learned that I have my own!" His voice lifted to the excited tone he'd always used when I used to share my mediocre light magic with him.

I smiled at him, glad he was happy.

"Plus, this is a whole new world to explore, and that's pretty rad," Finn's eyes sparkled. "I mean, Irish History is interesting, and being a professor was my dream when I was at Trinners, but . . ."

"Magic is cooler," I teased.

"Hell yeah! And being a major and prince isn't bad either." Finn raised a sandy blond eyebrow. "I mean, you can't really beat that, now can you?"

I laughed at the endearing look of incredulity on his face. So much had happened to him—to all of us—in the last two weeks. Our lives had totally changed . . . and I had a feeling those changes weren't going to stop soon.

"As usual, you're right, Finnegan Fairchild. Not much can beat that."

CHAPTER FIVE

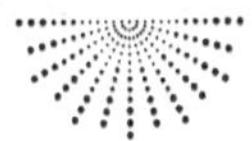

Winter deepened as New Year's Day passed, and a thin sheet of frost covered the ground each morning. My siblings and I had been training hard for nearly two months, honing our skills, both magical and military.

In a few cases, we had even discovered new types of magic. It should have thrilled me that discovering new powers was still a possibility, but it didn't.

In fact, the idea depressed me a little.

Because of tradition, we'd been given two weeks to settle into our inherited fae magics before the Successional. But for some of us, that length of time hadn't been nearly enough.

I couldn't help but wonder if Kate or Kumar would still be alive had our father damned the fae tradition of allowing only two weeks to prepare for the Successional, and pushed the tournament back a bit. Perhaps they would have discovered a power that could have helped them stand up to Nigel.

Despite the pain these revelations brought, I tried to find joy when Finn made magical breakthroughs. After all, he'd wanted this all his life, and I *was* happy for him . . . Happy and a bit astounded at the immense progress he'd made in such a short amount of time.

Thanks to his mixed witch and demon blood, Finn had the ability to access all four elements, but not all at the same strength. Before the Successional, he'd managed to use water, fire, and wind, but only recently had earth come to him.

His demon gift, the power directly from his demon line, was the only magic that remained a mystery. I figured it was just a matter of time before it appeared. The idea was exciting, but it also made me shiver. Demon gifts were usually quite powerful, but also dark.

Then there was Victoria, the half-vila who had, just the day before, gained the air magic her kind was known for in Eastern European lore. It was an improvement our father would be very pleased to learn about.

I strode through the white marble halls of Castle Phoenix to meet with the king while everyone else was at training, when I recalled another breakthrough I needed to report. One that annoyed me.

Crystal had recently conjured a tornado of epic

proportions. As much as I didn't want to admit it, the feat had been impressive. A triumph of that magnitude often took years for weaver witches to master.

Intellectually, I recognized that every skill someone gained would only help us on our future missions. Still, I couldn't help but feel annoyed with my redheaded sister. If I'd thought our first two weeks together had been hard, they'd been nothing compared to the weeks after the Successional.

Crystal had made it her personal quest to let me know I wasn't fit to be a general. Like I needed reminding. Every knife she threw straight into a bullseye, every magical win, and every insane physical feat she overcame with ease that I struggled through was a nonverbal confirmation that I was subpar.

Unlike my siblings, I hadn't experienced a magical revelation since the Successional. A part of me knew I was being a bit peevish about it. I had, after all, accessed *two* new spectrums of light since arriving in Faerie. Even accessing a sliver of the spectrum was a triumph after my years of stagnation. And yet, I yearned for more.

Just like when I was growing up, the lure of possessing an elemental power called to me, but was out of my reach. It was as if my elven blood—the blood that might have given me the ability to work all four elements, or at the *very* least, one—hadn't activated at all.

A long exhale escaped me, and I rolled my eyes at

myself. Yes, I *definitely* sounded whiny. Lightworkers were rare and highly valued in Faerie. I should be content with that.

Then again, having Prince Casimir around, possessing all the power I desired, and besting me in the manipulation of the electromagnetic spectrum made gratitude more difficult.

Although I didn't like him much, I had reasons to respect the prince. He'd grown up with the innate elven power over all four elements and had still decided to strive for more and conquer light. As a prince, he probably wouldn't have had to work for anything, but he had chosen to, and that was commendable.

I turned down the hallway that funneled directly to my father's chambers and forced my doubts and worries aside. I always strove to put my best face forward when I met with him. A few paces later, I was before the door inlaid with a golden feather, my hand raised and prepared to knock, when it flew open.

"Ah, yes. I forgot you and *Princess* Lana have your meeting today. No wonder you were so quick to toss me out." Meegra's tone was icy as she took me in with disdain.

Even her use of the term "princess" grated on my nerves. It was her way of subverting my authority.

Since the day I'd pushed pack, Meegra had refused to call me "general," even in the training room, where it would be appropriate. She hated that

I'd claimed my power over the guards and my siblings, a privilege she'd grown accustomed to.

She couldn't bully us anymore. Now the only soldiers she could rightfully lord over were the Feathered Fae.

"My apologies, Meegra, but yes, I have a meeting. And I will not keep my daughter waiting," Father said, his tone weary.

The Master Feathered Fae bowed shallowly and, without another word, stormed down the hallway, her black feathered cape billowing in her wake.

My father let me in, and then went straight for the alcove housing his wine, pulled out a bottle, and poured himself a glass. "It's a superior vintage produced by my favorite winemaker in the Free Realm. Difficult to get here because the dwarves drive a hard bargain, but worth it for situations such as these. Would you care for a glass?"

"Sure," I replied, not about to turn down a king's favorite wine.

My father filled another goblet and gestured for me to sit in what I now thought of as my chair. It was at the end of the table, directly to the left of his seat. Meegra had been so pissed when I sat there during our first group meeting that I figured it used to be her spot, although I'd never confirmed that idea.

I took the glass my father handed me, mimicking the way he examined it, then sniffed it, and finally sipped it daintily. An explosion of flavor darted across my tongue. My eyes widened. The aroma of green forests and the taste of plump wild blackberries tantalized my senses.

"Holy wow," I whispered, staring at the glass. I'd become used to good wines during our meetings, but I'd never had something like this.

My father smiled. "Your first experience with truly superior fae wine is one you'll never forget. Only very adept winemakers can succeed in putting a bit of their own magic in their product. And *this* dwarf is special. No doubt you tasted a bit of his earth magic from an elf ancestor? To have the pure strength and cunning of dwarves, as well as the magic of the elves, is to be blessed indeed. Would that I could get him to live here, but he declines. Then again, I can't blame him. My land is hardly suitable for vineyards."

I nodded, trying my best to ignore his comment on dwarf and elf mixes like Crystal being 'blessed.'

My father took another sip and lifted one hand to rub the nape of his neck, a gesture I recognized as one I performed often when stress got the better of me.

"I regret you had to witness Meegra's anger. She's having a difficult time adjusting to the new circumstances. It frustrates her that she has less access to me."

My skin crawled, as it always did when I thought of my father and Meegra together. Although he'd never said it outright, I knew they were a couple.

"It's an adjustment for everyone," I replied.

My father smiled warmly. "You're even learning how to speak like a royal. Have you perused your library yet? I had it stocked with books specific to your duties."

"I have. Thank you." I took another sip of wine.

I had, in fact, explored my library—the mystery, thriller, and sci-fi sections of it. Though I suspected he was referring to the translated versions of military tactic books that a fae had dropped off weeks ago. Or perhaps the massive *History of Faerie* tome he'd suggested that I hadn't yet cracked open. I had time.

"Wonderful. Now tell me, how is training going?"

I launched into a summary of what had occurred since our last meeting just days ago. As expected, my father was pleased that new powers were emerging in his children. Seeing his eyes light up every time I delivered positive news was one of the best parts of my day—even if it was about Crystal.

"This is all very good," he said as soon as I stopped talking. "And excellent timing. In fact, I think you have all earned a bit of a break. You have yet to have a day off since before the Successional, am I right?"

"That's right."

"Then it's high time you have another. Even guards get personal recesses once a week. I can't have my subjects thinking I work my children to the bone. Plus, I believe that you'll enjoy what I have in mind."

He leaned forward, as if we were sharing a secret. "Tomorrow is Ration Day. It's a day for those in the castle to mingle among the subjects of Lyonesse. I'd like my children from the Old Land to join in on the celebration."

Prince Casimir had mentioned Ration Day before. It was the day when the castle staff and royals delivered food allotments to the families of the Feathered Fae, guards, and even the kin of some servants like Tess who worked in the castle. The prince had alluded to it being hard work, but my father made it seem fun. Either way, it had to be better than sweating our butts off in the training room like we'd been doing for weeks on end.

"Sounds great. What time should we be ready?"

My father beamed and filled me in on the minor details. It warmed my heart to see a ruler who so clearly loved his subjects and being out among them. I was looking forward to getting out of the castle, exploring a bit, and meeting the fae too.

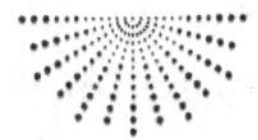

CHAPTER SIX

It was only my second time in the city, but I'd seen what constituted normal days in the firlon plenty of times. Save for the day of the parade, I'd never seen the streets of Lyonesse as bustling as they were on Ration Day.

Fae were coming out of the woodwork. Streamers lined the thoroughfares, children ran amok, and people sat atop rooftops, playing wood flutes and small horns that produced sounds similar to that of a recorder.

"They're having a whale of a time." Finn grinned from ear to ear as we followed Garret and Ebba, our arms laden with baskets of food.

Though the pair was no longer our daily guards, our father had insisted we pair up once again for Ration Day. He claimed it was how he and Prince Casimir traveled, and as royal heirs, we should too.

I couldn't argue with that, so we were back to being babysat. To be fair, I didn't really mind. While I'd grown more used to making decisions and being "in charge" over the last few weeks, it still wasn't my default setting. It was a relief to have someone else calling the shots for a few hours. Plus, realistically, we'd be totally lost without them.

An elderly fae hobbled up to Garret, stopping our group in the middle of the street, and spoke in a voice too low for me to hear. I tilted my head, and barely had a second to wonder what he wanted, when Garret burst into laughter. His gray eyes crinkled at the corners as his lips pulled up, creating devastatingly handsome lines in his dark stubble.

My heartbeat kicked up, and my cheeks warmed despite the winter chill that cut through the early afternoon sunshine. Mentally, I added "eye-candy" to the list of reasons I didn't mind being watched over for the day.

Finn nudged me. "Earth to Lana. What's up with the faraway look? All this too much for you?"

I blinked and tore my eyes from Garret. "Sorry."

I turned to gaze into the crowds so Finn didn't see my blush deepen. "Actually, I'm fine. Just taking it all in. Seeing the people of Lyonesse like this makes me wish we came into town more often."

"Who are you, and what have you done with my best friend?!"

"Oh, shut it." I whacked Finn on the shoulder and

nearly lost control of my basket of golden Faerie apples.

Two spilled from the wicker, and a little boy with dark purple skin and slightly clawed hands jumped out from the crowd to grab them. He looked up at me questioningly, and an image of the green-skinned girl I'd met the day of the parade popped into my head. I'd kept an eye out for her since the moment we exited the castle gate, but had yet to spot her.

"Go ahead," I said, gesturing to the fruit.

The boy beamed and ran off, disappearing through the winding streets of Lyonesse.

"What part of town are we in?" I asked when we began walking again. Nothing looked familiar from the parade. Too much time had passed since that strange day. But even if I recognized areas, I wouldn't have known what they were called.

"This is Market Street." Garret swept his arm up and down the thoroughfare that we'd been traveling on since we left the town square. "Fae sell their wares or buy food for their family here. Some live above the shops. They're usually the wealthier merchants, of which there are few."

That was interesting. I'd seen my father disappear into a large shop off Market Street with five guards and two Feathered Fae in tow. From what I'd heard, few wealthy fae families received rations. I wondered what other sort of business he had in there. A king's job was so layered that I was always learning of various duties my father performed.

"But our group is heading to Hob Hill," Garret continued. "Ryker and Sai will be there, as it's their day off."

"How'd they manage to get Ration Day off?" Ebba's expression was disbelieving.

"Their grandmother has been ill," Garret explained. "It was a last-minute request, but His Majesty granted it all the same. The woman used to work in the castle in her younger years. Perhaps King Oberon favored her." He shrugged.

Pride swelled within me. I loved that my father cared about his people so much.

"Hob Hill, you say? That wouldn't be short for 'hobgoblin,' would it?" Finn asked, intellectual curiosity evident in his voice.

"It is," Ebba confirmed.

Finn's face brightened, as it had been doing lately when Ebba paid him the slightest bit of attention. I bit back a grin. Although my friend had proclaimed to love me only weeks earlier, I suspected his heart might already belong to another.

Unfortunately for Finn, he had competition. Gio had been flirting shamelessly with the cute-but-deadly fae guard too. Both men were more charming than anyone had a right to be, but Ebba's standoffish nature gave no clues as to whom she favored—if she favored anyone at all.

"The area's name is a bit of a jab, to be honest," Ebba said casually. "It's a term that the first King of Lyonesse used in order to make it clear that hobgoblin families resided there. Nowadays, it's part of the vernacular. The current locals embrace it, but it wasn't always that way."

Garret gave Ebba a questioning look.

"I thought they should be informed," she said, her tone slightly defensive. "If something happens to Prince Casimir, Lana would inherit the kingdom. It's best that she—all of them, really—know of our local history. A lot of fae don't like to talk about the nastier bits, but that doesn't mean it didn't happen."

Garret shrugged. "You're right, of course. You just caught me off guard. I wasn't trying to censor the past."

"Thanks for filling us in, Ebba," Finn piped up. "A girl who likes history is a girl after my own heart."

Smooth move. I rolled my eyes at his remark, and Ebba turned away, ignoring him.

"How many districts make up Lyonesse?" Finn, never one to be deterred easily, pressed on.

"Besides Castle Phoenix, which is a district in itself, there are seven urban districts," Garret replied when Ebba did not deign to answer. "Or eight, if you count the few families who live outside the city walls. A dangerous choice, as Lyonesse has been at war for years." Garret swept his hand in the direction we'd just come from and to the right. "I'm from

Market's End district, and Ebba used to live in Meadows."

"Must be a lot of people for seven districts," Finn commented. "I always thought the population would be lower since there's less magic around."

Garret nodded and gracefully sidestepped a deep crater in the street. "While the fae of Lyonesse have had trouble conceiving in recent years, we can have children for much longer than humans can. It's not unheard of for families to have five or more kids over the course of centuries. Many keep trying to expand their families, hoping one may enter the guard or Feathered Fae and support the rest. It's a vicious cycle."

All brought on by Pari, I thought, though I stopped there. I didn't want my mind to wander down that path, not today when there was so much new stuff to see. We rarely left Castle Phoenix. I didn't want to miss a thing.

"Here we are," Ebba said, stopping before a brightly colored purple door that would not look out of place in Dublin.

She knocked, and a cacophony of noises erupted inside the home. Laughter and shrieks hit my ear until loud instructions to open the door were issued, shutting the rest up.

"Is this Ryker's family?" I asked, recognizing the booming voice.

As if on cue, the door opened. There Ryker stood,

taking up nearly the entire doorway and grinning broadly. Though he was off duty, he was still dressed in his guard uniform.

"They're all too scared to open the door. Not even Kyla would do it." Ryker gestured behind him to a small girl with oversized, pointed ears, amethyst eyes, and skin the color of onyx.

Aside from her tattered dress, Kyla was the miniature of Ryker's cousin, Sai. I wondered if she was the little sister Sai had mentioned before.

"You know that girl isn't shy about *anything*." Ryker teased the girl, who then hid her face. "But apparently when a princess and a prince come calling, she acts like she's never spoken a word in her life."

"Aren't you going to let us in so they can meet Princess Lana and Prince Finn?" Garret shoved his basket into Ryker's arms and pushed his way through the door.

It was obvious that Ebba and Garret had been here before. Ryker and Sai's family hugged them both warmly and exclaimed over their good health. Only when Finn and I crossed the threshold did the revelry dim a bit and the family cheer fade to quiet reverence.

Kyla performed a sweet little curtsey in our direction. When I returned the gesture clumsily, her eyes bulged, and a few people gasped. I made a mental note that a royal curtseying to their subjects was odd.

The house was as unlike the castle as two structures could be. The interior was made of a pale green wood, bits of which seemed to be in the early stages of rotting.

In lieu of stark white marble, photos and portraits of family members lined the walls. Sai's and Ryker's stuck out most. It was clear the family didn't have much money, even with two elite members of the Lyonesse guard as kin.

Someone cleared their throat. I followed the sound to find a woman who looked to be in her eighties, with a bright red headscarf tied over unruly black hair that rivaled Ryker's wild mane.

"Princess Lana. Prince Finn. May we offer you a drink? Some food?" She gestured to the basket of apples we'd brought.

My heart clenched at her generosity. We were bringing these people food because their family members served in the military. There was no way in hell I was taking any of it.

"Just water, please. We had a late breakfast, so I'm quite full, but have worked up a thirst after climbing that hill." I hoped that would keep them from offering anything more as we settled in for a chat.

We left Ryker and Sai's family home a half hour later, which, according to Ebba, was twenty minutes behind schedule.

"We were given ten minutes per household. That's five more than usual, as we're escorting you two. King Oberon knew his subjects would want to socialize. We must hurry back to Market Street and pick up our next allotment."

"It was worth it. They were a lovely family. Especially Kyla." I grinned. The girl had been slow to warm up, but once she had, the chatter hadn't stopped for a second. "She swore up and down that she was going to crush all of Ryker's and Sai's records and become the first Feathered Fae in their family."

"I bet she does it too," Finn grinned. "She has spunk."

"Let's *hope* she succeeds," Garret added. "That way, Ryker will have to stop bragging."

Ebba snorted. "He'll only find something else to blather on about. Still, I hope the girl makes the cut."

It was impossible to carry rations to multiple families in a neighborhood in a single trip, so the food was kept under guard in a centralized location called the ration ring. It wasn't the most efficient system, but Ration Day wasn't about efficiency. It was about connecting. Even though the king couldn't come to everyone's home, they were in the presence of someone who had his ear.

As we approached the ration ring, I glanced down the street to the shop that my father had entered. There were no longer any black cloaks or guards waiting outside, so I assumed the king and his Feathered Fae had moved on. He was probably already on the outskirts of the city, where he paid visits to the few fae nobles of Lyonesse every Ration Day.

I shook my head. I'd heard that the nobles kept villas on the edges of the city despite the brittle and dry land that surrounded their homes. While the city, with its run-down homes and rutted streets, wasn't a great beauty, it was certainly better than what lay outside its walls. At the very least, a fae could take pleasure in the shimmering blue-green waters of Choral Bay. I had a hunch that the nobles kept themselves separated from the more downtrodden masses who lived near the city center as a status symbol.

It was something I wasn't able to understand. Then again, I couldn't fathom spending hundreds of quid on a purse in the Old Land, and people did that every day.

Movement flashed in the corner of my eye, and I glanced down a dark alley. A woman with her back to me was leaning close to a man, who was transferring a basket of fruit and loaves of bread to her.

"Princess Lana?" Ebba prompted a few steps ahead of me.

"Sorry, I—"

I stopped talking. The woman I'd been watching had turned around and, surprisingly, I knew her.

She was the green-skinned girl's mother. Or at least, I thought so—with her face smeared heavily with dirt, it was difficult to tell. But when her eyes widened in recognition, I was positive I was right.

"Hi, there! Do you remember me? I met your daughter at the . . ."

I trailed off as the woman pushed past the man who had just given her the food, and ran down the alley, out of sight.

"Who are you speaking to, Lana?" Garret asked, coming up beside me.

I wasn't sure why, but the woman's reaction told me she didn't want to be seen.

Instead of answering honestly, I shook my head and pointed to the man. "No one. I thought that I'd met that man before, but I was wrong."

Garret followed my finger down the dark nook between buildings. Unsurprisingly, the fae looked baffled by what had just happened, making my excuse more believable.

Garret chuckled and patted me on the shoulder. "Dark alleys have a way of making us see things that aren't there. Come now, Princess Lana, we must move on. There are many more homes awaiting their rations."

I nodded and followed him to the ration ring for our next pickup, the vision of fear on the green-skinned woman's face burning deeper into my mind with every step.

CHAPTER SEVEN

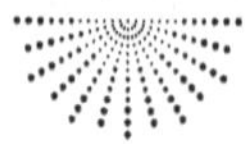

"Y ou're late," a heavyset guard remarked when we approached the ration ring. "This is only your second pickup."

Ebba's lips tightened at the corners. "Where's our next drop off?"

"Any reason why the others have already been back three or four times, but not you?" the soldier pressed.

"People want to speak with Princess Lana and Prince Finn," Ebba explained unapologetically. "Our royal heirs enjoy the conversation. Who are we— mere guards—to stop them?"

The guard grunted, but his eyes darted to Finn and me, as if wary that we were about to tell him off. "Just try to make this next round faster. We can't leave until the last of the food is distributed. I don't want to be out here all night."

I glared at him, and he had the good grace to lower his face to the ground. He lived in a comfortable castle, but these families sometimes went days without proper food. I didn't like that he thought his needs were above theirs.

"And of course, the families waiting for their rations shouldn't be kept long either," he mumbled as an afterthought.

Although I had half a mind to extend our visits even longer, just to spite that soldier, he was right on the last count. Many families still waited for their rations. So instead of giving the soldier a piece of my mind, we simply got a move on. We went door to door, dropping off rations.

Three hours and many quick visits later, my legs ached as we climbed Hob Hill yet again. Despite being filled with only fluffy bread, my basket quaked in my arms. When we returned to the castle, I planned on enjoying a long, luxurious soak in my tub.

Garret knocked on the next door, and a moment later a fae with the pointed ears of an elf, and gossamer wings of a pixie, opened the door.

"Oh, welcome, Princess Lana and Prince Finn," the male fae said, his voice high and bewildered. "We weren't expecting—"

"If you do this every month, there should really be a better system." A voice inside cut the fae off. "As you can see, we've got this house covered."

I peeked past Garret's broad shoulders to find

Crystal, Victoria, and their guards already inside. Crystal met my gaze, her eyebrows arched. Honestly, the last thing I wanted to do was be in the same room as her, so I turned to Garret.

"They can keep the extra food, but we shouldn't impose."

Garret opened his mouth to respond, but the other fae stepped forward, stopping him.

"Please don't leave. It's a delight to have you join us!" The fae opened the door wider. "I beg you, please come in and sit."

Like most of the other homes I'd been in that day, the general air of the abode was barren. The poverty chipped away at my heart every time I witnessed it, and I'd learned to focus on the small, simple touches to lift my spirits. Here hand-drawn pictures decorated the wall, a soft-looking, hand-knitted blanket lay over the back of a chair, and a few simple wooden toys littered the floor. It was easy to imagine a loving family living in this home.

"Might we offer you water to quench your thirst. Or perhaps an apple?" The fae gestured to the basket nearest Crystal, brimming with two dozen apples.

It was the same at every home. The fae of Lyonesse offered us food that they desperately needed for themselves.

I shook my head as I took one of the dilapidated wooden chairs his wife pulled out for me—the only furniture in the room, save the seats that Crystal and

Victoria perched upon. "Just water would be wonderful."

The young couple nodded and bustled into the kitchen.

Crystal's eyebrows rose. "Funny. I haven't been offered any food. I guess they only offer it to the most *elite* princess." She didn't even bother to keep her voice low as she spoke. "Didn't those idiot guards at the ration ring tell you we were coming here? They decided we needed to pick up your slack, because apparently you're super slow."

I rolled my eyes. "Perhaps the fae you visited simply didn't take to your charming personality, Crystal."

Her lips flattened, and I sensed a retort coming, when the couple flew back into their living room to present us with water and crackers.

"We added extra." The female fae—who, with her bark-like skin and short stature, looked to be of dryad and dwarf heritage—gestured to the plate.

I thanked them, and we began to chat merrily. Eventually, their two children, after peeking around the corner for ten minutes, ventured into the living room timidly and joined us.

The mother situated the smallest child on her lap, and Crystal eyed the boy.

"Are they going to take part in the Harvest to become a member of the king's army or Feathered Fae one day?"

The couple nodded eagerly, small smiles on their faces.

"How much longer do they have?" Ebba asked, as she watched the older girl with interest.

"Our eldest will take the test next year. We think she has a good chance at the guard. She's small but very quick, which we think will earn her a spot." The mother beamed at her daughter, who was quietly playing on the ground with her toys, before ruffling her son's hair. "He still has two years."

Crystal sniffed. "I just don't understand why everyone here wants to ship their children off. Don't you want to see them grow up? My guard swears it's an honor, but my mother never would have given me up. And that's saying something, considering all the shit I put her through."

My face burned. I might have wondered the same in private, but how could she say such a thing out loud? This was a different culture—an entirely new world, with standards, expectations, and challenges we'd never faced.

Sometimes I couldn't believe that Crystal had been training to be a physician before she came to Faerie. Her bedside manner really sucked.

"Er . . ." The mother shifted uncomfortably, and I jumped in to smooth things over.

"Your mother wasn't in the same situation as these people," I admonished my sister, then turned to the parents. "However, I would love to hear what you think of the testing and choosing of the royal guard. It's always good to get an insider's opinion."

The husband gave me a soft smile. "It's an honor to give your child to assist and protect His Majesty. Without your father's line, we might not be here."

"But you didn't have to do this sort of thing before our father became king, did you?" Crystal pressed. "So why would you do it now?"

Her tone had softened a bit, but the question still stunned me, although in a different way. I hadn't realized that our paternal grandfather, the first king of Lyonesse since the creation of Faerie, had not selected his guards and closest advisors in the same manner.

"It's true that Harvest testing didn't exist in previous generations." The mother stroked her son's head gently. "And you're correct in thinking we'd enjoy keeping our children with us longer."

"But it's worth it if your child is chosen to protect the king," she said softly. "It means that in some small way, our family line is repaying the debt we owe the Fullfeathers. The sacrifice of our Sinker. They helped create a home in which all fae could live as they were, without threat."

"But you're receiving rations, so clearly you're doing *something* for your kingdom already," Crystal pointed out. She was right. Rations were given to those whose family members served the crown.

"Yes. My sister works at the castle," the mother said. "She has no family of her own, which is why we are given rations. But we hope to do *more*. Not only was your line instrumental in the Great Sinking, but King Oberon keeps us safe from the evil queen. It is a fair trade, I think. One that empowers our children to be more, and to serve their community as best they can. Once the evil one is defeated, our lives will return to normal. I am sure of it."

"*Hmph*," Crystal grunted.

"Well, we thank you," I said before Crystal could ask anymore prying questions. "I can't wait to see your children compete to be guards. Or will your son try for a spot with the Feathered Fae?"

The father beamed. "Guards. We have no shifter blood in our line. Although, of course, we wish we did."

"We can't all be so lucky," I agreed and handed my empty cup to the father. Crystal seemed semi-placated, and I felt we could safely move on. "We should be going. Other families will be waiting."

The fae waved at us until we were down the street. Once we were far enough away, I exhaled. That had been a lot.

"A few weeks in and you're already a pro at this princess thing," Finn said, coming up to my side.

I snorted. "Yeah, right."

"I'm serious, Lan. How you handled making those fae feel understood after Crystal's negative attitude . . . not everyone can do that."

I sighed and shook my head at what had just

happened. Why couldn't Crystal just keep her trap shut from time to time? Even if she was jealous of my rank, there was no need to make others feel bad about their experiences. I didn't understand her at all.

"If it were Ryker, he'd have made a joke of it to lift the families' spirit," Garret added. "Which works sometimes, but other times it's just uncomfortable."

I spared him a smile before turning back to Finn. "Let's be real. I only piped up first. You could have smoothed things over much more eloquently."

"While I agree I am far more charming—" Finn jerked as I shot a palm at his shoulder, shoving his tall form into the side of a building playfully. "Hey now! You said it, not me!"

I chuckled and shook my head.

"But to be clear, I disagree that you didn't do a good job," Finn continued. "If I'm convinced of one thing after seeing the city of Lyonesse again, it's that someone needs to bring a bit more light into the kingdom. Sounds like a job for an illuminator witch to me."

"Thanks," I mumbled, pleased by his kind words even if I wasn't totally convinced. Maybe it was the exhaustion talking, but I didn't think so.

Finn could wield fire, which meant he could beat back the darkness too. Still, I'd take the compliment. Maybe one day, I'd even believe it.

We arrived back at the ration ring to find it nearly depleted of food and manpower. The few soldiers who remained to protect the meager supplies checked the list to see who had been missed. Garret beamed when a guard read off a name and urged us to grab armfuls of food.

"We should bring these two with us on every Ration Day," Ebba commented as we set off. "They're bringing us all sorts of luck."

"I volunteer," Finn volunteered quickly, like a too-eager puppy.

I had to refrain from rolling my eyes.

"Do you know who we're delivering to next?" I asked.

"You could say that," Garret replied as he turned down a narrow, stone-paved side street that I hadn't even noticed, and stopped before the first house on the right. "Here we are."

The cottage was weathered and small, though undeniably well kept. It seemed that a fresh coat of paint had been recently applied to the door, which shone peony pink against the battered brown wood. Flowers resembling irises bloomed on the sill outside the window, even in the cold of winter. I yearned to touch them, to feel the velvet of a petal beneath my fingers, alive and soft.

"How did they do that?" I asked, pointing to the flowers. The temperatures hadn't dipped to frigid yet, and there'd been only a couple dustings of snow, but it usually took much less to kill off such delicate beauties.

"The fae who lives here can wield all four elements, but she finds air, water, and fire uncomfortable, so she channels mostly earth magic."

I furrowed my eyebrows. Garret sounded pretty familiar with whoever lived here. And judging by the eager smile on his face, he liked her too. A girlfriend, maybe? I frowned as a feeling of possession rose in me, and then I stiffened, shocked by the sensation. Quickly, I squashed it down and glanced at my friends to see if they had noticed.

I breathed a sigh of relief. No one was paying me any attention. Garret was crouching comically behind Ebba, who beamed as she knocked on the pink threshold.

What was he doing? I shot a glance at Finn, who looked confused too. Though the pair had been jovial all day, Garret was acting like a total goofball.

The door opened, and a tiny woman with glossy black hair and light brown skin answered the door. Her gray eyes widened at the sight of Ebba.

"Darling, girl! Come in, come in! I was wondering where my allotment had gone to."

Garret sprang up from behind Ebba. "Surprise!"

The woman let out a startled gasp and swatted the air. "Garret! I can't believe it! Two times in one week! Oh, you little sneak, why didn't you mention I was on your route?" The small woman clasped her arms around Garret.

"Good to see you, too, Mother. And you weren't

on our route until just now. It worked out rather well, actually. You're our last run, so we can spend more time here than usual."

Mother? We were meeting Garret's family? I brushed my hair out of my face, hoping it still looked as good as it had when we left the castle. Considering I'd been wearing a fur hat most of the day, I sincerely doubted it, but a girl could dream.

"That *is* good luck." Garret's mother peered around Ebba curiously. Her eyes, which were the exact same shade as Garret's, latched onto Finn before shifting to meet my gaze and holding there.

"Mother, this is Princess General Lana and Prince Major Finn. King Oberon's children from the Old Land. If you recall, I told you that Lana—"

Garret's mother's lips turned up in a sly smile and she patted Garret on the chest. "Yes, yes. I remember *everything* you told me about Lana, dear. And Prince Finn, too. What do you say we head inside and serve the royal family refreshments?"

What had Garret told his mam about me? I shot him a questioning glance and blinked. His cheeks were tomato red. Weird. He never blushed. Then I remembered how all the homes we'd seen so far had been in bad shape and the families poor. Was he embarrassed about that?

I cleared my throat. "Garret, if you'd like some alone time with your Mam, we'd completely understand."

"Oh, please, Princess Lana!" Garret's mother waved her hand dismissively. "My boy would like nothing of the sort. Come in, come in!"

She ushered us into the cottage, down a short hallway boasting two massive portraits. One of the fae depicted looked a lot like Garret, but a little older. The other showed a fairer male of around forty. His older brother and father, perhaps? I made a mental note to ask Garret about them later. Unlike many other homes we'd been in, this one smelled pleasantly clean, not like dirt or of strong astringent. It seemed that Garret's family was slightly better off than the others we'd visited that day.

The matriarch led us into the kitchen, which was overflowing with plants. A four-person dining table was positioned between pots of flowers and shrubs with leaves that resembled butterfly wings. Garret's mam gestured for us to sit. Only once she was assured that we were settled did she go about making an infusion of pungent herbs and water called caj. This blend of drink was the closest thing I'd experienced in Faerie to black tea, and that was mostly down to the addition of fennel, which I'd tasted in many black teas. Caj was considered a treat.

I protested, not wanting our hostess to use up her best foodstuffs on us, but Garret waved his hand as if to say it was fine. Once his mam finished making the caj, he helped her serve and then offered his mam the final chair and moved to stand behind me.

"So, Princess Lana and Prince Finn, tell me all about yourselves." Garret's mother's eyes crinkled at the corners as she smiled warmly. "I have a bit of an obsession with the Old Land. Sometimes, Garret brings a book from there and reads a chapter or two out loud while he visits. He tells me most of the stories are imagined, but still . . . they're fascinating."

I liked that Garret read books from the human plane. I'd have to ask him if he'd read the one I was currently devouring.

"Just Lana, please," I said, picking up my cup and savoring the warmth spreading through my cold fingers. "I know your son so well, it's strange to hear such formality from you."

Finn echoed my request that only his first name be used.

"That's sweet of you, dears. I'm glad you hold Garret in such high esteem." Garret's mother smirked up at her son, who cleared his throat loudly. "My name is Alvina. Now please, humor an old woman. I'd love to hear of your life in the Old Land." She looked at us expectantly.

It was refreshing that Alvina didn't bow or attempt to entertain us as others had, but I was already knackered from a full day of delivering rations. I nudged Finn, who took the hint like a pro and launched into his life story. I leaned back, content to listen as he wove my tale expertly with his.

Alvina filled our cups again and again and eventually pushed almond biscuits on us that smelled so divine they were impossible to resist. Even though Garret's mam was sweet and entertaining, I was soon ready to head back to the castle. It had been a long day, and the introvert in me felt quite drained. The moment there was a lull in the conversation, I took my chance to exit gracefully.

"I think we should get back so we can wash up before dinner. Thank you for your hospitality, Alvina. It was a pleasure. I can see where Garret gets so many of his good qualities—you raised him well. I don't know where I'd be without him."

Alvina beamed. "You don't know how happy that makes me. It was a pleasure meeting you, too, Lana dear. I hope to see *much* more of you in the future."

I stood to find Garret, still red-faced, standing stiffly behind me. He'd been acting strangely since we'd arrived at his family home. Coughing and sputtering when his mother regaled us with the embarrassing childhood tales that we all had, or asked how I felt about leaving the Old Land. But perhaps his strangest reaction had come when Alvina asked about the morning I'd woken up to find a knife laying on my pillow, and Garret had rushed into my room to defend me. He'd acted like his mother was giving him up for revealing royal secrets—even after I assured him I didn't mind that he'd told his mam. Thankfully, his annoyance passed quickly, but still, he was acting rather odd.

CHAPTER EIGHT

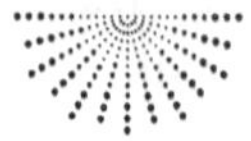

My stomach rumbled as we made our way down the streets of Lyonesse. Though everyone had offered us food, we'd always declined. So now, I was starving and ready to get back to the castle.

Unfortunately, things were slower going now because the streets were absolutely filled with fae. Everyone had received their rations and could now walk around without the anxiety of missing their drop-off. As we trudged through the crowds, heads turned as the people stared and pointed. A few approached for a chat. I tried to smile through my exhaustion, but truth be told, I really just wanted to go sit in my room and be alone for a while. I'd enjoyed the visits, even more so than I thought I would, but now it was time for some self-care.

We were nearing where the ration ring had been

located, in the middle of Market Square, when a cloaked figure ran out of one of the shops and headed straight for us. By fae standards, he appeared ancient, and his arms flapped strangely with each step.

Garret and Ebba stiffened and placed their hands on their swords. It was only when the figure stumbled that they eased up, recognizing he was drunk.

"You there! Princess! Prince! Cap'ns!" the man slurred his words slightly. "A word, if you please?"

Garret and Ebba stepped forward, ready to act as a shield, but I stopped them.

"It's fine, guys. He's just drunk and probably wants to chat." I sighed. Just one more person. I could do this.

"About time I caught one of you." The fae wheezed as if he'd run much farther than just across the street.

He was younger than his stooped back and long, white hair had originally led me to believe. While I'd seen old fae before, I'd never seen someone like this guy—a young fae who looked like life had gotten him down. The scent of ale rolled off him in waves, and I wondered if alcohol was a factor.

"What can we help you with?" Finn asked jovially.

"Prince! It is *I* who am helping *you*. I bring you a warning! You must leave the castle. Your father is a bad man. He brings the darkness with him and will drown out your light." The fae turned to me. "Especially yours, princess."

"Watch your tongue," Ebba hissed as she moved forward. "You're speaking treason."

The fae pulled a dagger from beneath his cloak and pointed it at Ebba's throat.

I tensed, and Ebba's lip curled dangerously, which strangely seemed to strengthen the drunk's resolve.

"It's not treason if it's the truth. I speak of what I've seen with my own eyes."

Anger surged within me. Clearly this guy had lost it. All day long, I'd heard testimonials to my father's goodness, and seen what he would do for his subjects. Who did this guy think he was, spreading such lies?

"I won't stand here and let you insult my father." I stepped past Finn and Ebba to face the man, a flare of searing infrared light in my hand. "Did you not see the pile of food out here earlier? Did you not witness the king walking amongst the fae, interacting with and greeting old friends?"

Startled, the man dropped the dagger and leapt back, his eyes locked on the light in my hands. He may not have seen a demonstration of my powers at the Successional, but he'd clearly heard about how deadly light magic could be.

"Nothing against you, princess. We can't help who our families are, can we?"

My jaw tightened, and the light pulsed like a

snake ready to strike. "If you were smart, you'd leave now. Go sober up and consider yourself lucky."

Instead of running off, the drunk stood straighter. "Perhaps you're right that I've had too much ale. But I won't go back on my word. King Oberon is bringing the darkness . . . maybe Queen Pari, too. I wouldn't be surprised if they're all in it together! I tell you, princess, he took my magic once! I was in that very tavern." The man pointed wildly to the building he'd darted out of and nearly toppled over. "Came in during a Ration Day just like this one to have a chat with the owner. Well, I don't get many chances to tell a king what I think of him, so I did it right then and there. I couldn't do any magic for a week afterward!"

The light pooling in my hands flickered and disappeared as the situation became clear. This man was on the outs and paranoid. He obviously hated the king for having what he didn't.

There were plenty of people like him in the Old Land: haters who wanted to bring down someone who'd worked hard and was loved by others. He'd probably overindulged that day, too, and had incapacitated his magic. He stank so strongly of alcohol and sweat that I wouldn't doubt it.

Garret smirked and sheathed his sword. "Perhaps if you'd lay off the elven wine a bit, you'd have a better chance of performing magic. Why don't you go back to the tavern and ask for water? We have somewhere—"

The drunk lunged at me, his fingernails scratching across my neck before his hands grasped my shoulders.

A scream ripped from my throat as I yanked away from him, turned, and promptly tripped over my own feet.

Ebba, not quick to take her hand off her sword like Garret, swung her weapon.

The drunk's screams mingled with my own, and hot blood spurt onto the nape of my neck, raising the hairs on my arms as the man's body crashed to the ground.

"I only wanted to take her into the tavern! Have her talk to the barfae!" The drunk's voice was garbled.

"You'll do nothing of the sort," Ebba said. "Garret, take Princess Lana and Prince Finn back to the castle. I'll deal with this."

Garret's hand landed on my shoulder as he helped me to stand. Only when I was upright did I see the carnage Ebba had inflicted. Her sword had cut deep into the man's torso, and his guts fell onto the street.

I was no healer, but I knew there was no way to save him. She was staying behind to put him out of his misery.

A lump rose in my throat as I took in the carnage. I was grateful that Ebba had been there, ready to protect, but a loud voice in my head quickly drowned out the gratitude. It screamed over and over that I shouldn't have needed her aid. That I should have taken command of the situation and ordered the fae to leave to avoid unnecessary bloodshed. And if that hadn't worked that I, as a general, should have been able to protect myself.

WHEN MY FATHER HEARD WHAT HAD HAPPENED IN THE square, he demanded that the drunk fae be brought to justice. His angry bellows had echoed through the walls of Castle Phoenix, seemingly vibrating the marble itself, until Ebba returned and informed him she'd already taken care of it. Father increased her earnings and family's ration allotment on the spot.

Once he'd calmed down, my father suggested I rest for three days. It was strange, since I hadn't really been harmed in the incident—just a little scratched up and scared. But I figured he was taking proactive measures to ensure that I didn't jump back into things like nothing had happened, only to suffer from PTSD later. As the leader of a kingdom, he'd probably seen officers fall prey to such tendencies many times.

Whatever his reasoning, I took the days off with glee, contenting myself to walk the castle grounds with Naela, and read. The most strenuous activity I'd partaken in was deciding which of the rugs in my room to send Ebba as a personal thank you gift. It wasn't much, but after Naela ripped one apart, Tess had mentioned that they were extremely valuable. As I didn't make money in Faerie, a valuable possession was the best I could offer.

Nearly a week after Ration Day, things were back to normal. I'd just arrived at my father's chambers for our first meeting since my attack, and like usual, the door opened on its own accord.

I shut it behind me and looked around. My father wasn't there, so I went to the table in the back of the room and waited, knowing he would arrive from the sub-chamber. Sure enough, minutes later, the sound of stone grinding on stone filled my ears.

"So good to see you, Daughter," my father said as he rose through a circular hole in the ground. "I'm sorry to have kept you waiting. I was just finishing up with a pet project." He gave me a wry grin.

I'd asked him once what he did down there. He had replied that it was private and that his sub-chamber was the only spot in the castle that he kept for himself. Not even a maid was allowed in to clean it. I figured that a ruler who ran a kingdom constantly on the brink of devastation deserved a space to be alone, so I didn't ask again.

"How are you feeling?" my father asked, stepping off the stone dais as it clicked into place.

"Well. These last three days off were exactly what I needed," I replied truthfully.

The previous weeks of nonstop training had taken

a toll on my body. And while I was stronger than I'd ever been, my muscles had relished the break.

"I'm glad to hear it. You must take rest when you can. Plus, it is beneficial for your Major First Order to lead the forces without you every once in a while. Much like when I let Casimir orchestrate Ration Day."

My father moved toward the firlon and waved his hand over it. The blazing fire transformed from a blend of dancing reds, oranges, and yellows to a bright, electric blue and then back again.

"Would you come here, Lana?"

I rose from my seat, excitement coursing through me. The firlon was one of my favorite enchanted objects.

"While you were mending, Finn and I met. I hope you don't mind him taking on your responsibilities, but I will admit it was good to speak to another one of my children. I must try for more one-on-one connections in the future."

I shook my head in answer. I didn't mind if he talked to his other children. In fact, I preferred it. Recently, I'd detected hints of jealousy from some of my siblings, and I had a hunch that my growing closeness to our father was the reason.

He seemed pleased by my reaction. "I didn't take you for the jealous type, but you never know. You wouldn't be the first of my children to have such a streak."

Like Prince Casimir, who I'd barely seen since the Successional. The prince was keeping himself busy, training for who-knew-what in a separate training area. His personal guards and the Feathered Fae were the only ones allowed to see his sessions, so the rest of us had no idea what they were doing. I'd felt awkward around him since he brought up marriage, so I preferred this arrangement to trying to smooth things over.

"Finn is a charming young man," my father continued. "I can see how you were friends before you arrived in Faerie, and I'm proud to call him my son. He, like you, informed me that training was going well. Since you both seem confident with the progress the group has made, it's time to send you on your first assignment."

My eyes widened. I'd been wondering when my siblings and I would undertake a mission, but I hadn't expected we'd talk of it today.

He gestured to the firlon. "This is Zatus—the largest city in the Free Realm, and your destination. As you can see, it is a coastal settlement on the other side of Faerie."

I studied the flames. The vast city reminded me of photos I'd seen of small Italian fishing towns, though much larger and with no vehicles clogging up the streets.

"The journey itself will be difficult—a week long one-way—and your first test. Your second will begin when you get there. I require hired swords for when we march on Buyan. That is some time away, but these things must be arranged with Masters of Swords far in advance to allow armies the time to travel." My father paused, his golden eyes boring into mine, assessing me.

"Lastly, I wish for you to make one more stop after you have secured our hired swords. It will be dangerous."

"We can do it, Father," I assured him.

His lips curled up. "Very well. I would like you to lead a team into the False Realm and persuade at least one giant clan to fight for us. When fae battle, it is best to have a varied force."

My mouth opened and closed and then opened again. Giants? An image of the giantess from the Successional flashed in my mind. I gulped as my confidence plummeted.

"I'm not going alone, right? Finn will be there? And some guards?" This was *exactly* the type of scenario where I preferred Finn by my side. Meeting new people and persuading them to do what he wanted was his specialty.

"Naturally. Finn, Crystal, all of your siblings, if you so desire—except Casimir, of course." A weary sigh gusted from him. "Although I'm sure he would like nothing more than to join, the heir and the second to the throne cannot travel together, for obvious reasons. You will also have a retinue of guards of your choosing."

I glanced into the firlon. A thousand lives flashed before me. Zatus was a city unlike any I'd seen, a true adventure. Butterflies rose in my stomach in a familiar mixture of excitement and nerves.

"When should we leave?"

"Once the horses are prepared and enough food is packed, you may depart. The true question is, when will *you* be ready?" He eyed me cautiously.

It was clear he didn't want to force me into a situation for which I wasn't prepared. But I was ready to prove myself.

"When I return to the training room, I'll ask my siblings and a few guards I trust if they'll join me. We'll leave in two days, if that's all right with you?"

My father nodded, a smile brimming. "Ambitious and eager. The Masters of Swords in Zatus won't know what hit them."

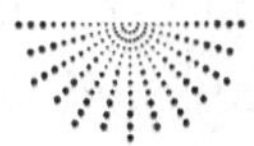

CHAPTER NINE

I f Garret lied about this being the last mountain, I may just have to shove him off a cliff, I thought, pushing my horse forward. The burn in my thighs had gotten so bad in the last couple of hours that I prayed they'd go completely numb to save me more pain.

Horseback riding had never been my thing. My only small comfort after a week of riding was the knowledge that I wasn't alone.

Out of the group traveling to Zatus, only the ten guards I'd chosen to accompany us, and Crystal were not complaining that they'd be walking bow-legged for months. In fact, those equestrian-loving arses were all laughing up a storm in the front of the group. Each one guided their own horse, *and* another beast weighed down with supplies, while my siblings and I languished behind.

As had become my routine when my hands needed a break from gripping the reins, my hand dipped into my side satchel. I fingered the cool, white bones at the bottom. Although I hadn't delved into the powers that the fae insisted Kate's and Kumar's bones held, I also hadn't been able to stomach leaving them behind while I explored Faerie for the first time. So they'd journeyed with us. During the exhausting, week-long trek west, they'd comforted me. A part of me wondered if Kate's healer magic was keeping me from passing out across my horse.

I bit my lip, trying to hold back the emotion that thinking about Kate and Kumar always brought to the surface, and moved my hand unthinkingly to the other side of the satchel. Pressed up against the leather, so as not to muss its fringe, was a feather. I stroked the soft plumage on autopilot, hoping it would calm the tide of sadness rising within me.

Before we'd left Lyonesse, my father had handed me the token—one of Xerxes' black tail feathers—and mentioned that it would allow me to withdraw gold from Zatus' coinary, the fae version of a bank. It was an odd way of doing business, but this was Faerie, and I'd much rather carry a feather across Faerie than multiple chests of gold. The extra horses were already bogged down with supplies that we'd need for bargaining with the giants.

A screech came from on high. I glanced up to find that Naela and Kane had joined us once again.

"They look like they're having a grand time," Finn commented, riding up beside me to watch our hawks swoop and dive in the wind. "I miss going out with you, Naela, and Kane. I know we don't get a lot of free time, but we really should try to make more of an effort when we return to Lyonesse."

I nodded. Although Naela and I had walked the castle grounds together on my three days off, it hadn't been enough. Hawking was an activity I would do daily, if given the chance. However, since I had arrived in Faerie, I was pleased if I managed once a week.

"I agree, we need to make the time."

The horses ahead of us crested the mountain and halted.

"Geez, you guys, hurry up!" Crystal called back, walking her horse along the snow-dusted ridge and twirling the reins in her hand. "Thank goodness we didn't put you oafs in charge of guiding the extra horses. We'd *never* make it to Zatus."

God, sometimes I wanted to strangle her.

Behind us, Maria, Gio, and Dak muttered about where Crystal could stick her reins. Someone else groaned from the jostling of their horse on the uneven road. I urged my horse forward and did my best to refrain from whimpering.

Arlo, Himari, Wikolia, and Victoria had probably been smart to decline my invitation to join us. Especially considering that none of them had ever ridden

—or in the case of Wikolia, *touched*—a horse before. Even if they had to put up with Meegra, at least they wouldn't be enduring weeks of sitting funny, which was more than I could say for myself.

When Finn and I finally caught up, the guards had dismounted and were already pulling out lunch.

"I'll grab our meal," Finn said, redirecting his horse toward the food.

Sinkers be praised, I thought, and then smirked at my use of the fae phrase. Their lingo was growing on me.

I dismounted carefully, my legs shaking like jello when my feet hit the ground. Slowly, I shuffled over to join Gio and Dak, who had basically collapsed off their steeds, to sit on a snow-dusted log.

Gio winced as he shifted to make room for me. "Does anyone else's ass feel like it's covered in blisters?" His hands gesticulated in the stereotypical Italian fashion as he spoke.

Dak chuckled without humor. "You're not alone, brother."

"No, you're definitely not. I'm not sure that I'll be able to sit right ever again," I whined.

Gio patted my shoulder sympathetically. "Well, at least we're almost there. Thank goodness Zatus is a port town."

As a diviner witch, Gio's magic and body would gain strength as we drew closer to Zatus. Although no one else would benefit from the proximity to water, the rest of us were still looking forward to visiting the foreign city. Not only was it somewhere new, but the town was rumored to be divided and run by fae mafias, which was pretty interesting.

"I heard they have the *best* taverns in Zatus," Dak added, prompting a grin from Gio. The pair had frequented the taverns in Lyonesse a couple of times, usually with Ryker and Ronan, Kumar's old guard, escorting them.

"What do you mean by the best?" I asked.

"Hot fae ladies, good drink, and music is what my boy means!" Gio twirled his arms around like a belly dancer and wagged his eyebrows.

I laughed. "You dance?"

His bottomless brown eyes widened. "It's one of my favorite things. Especially if I have an attractive and talented partner." Gio's gaze sought Ebba, who was brushing off her horse and chatting with Sai and Ronan.

Poor Ebba was *always* fending off either Gio or Finn.

"Well, I can't say I'll be able to dance after all this riding, but getting out sounds fun. Can I join you guys?"

My brothers' mouths fell open, which I should have expected. I rarely socialized outside of training sessions and meals. Many of my siblings, however, were involved in the weekly card games with the guards, trips into the city of Lyonesse, or faeball matches on the castle grounds. I just didn't know how they had the energy for it all. But traveling through Faerie kind of felt like a vacation—even if it was for diplomatic purposes. I wanted to explore a wee bit.

"We need to get out of town more often!" Gio exclaimed. "Lana's bar hopping? Zatus isn't going to know what hit them!"

"What's that, now?" Finn asked, joining our trio and handing each of us a sandwich and an apple.

"Lana wants to get crazy tonight. We're going out, bro!" Gio shouted, his eyes twinkling with mischief.

I rolled my eyes, but couldn't stop my lips from quirking upward. Gio was such a ham.

"It's a bloody miracle!" Finn's hand covered his mouth in exaggerated shock. "Do you blokes know how hard I had to beg to get her to go to a pub with me when we were at university? I had about a five percent success rate. Clearly, she likes you two better."

"Can't say I blame her," Gio quipped.

"I just want to see Gio dance," I said, trying to steer the conversation away from my hermit nature.

It worked, and the conversation flowed naturally to speculating on what we'd find in the town. Too soon, Garret informed us that we needed to hop back on our horses if we were to make it to Zatus before sundown and find a decent place to stay.

The next day, we'd do what we came to do and hit the streets of Zatus to purchase an army of hired swords.

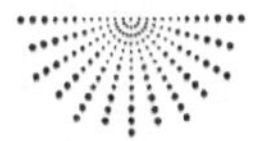

CHAPTER TEN

My heart rate kicked up the moment we entered the tavern.

For a moment, the music, lively and fast, like the Celtic reels I'd grown up hearing in the village pub, transported me back home. But one scan of the room assured me I was still far from home.

The tavern by our inn was packed with all types of fae. Those with blue scales and wings. A few were indistinguishable from people from the Old Land, until you took in their attire, which was not modern at all. Some were short as a child, others brawny as a bodybuilder. Even a few chimera, half human, half animal, all in one form, milled about.

A dozen people swayed on a dance floor. Although I'd proclaimed early that I wasn't a dancer, which was true as the sky was blue, the tune was so familiar it made my tender legs yearn to join them.

"Feels like home, doesn't it, Lan?" An easy grin lined Finn's face. He was in his element, having fun and letting loose.

Though it was undeniably strange, there *was* a lot about this tavern in the heart of Zatus that eased me. I inhaled deeply. The scent of malty ale and fruited booze filled my nostrils.

"Aye, it does." My tone took on the cadence of rural Ireland. Four years in the city had tried, and nearly succeeded, in training it out of me. Nearly—us country folk were stubborn.

Gio and Ryker detached themselves from the group and beelined toward the bar, and I followed them. In the past, frequenting pubs was an awkward experience. Being in a tavern in Faerie when we looked so thoroughly human would probably be even worse. Still, something propelled me to join in on the fun, to bond with my siblings and make memories. I was going to make the best of the night, and a wee bit of liquid courage never hurt in that department.

I sidled up to the bar with Finn, and we took in what was on offer. Many of the bottles looked far more elaborate than your normal whiskey or gin. Some bottles even had tiny wings floating inside, the sight of which wracked my spine with shivers. No thanks on that one.

"What do you think the chances are they have tequila?" Maria joined us, the yearning in her voice obvious.

Finn wrapped his arm around her and pulled her closer, so that she stood between us. "I'd say slim to none, Sis. But whatever they have—whatever you want—is on me."

"He always was the generous sort," I quipped.

Maria snorted delicately. We did not earn money in Faerie, but Father had given us all pouches of gold for our travels. I wouldn't be surprised if Finn spent his entire pouch tonight. Easy come, easy go.

"Correction," Garret's voice boomed over the music. "The first round is on me."

I turned to find him standing directly behind me, mercurial gray eyes twinkling. "You sure?"

He actually worked for his money. I didn't want him to feel obligated, but also knew that sometimes people just liked to treat others.

"It isn't every day I get to enjoy an evening out with so many royals," Garret replied, his fingers tapping on the bar with the beat of the music. "And as you say in the Old Land, 'we're not here for a long time, we're here for a good time'."

I burst out laughing. "Where the hell did you hear that line?"

Garret shrugged. "I don't know. One of those books the Feathered Fae brought back from the Old Land. Does it matter? It got a smile out of all you three, and that was well worth it."

"Smooth," Maria purred, her gaze flashing up at him between lowered lashes.

Garret's cheeks turned bright red, which only made Maria's smirk grow. She liked getting the best of the men and it didn't matter much how she did it either.

"So, what's good here?" I asked.

Garret rattled off a list of drinks he enjoyed. Maria and Finn ordered first. Both let me try some of theirs, which I promptly declared too strong and settled on elven wine, a staple at every feast at Castle Phoenix.

Once everyone ordered we got to chatting about our journey and how happy we were not to be sitting horseback any longer. Maria, always one to be on the move, soon grew bored with standing around and yammering. She beamed when a hot fae, definitely pixie judging by the wings, made eyes at her. My rumbler sister had spotted her target.

"It's been fun, but I see something that could be a lot *more* fun. See you around." Maria begged off, her ample hips shaking with the beat of music as she left.

"Bloody hell, have you ever seen anyone dance like that, Lan?" Finn asked, his eyes wide.

"How does she make folk music look sexy?" It was a mystery to me, the woman who struggled to make anything look sexy.

"You know, for a rumbler she rather resembles a diviner. Wouldn't you say?"

I smirked. Finn had only known he was magical for a couple months, but already he was slipping into the supernatural world like he'd lived there all his life.

"You're right there," I replied. "Most rumblers aren't nearly so graceful. Too heavy footed."

"That's interesting," Garret mused. "That's not the case with earth fae. Many are graceful."

I rolled my eyes. "Surprise, surprise. The fae are great at *everything*. You get all the elements and other magic, which is already ridiculous, but then you get grace too?! Way to rub it in."

Garret's eyes crinkled at the corners. My stomach did a flip, and I looked back over the bar at the bottle containing wings. Instantly, the flame of desire that had sprung up was doused.

"Speaking of the fae getting everything," Finn finished his drink and set the glass down. "I see a lovely lady who seems to be getting some rather unwelcome attention. I should go save her."

He strode off, straight for Ebba and Gio, talking in a far corner. Ebba was not a woman to need saving, but Finn just couldn't help himself. When it came to the blonde guard, neither he nor Gio seemed to think straight.

"Will they ever give up?" I asked Garret with a chuckle.

"I'm surprised that Ebba hasn't demanded that they leave her alone already," Garret replied, his mirth equaling mine. "Maybe that's saying some-thing," he added after a moment's pause.

"What do you mean?"

"Maybe . . . Ebba is only playing hard to get and she actually likes one of them."

I cocked my head. It didn't seem likely, but since Garret knew Ebba better than me, maybe it was true.

"Perhaps." I took another swig of my wine. Compared to the wine father served during meetings, it was not so tasty. Actually, it burned like hell going down, but I took it as a cultural experience.

"So, the crowd here is . . . lively. What do you think they do with their time?" I pivoted to face the crowd. This was a game Finn and I often played at uni. It was always good for a laugh.

"You mean, their jobs?"

"Or their lives. Whichever. It's fun to make up stories about them." I grinned at Garret.

"I see. Well then, that fae," he leaned closer, so that I could feel his breath on my ear. A shiver tore up my spine. "She must be the wife of a mob boss. Her clothing screams status, and she holds herself like she's better than everyone else in the room, including our group — which she undoubtedly knows is full of important people."

My mouth had gone dry as he talked, so I whetted it with more wine. "How would she know that?"

We looked pretty haggard after a week of riding. Not to mention, none of us bore a Fullfeather crest. That had been intentional. We did not want to draw eyes in Zatus before we approached a Master of Sword.

"Only royalty, mafia bosses and their families, or Masters or Swords travel with guards. She might assume we're part of a mafia ring in another free city, but they all know each other well. If she's intelligent, which those shrewd eyes say she is, then she knows your royalty or someone very important."

"Hmm." I studied the woman. I had to agree with his assessment. The fae looked like she could read a room well. "Is there anywhere in Faerie where your rank does not matter?"

"Not really. Even among the most feral tribes in Beast Realm, there are leaders for every group." He turned to face me and set down his glass. "Is your home different?"

"It's the same, but yeah, a little different. Here the division feels more stark. Like I imagine how it was a few centuries ago in the Old Land. In those days, if you were born in a social class, you stayed there until death."

"It is kind of like that here too." Garret nodded. "Although there are exceptions. "

"Like what?"

"Fae can work their way up if their magic is powerful enough, or if they please someone high up enough. And of course there's marriage." He trailed off and then burst out laughing. "It seems we've attracted a bit of attention."

I followed his gaze to where the mafia wife sat. Her ice-blue eyes were narrowed on us. Her lips pursed with disdain.

"She doesn't like us being so close," Garret said.

I bristled. "Oh, yeah?"

Garret inched away from me, but I grabbed his hand before he could widen the gap. Something inside me did not want him to pull away.

"That's her problem, isn't it?" I gripped my glass tighter and slammed back the rest of the wine. Fire burned through me, as hot as the woman's gaze. I'd seen that look before on other women, those who thought Finn and I were together and that I wasn't worth his time. I gestured to the dance floor. "What do you say we go for a spin?"

Garret's eyebrows rose in shock. "You said you don't dance."

"I don't, but if she's going to stare, we might as well make it worth her time." With that, I grabbed his hand and dragged him across the room.

A low chuckle left his lips as we zigged and zagged between fae. The sound sent a shiver down my spine. Garret's large hand made mine feel so deliciously small. My heart thrummed excitedly. This was so unlike me, so impulsive. I didn't even mind that I'd soon be dancing in front of others, probably making myself look a fool. It felt amazing.

We passed where Ebba and Sai danced, drinks in hand. Either Ebba had removed herself from the

Fullfeather love triangle, or Sai had. My money was on the former. From the side of the room Gio and Finn watched, both clearly trying to get up the courage to ask about if they might cut in.

At that moment Finn caught sight of me. His eyes widened as a smile crossed his face. I looked away, slightly embarrassed, but also enthralled. Maybe it was the wine, but something about this tavern made me want to let loose. Something more than sticking it to the mafia wife. When we reached the dance floor, I twirled toward Garret and began to sway, somewhat awkwardly, but I couldn't help it. I wasn't a dancer!

"I'll show you the dance. Take my hands." His tone was low, raspy. It sent my heart straight into my throat. Oh, Sinkers . . .

Perhaps I'd been too brash. Too forward. I did not want to look like a fool in front of him, or anyone else here. Gentle swaying, I could do. But a real dance? Well, that was asking an awful lot.

"Garret, I have no idea what I'm doing."

"That's new," he teased. "I thought you knew what you were doing all the time."

I stuck my tongue out at him and was about to retort when he took my hands in his. And then we were off. My breath whooshed out of me as Garret led me around the dance floor in a lively jig. It was nothing like the club dances of the Old Land, more like traditional Irish dance with less jumping. We spun and twirled. At one point I got so dizzy that I collapsed into his chest with a laugh.

"You okay?" he asked, softly.

I looked up. His gray eyes bore down on me, hot as fire. Somewhere deep inside me, something quintessentially female begged me to reach up, take his lips and mine.

But I couldn't. Not here. Not now. Maybe never? I didn't know the rules of royalty dating a guard. Or if there even were any. I was too scared to ask. The fantasy of us was safe in my mind, but in the real world, it could shatter. Plus, I was nearing drunk.

"The elven wine is strong," I said, my voice cracking slightly.

Garret backed away. "Is this —"

"I-it's fine." I stammered, unable to help myself. I was having fun, even if I wasn't sure what we were doing was appropriate. But did it matter? Hell, it felt so damn good. "Teach me another dance."

A smile lifted his full lips. I could tell he was about to ask again, but I shook my head. "I should know how to dance. I'm a princess."

"You should know the *formal* dances," Garret replied.

"Oh yeah, because there seems to be a lot of formal dancing going on in here."

"What's going on in here is . . . slightly improper." He gestured to the mafia wife again. Now she was flirting with two men, her hands on one's thigh and the other's cheek.

"Is one her husband?"

"I doubt it. Maybe she's trying to show us up. Show who can be the most daring."

"Daring? Is that what we are?" I chuckled and turned my attention back on Garret only to find him staring at me, his gaze full of desire. Heat flooded my cheeks.

Slowly, his hand lifted to cup my cheek. I thought he might want to kiss me, and while I had so many doubts and questions, I could not help but hope that he did. Time stilled as the bar swirled around us.

Then his lips drew nearer, making my breath hitch. My nostrils filled with his scent, tinged with sweat from dancing. Unable to stop myself, I eased closer too.

"Garret, I—"

"Yeah, Lan! Show us that dance again!" Gio's voice rang from the sidelines. I could hear the humor there. People were watching.

I nearly turned away, embarrassed, but Garret caught me and eased me back toward him.

"Forget them," he whispered. "Let's dance."

I couldn't say no. Not with his eyes pinning me, his hand clenching me and making every cell in my body tingle. So I didn't.

And we spun once more.

CHAPTER ELEVEN

Rap! Rap! Rap!

"No one is home," I croaked, and then winced at the sound of my voice. So loud! "Go away!"

Three more knocks came in rapid succession. I covered my head with a pillow, attempting to block out the offending light streaming in from the window just as much as the damnable knocking. What a day to wake up with a case of drinker's remorse.

Blessedly, whoever the annoying person was, stopped making a racket. Footsteps led away from my room. I exhaled. Thank all the Sinkers and baby Jesus and Buddha, I thought as my eyelids fluttered closed. I'd only had three drinks at the tavern, but it had been enough to make me feel like death. It wasn't right. I shouldn't be feeling this terrible.

I closed my eyes, trying to reclaim sleep. I'd almost

succeeded when the door creaked open. I stiffened beneath my covers as Sai thanked the innkeeper.

My jaw tightened. Sinkers alive. Go away.

"Good morning, General!" Sai chirped and yanked the pillow off my head.

I whimpered and batted her away weakly. If it had been almost anyone else, I probably would have raged, but Sai had saved my butt many times. This rude display deserved a pass. After all, I would have been toast during the Successional without her and Garret.

Garret . . .

My right hand twitched as a memory from the night before flashed through an alcohol muddled haze. His hand brushing mine. The pair of us holding tight for a moment before pulling away.

Had that really happened?

"How are you feeling?" Sai perched on my bed and handed me a glass of water. Her violet eyes looked especially bright today. Clearly, *she* hadn't overindulged last night. "You had *a lot* of fun at the tavern."

I bolted upright and my head spun as water sloshed onto the blanket. "*Meaning?*"

Sai cocked her head and her white hair, which she usually wore pulled back, cascaded over her shoulder in soft waves. "Just that you were more outgoing than usual. Talking to everyone, singing with the rest of the tavern, dancing for hours.

Sinkers, you even got Garret out there to dance. I've *never* seen that."

I closed my eyes and chugged the remaining water. Memories prompted by Sai's words trickled back with each gulp. Garret and me dancing alongside Finn, Ebba, Gio, and an attractive fae girl. Garret holding me tight, me twirling his silky, black hair in my fingers, his lips coming closer.

My gut flip-flopped, but the visions faded to black before I could catch how it ended. I tried to recover it, but in the next flash of recollection, we merely sat at a table. Dak was there too, chatting with a group of fae. Everyone else was dancing or at the bar. Garret brushed my hand and held it.

"I have to talk to Dak." I lunged out of bed. My head swirled, and I blinked, disoriented for a few seconds. "Wait. Is Garret up yet?"

There was no way I was going to question Dak with Garret around. Talk about awkward.

"Ha, not yet. He's nearly as bad off as you. Ronan is rousing him. Dak's already downstairs eating."

I rushed to get ready, and fumbled down the stairs to find my brother, who looked as chipper as Sai, sitting alone at a table.

"Morning, Dak. How are you?" I tried to seem natural, though my persistent blinking at the bright lights almost certainly suggested things were off. Acting was not my calling.

"Hey, Lana. I'm good. You?" There was no judgment in his voice, none of the teasing I would have expected from Gio or Finn, which made my next question easier.

"Um . . . I'm okay. Hey . . . so last night—Garret and I were dancing and then joined you at the table. I can't really remember what we were talking about, but something tells me it was important. *Super* important. I think I had too much bloody wine. Can you help me . . . errr . . . fill in the gaps?" I rubbed the nape of my neck, fully recognizing how ridiculous I sounded.

Dak gestured at the rickety chair across from him, and I took a seat. "To be honest, I wasn't really listening to your conversation. I was surrounded by fae who were mesmerized by me. Apparently, they've never seen an albino."

He took a drink of his beverage—juice, by the sickly sweet smell of it—and set the cup down, his eyes leveling me. "But I know what you're getting at. You and Garret held hands for a while. You guys seemed into each other. And happy."

He shrugged as if to say 'hey, you could do worse.'

I groaned. Of course I could do worse. I could do a *hell* of a lot worse. Garret was a great guy and undeniably attractive. But now?! *Now* is when I find someone I'm attracted to, and he seems to like me back? Talk about shite timing!

Things were hard enough with me not knowing

what I was doing as the General of Lyonesse half the time. And Garret was a subordinate in my army. Would that cause issues? Was it legal? Or smart? Sinkers, why had I given into desire when surely there were rules about this sort of thing?!

I grabbed a pastry shaped like a sea monster from the platter in the middle of the table and put it on a plate. Maybe if I ate it fast enough, none of my confusing feelings could bubble up.

"I wouldn't worry about it," Dak assured me. "You weren't the only one flirting with a guard. Crystal and Ryker have been getting pretty close. And of course, Finn and Gio wouldn't leave Ebba alone."

While that was true, it didn't make me feel much better.

"Morning, General Party Animal." Gio's lively Italian accent shot through me.

I turned around to find him grinning so hard that someone could probably lose a euro in his dimples. I was about to tell him to shut it, when I caught sight of two others.

Ryker and a crimson-cheeked Garret followed my diviner brother. My stomach sank.

"Morning," I mumbled, embarrassed by my ex-guard's discomfort.

"An enchanting white-haired fae tells us you aren't feeling so well, Lan? It seems you and Garret here took it too hard, too fast last night, huh?" Gio wagged his eyebrows playfully.

Oh no, I was so not doing this.

I shot out of my chair and marched from the room. Finn was descending the stairs as I strode past, but I charged right by him, needing fresh air.

"Lana?"

"Not now."

I shoved the inn's front door open. The city's stench of fish and rotted fruit assaulted me. My stomach heaved, but that didn't stop me from running down the street to a crumbling fountain in the middle of an abandoned square and sitting on the edge.

My face flamed as embarrassment threatened to drown me. I could not handle this right now. Not with all the other crap I had going on. I was trying to get a grasp on not one, but *two* leadership roles in Faerie culture. Me. Someone who was no natural at taking charge, or even interacting with others.

I released a frustrated sigh. The bloody deck was completely stacked against me. No wonder I was having issues. Something had to give.

I shook my head. Garret was great, and I was totally attracted to him, but now was not the time for a relationship. I needed to focus on myself.

My stomach rumbled. I regretted that I'd stormed out of the dining area without my pastry. Maybe I could find something in the square? Father had given us each a small allowance of coin to carry. Mine jingled in my pocket, ready to spend. I stood and took in the dingy square, my hand on my stomach, trying to calm its persistent growls.

"You left this."

I turned to find Ebba holding out the sea monster shaped pastry, wrapped in a cloth napkin.

"Thanks," I mumbled, taking it and sitting down on the fountain's edge again.

Uninvited, Ebba took a seat next to me. "Don't be embarrassed, General. Elven wine gets the best of everyone sometimes. And as for Gio, he *never* knows when to stop. Not to mention he has absolutely no room to talk. Did you see how shamelessly he was flirting with me last night?"

A cough-laugh flew from my mouth, causing me to choke on my pastry. Ebba unhooked a canteen from her hip and handed it over. After a few sips, I could breathe normally again.

I turned to face her. "You know, I'm not really good at this sort of thing. Relationship talk . . . mostly because I have almost no experience. But something tells me you can relate to me on that." I paused and took another sip of water while I tried to sort through the hundreds of thoughts tumbling around in my mind.

"I guess I feel like what I did last night was out of line. I'm supposed to be a general in charge of an army. How can I be taken seriously if I get wasted and flirt with my guard?" My mortification swelled once more and my head flew into my hands.

"This is just another complication I brought on myself."

There was a pause, and I peeked up to make sure that Ebba, unwilling to deal with my moaning, hadn't simply left.

She was still there, her dagger-sharp green eyes taking me in cooly. An uncomfortable minute later, she finally spoke.

"You're right. I'm not great at this either. Being a soldier means I'm around a lot of guys, and they tend to avoid relationship chat. But I have to ask . . . do you like Garret? Or was it just a drunken night?"

I ran my hand over the nape of my neck. At the rate I was going, I wouldn't have skin there soon. "Does it matter? Is that sort of thing allowed?"

Ebba shrugged. "It would be unusual for a royal to end up with a commoner, but it's not totally unheard of."

I bit my lip and shoved down the hope that had surged upward at her words. "I'm attracted to him, but I really believe that now is not the best time."

My stomach hardened, my body revolting against my brain, but I pressed on. "I'm struggling to find out how I belong here. I feel like I should focus on that."

Ebba stood and brushed off her pants. "Well then, I guess you've already decided. You do you, General."

I cocked my head at the phrase. It was so not fae.

"I read it in one of the books from the Old Land. It's catchy," Ebba said with a shrug. "Anyway, I don't see Garret going anywhere. Later, if the time is right, perhaps it will happen."

I nodded, unsure of how to respond or how to proceed.

Ebba studied me intently, as if she was trying to read my mind. "I'll tell you what, I'll head back and tell the men to shut it. In the meantime, you pull yourself together and meet us outside. If you truly want to discover your path as general, we'd better get going."

She walked away, leaving me sitting on the fountain, my mouth hanging open.

THE LARGE SIZE OF OUR GROUP WORKED TO MY advantage as we rode through the streets to meet a Master of Swords named Gory. Garret and Ryker, who had both been to Zatus before, led the group. I happily took up the rear with Ebba and Maria at my sides. Even with the distance between us, I could see the nape of Garret's neck, as bright red as Crystal's hair. We'd barely looked at each other since I returned to the inn.

Our troop had arrived in Zatus late the night before, and after a quick dinner at the inn, we'd walked to the tavern in the dark. The same bloody tavern where I'd gotten wrecked. Ugh! So, today was my first experience really seeing the city.

While it was a welcome distraction from my

conflicted thoughts and emotions, it was also decidedly unpleasant.

If Lyonesse was shabby, Zatus was ten times worse. Rats ran through the streets. Litter and decaying fruit lined the gutters. Most of the buildings had clearly once been impressive, but were now in various states of disrepair. While our inn had seemed subpar the night before, compared to what I was seeing now, it was absolutely grand.

The creatures who lived here were harder, too. Unlike the subjects of Lyonesse, the fae of Zatus did not seem to like us one bit. They watched our retinue walk by, their eyes narrowed and lips down-turned.

"Why does everyone look pissed off? And why is the city so dirty?" I asked, leaning toward Ebba so none of the onlookers could hear me.

Maria had clearly been wondering the same thing, because she inched closer to hear Ebba's answer.

"The Free Realm cities each have a different governing style. Some have a true democracy, where the fae vote for their leaders, and every vote is considered. Others are more in the style of a republic—like I've read that humans had in ancient Rome." Ebba paused to glare menacingly at someone who walked too close to our retinue. Her hand strayed to her sword, and the person scampered off.

Ebba smirked and continued. "In Zatus, their governing style failed terribly. It used to be a true democracy until gangs rigged the system and took it over. Now warring factions control various parts of the city and its surrounding areas. It's anarchy here most of the time, which makes the people hard and distrusting."

"Wow, that sucks," Maria said, wrinkling her nose. I had to agree.

"Yes, it does, but it also makes it a great place for leaders from other kingdoms or free cities to purchase hired swords." Ebba quirked an eyebrow. "There are nicer places in the Free Realm, where you'd receive a more appropriate welcome. A couple cities you might even call utopian. But we would have no hope of hiring soldiers there."

I frowned. I didn't love the idea of buying hired swords from gangs, but to save the people of Lyonesse, the people I was very fond of, I would do it.

"They aren't given ranks in our army, are they?" Maria asked, crossing herself as she glanced warily at a group of haggard male fae who were staring her down.

Ebba laughed. "Sinkers no! The hired swords are the first soldiers we send into battle. Because of the risk, the price for their service is extremely high. Though, all of them understand what they're getting into. Many have been doing this for years. Some are second generation swords. This is the work that feeds their families."

Like a job, then, I thought, reframing the idea of a gang member to something more palatable.

Ahead, Ryker turned down a narrow side street. We rode almost to the end of the lane, when he stopped before a nondescript door riddled with holes. He caught my gaze pointedly.

"I meant to bring this up at breakfast, but . . . it didn't seem the right time. So I'm going to warn you now," Ryker said when I joined him. "The Master of Swords you're meeting with, Gory, is a spriggan. He's rough around the edges, but notoriously cunning. He'll take us for as much coin as he can get."

I knew about spriggans from the Successional. I didn't look forward to dealing with one again.

"King Oberon has assured land rights to the masters of swords who assist Lyonesse," Ryker continued. "He's also given us five chests of gold with which to bargain per Master, not to exceed twenty chests total. As someone who's witnessed these negotiations before, I counsel you to start with two chests. Try not to go over four for anyone, Master—we don't want to set a precedent of over-paying. It's traditional for half to be paid after an agreement is reached, and the other half after the mission."

"Understood," I said. "Anything else I should know?"

Ryker exhaled a long breath. "It's our hope that we can strike a favorable deal with Gory. He has a large band of experienced swords. Hiring them would eliminate the need to speak to any other masters of swords. The fewer ears who hear of our mission, the better."

So I needed to seal the deal quickly. No pressure.

"That being said, don't tell them the *details* about the expedition," Ebba added, sidling up next to me. "All you have to say is there will be a skirmish, lives surely lost, and that it is a matter of one kingdom against another. We don't need people spreading word that the Princess General of Lyonesse is walking about Zatus, spouting off plans to assassinate the Queen of Buyan. They might guess, probably will, but we don't have to be forthcoming."

Ryker nodded his agreement. "Be aware that masters of swords generally will only speak to the highest-ranking person in the room—or royalty. They also don't allow a full regiment inside their chambers."

I tensed. "What? I thought we'd all be together."

"Most of our troop will remain outside and guard the cache of supplies and horses," Ryker replied with an understanding smile. "Naela and Kane won't be permitted inside either. The fae of the Free Realm don't trust familiars."

I turned to Naela, who had been riding on her specialized perch rigged to the back of my horse.

"Naela, up." I pointed to the roof, and she launched herself off the perch and flew high to land on a crumbling statue.

Finn gestured for Kane to do the same, and a

second later, both hawks stared down at our group. This way, we would be assured they were out of harm's way if a mob fight broke out—something I wouldn't be surprised to hear, after riding through the city.

Ryker nodded approvingly. "Garret, Ebba, Ronan, Sai, and I will accompany you inside, but like I said, we shall remain quiet." He swung off his horse.

I gulped and dismounted too. "Finn? Will you stand by me? Help, if I need it?"

Finn nodded and moved toward the door alongside me. Ryker positioned himself at my other side, and Garret winged Finn. Garret's nearness, the unsaid words, vibrated between us. I pulled in a trembling breath. Thankfully, Ryker's hand pounded on the door, announcing our presence before I could blurt out anything stupid.

We waited as footsteps approached, echoing from what seemed to be some distance away.

I gulped softly and straightened my shoulders. It was time to show Faerie and Father that I was a capable leader.

The hole-riddled door squealed open, and a wizened fae with a hunched back and gnarled hands poked his head out.

"Princess General Lana Fullfeather of Lyonesse is here to see Gory," Ryker boomed, his chest puffed out.

If I didn't know how big of a teddy bear he was, I would have cowered.

The old fae nodded and opened the door wider, allowing us into a space that smelled like mold and smoke. My nose wrinkled as we followed him down a dank hallway. Every ten meters or so, a guard appeared out of nowhere, hidden perfectly in an alcove until we drew up right next to them. Gory was well protected . . . probably a fae with many enemies.

My hand found the phoenix feather in my side

satchel. I stroked the reassuring plumage, and my racing heart slowed.

Finally, we came to a door with a raven etched into its gleaming wood. Upon first glance, the image of the non-magical bird surprised me. Then again, ravens were known for their cunning. As were spriggans.

Perhaps it wasn't such an odd choice.

The hunched fae knocked, and immediately, the portal cracked open. A massive soldier filled the doorway. It took everything I had not to recoil at the sight of him.

His face was littered with scars, and his lips were little more than burned bits of skin. Muscles bulged beneath his leather tunic, and a sword gleamed in his twisted hand. This fae had certainly seen a battle or two.

"Princess General Fullfeather of Lyonesse is here for Master Gory," the old fae wheezed.

A pleasant scent filled my nostrils. I blinked as my eyes adjusted to the light. The room before me was grand, with blue, green, and white tiling reminiscent of southern Spain, and a large fireplace. A man in a huge red chair sat next to the fire, drinking a goblet of wine despite the early hour.

I'd seen a spriggan during the Successional, yet Gory's appearance still caught me off guard. With a child's head atop a withered old man's body, a spriggan's appearance was a gruesome juxtaposition.

Gory's face looked like he'd be about eight, although his gnarled hands and stilted gait suggested he was much older.

"Princess General Lana, correct?" Gory's voice was deep and rumbly.

I pulled my shoulders back and stepped forward. "That's right."

Gory nodded appraisingly and gestured to the seat across from him.

I made my way to it, my feet feeling as if they were traveling through mud. Finn followed me, content to hang his arm over the top of the chair that I occupied, like a hawk over his kill.

"This is my brother, Finn Fullfeather, third in line for the throne of Lyonesse, and Major First Order."

Gory snapped his fingers, and five guards emerged from the darkness of the room. "Bring more chairs. I assume those not in soldier's attire are King Oberon's children. I will not have you standing as the help does."

The Master of Swords ensured that my siblings and I had all we needed—drinks, blankets to cover our legs from the cold, and even snacks. Once we were settled in, we got down to business.

"Princess General, tell me why the King of Lyonesse has sent you." Gory leaned back in his chair and smiled like we were old friends. "What damage would he like done for him?"

His aura was nonthreatening, but Ryker had

warned me that this spriggan was cunning. I sat up straighter, hoping to project the illusion that I'd done this a million times before. Negotiations always made me nervous, and this one had high stakes.

"The King of Lyonesse requests an army of swords for hire."

"An entire army, then? Not simply an assassin?" His eyes hardened, and Gory set his wine glass down with a thunk.

I stiffened. The abrupt change in his attitude was jarring. His guise was already down. Thank the Sinkers the guards had prepared me for it.

"An army," I reiterated. "There's no need for an assassin."

At least not from you.

Gory's eyes narrowed. "Very well, then. Tell me, how much is the King of Lyonesse willing to pay for this army? It had better be more than the last time he made me an offer. My worth has increased since then, seeing as I provided such excellent results."

Last time? Why hadn't my father, or anyone else, told me the crown had approached Gory before?

I shot a look at Ryker, whose eyebrows were furrowed. It seemed he, too, was in the dark.

"Two chests of gold?" My voice rose into a question, and I cringed internally.

The spriggan smiled, sensing my weakness. "During her recent visit, Meegra and I settled on two chests. And all she desired were a few of my best soldiers on retainer. She hasn't even collected yet. It's the best deal I've ever made."

My lips pressed together. What in the world was he talking about?

"But *you*, Princess General—you need an entire army, and you condescend to offer me only two chests of gold? Why must you mock me so?" He paused and fiddled with his glass of wine. "For an army, I'll be needing at least seven chests of gold."

Meegra had been here asking for soldiers lately? Why hadn't my father just asked her to do this when she was here?

It wouldn't be a trial for *you* then, a small voice in the back of my head whispered. I clenched my jaw and wracked my brain for what to say next.

Apparently, I'd been silent for too long, as Crystal piped up.

"Seven chests of gold. Are you a madman? You're saying your band of hired swords is of higher caliber than the chimera army Poplin the centaur king purchased to save his lands from the pooka of Brazir? That's *quite* a claim."

Gory's eyes widened. Whatever Crystal was talking about, she'd hit the nail on the head.

"Of course not. I will not be supplying King Oberon with an army quite that large, nor half as brutal as the beasts."

"Brutal?" The word slipped out, and I cringed when Gory popped an eyebrow at me.

"Totally *savage*," Crystal said. "The chimera slaughtered all the pooka *and* ate them. Then they went to Brazir, the largest pooka kingdom, for vengeance because the pooka had killed King Poplin in battle and ravaged the areas. Of course, their reaction instigated the descendants of those pooka to become vengeful and vicious. That's why the fae talk about the famed pooka army of the *next* generation, but it all started with the chimera and *six* chests of gold." Crystal's brown eyes seared through Gory, who squirmed.

"Brazir . . . I've heard that."

"It was discussed in a general class our first year at Trinity." Finn grinned enthusiastically, unable to help himself from slipping into his teaching persona. "Brazir was more commonly known as Hy-Brasil, a mythological sunken land off West Ireland."

Gory coughed, and all eyes shifted to him. He'd pulled himself together, and instead of looking uncomfortable, annoyance flashed across his face.

"If you're done with the history lessons, I'd like to be getting back to our negotiations." He turned to me. "Princess General, as your sibling has rightfully pointed out, I will *not* be supplying King Oberon with an army of the same caliber as the chimera. Therefore, I'd like to renegotiate." His dark eyes bore into mine. "Five chests of gold."

"You said your army wasn't even half as brutal. But if anything is brutal, surely an army should be?" I challenged. "Three chests of gold, and land rights for yourself once your army wins. We'll give you two chests when you agree, and the other once the battle is over."

"They'll be following *you* into battle, isn't that right?"

I nodded.

Gory stood and went to a table at the side of the room, then pulled out a drawer and removed a roll of paper. "Would you join me, General?"

I approached the table with my shoulders square but trepidation in my heart. I did not trust this spriggan.

Gory unrolled the parchment.

It was a map of one large island and many other smaller ones surrounding it. Faerie, I suspected, although I'd never actually sought a map of my new home or studied one. There were no words on the map, only dozens of symbols.

"Tell me, General, if you expect my men to follow you, where is, say . . . the capital city of Buyan?"

Heat rose in my face. Clearly, Gory was on to us. But more than that, without words on the map, I had no idea where *anything* was located. Hell, even with words, I would have had to study it for several minutes before being able to find Buyan. And that was if they were in English. I knew the location of Lyonesse, vaguely. Buyan was a part of Sinkers Realm too, which meant it couldn't be that far away. But that was the extent of my knowledge.

Without my even asking, Finn joined me at the table. For once, he didn't look sure of himself. Although my embarrassment was mounting, it was a small comfort to know I wasn't alone.

Finn spread his hand over the map, flattening the curled-up edges and filling the room's deafening silence with the sound of unfurling paper. I knew he was just making a show of the motions while he quickly attempted to figure out where Buyan was.

"It's here." Crystal stepped forward and pinned her finger to a symbol of a leaf.

"As I thought." Gory nodded at Crystal before sliding his eyes back to me. His gaze roved over my tense jaw and bright red cheeks, sending chills up my spine.

Rolling the map back up, Gory replaced it, shut the drawer, and went back to his chair. After another tenuous minute of staring into the fire, he spoke.

"Princess General, it's clear you're as green as summer grass. Luckily, you seem to have subordinates who you can lean on . . ." He gave Crystal a curt nod. "Seeing as I look after the welfare of my men, this is my final negotiation. I'll be needing three chests in advance and two after the battle, no matter whether King Oberon's side wins or loses."

"But that's outrageous," I sputtered, my cheeks warming. "You—"

"*Also*," he cut me off. My fists clenched at the slight, but I said nothing. It would only draw attention to him not respecting me at all. "I require land rights within Lyonesse proper, not the surrounding wasteland. *All* of those stipulations will be met—that is, if my men decide to follow you at all."

His eyes bore through me. "You understand, don't you? We are but hired swords. As a respected Master of Swords in Zatus, I cannot commit lives to a general who knows so little. They must also agree. If they do, I expect the first payment to be made within two weeks, or the terms are void."

My hand found the nape of my neck. Gory was asking a lot more than Ryker had specified. But after the embarrassment of this morning and now this, I had to do *something* to ensure that I was in control.

Even if I didn't feel like that was the case.

"Deal," I said. "Speak with your men and send word to Lyonesse. If you agree, we'll transfer the gold then."

"I'll let you know," Gory said, his tone low and slightly menacing.

Can't wait, I thought, the pit in my stomach growing as I stood to leave.

MY FAILURE TO SEAL THE DEAL WITH GORY MEANT WE absolutely needed to seek an audience with another Master of Swords before leaving Zatus.

As we marched through the city, I was shocked to find that the other districts were even seedier than the area around Gory's headquarters. At one point, I saw words written in fresh blood on the side of a dilapidated building.

I should have been terrified, but the overt violence actually gave me hope that the next Master of Swords would have lower expectations.

As it turned out, I was fated for disappointment.

While none of the masters were as calculating as Gory, they didn't commit to my terms either. They all seemed to sense that something was off. They acted as though I wasn't good enough and tested me accordingly. Worst of all, it was usually Crystal who came to my rescue.

My brazen sister spewed facts about Faerie's history and wars. She impressed each leader of Zatus' districts, especially the dwarf Master of Swords, who eventually simply ignored me for her. Crystal gave them the impression that even if I didn't know what I was doing, *someone* did.

When we left the sixth and final hideout in the early afternoon, my soul felt battered from failure. My bad mood was obvious, and most of my siblings left me alone. All except Maria, who rode at my side, initiating small talk, presumably to take my mind off the day. Ebba, on the other side of her, led the group through the streets. I wasn't sure where we were going, but it didn't matter.

Clearly, *anyone's* guidance was better than mine, so I didn't need to know.

I sighed, and my hand sought the feather in my side satchel—the one I hadn't needed to present to anyone since I'd done so poorly. Suddenly, the item that had felt like a token of faith from my father made my stomach harden uncomfortably. I retracted my hand.

"God, that last hideout smelled so rank. I'm relieved we got out of there quickly." Maria switched gears after realizing that I was not responding to quips about the hot guards in the second gang den we'd visited.

"Yeah, good," I replied.

Maria sighed. "Dios mío, Lana, you're worse than mi madre when she is intent on suffering. You're not even listening to me, are you? Should I just shut up and leave you to wallow in your misery?"

I looked away and nodded. On the other side of Maria, Ebba chuckled hollowly.

"Fine," Maria huffed, before turning to Ebba and bringing up the night before.

Sinkers, not the tavern again. If there was one thing I wanted to think of less than my failures, it was *that.*

I veered my horse slightly right, just to put a little

space between my ears and Maria's loud mouth. Trying to block her out, I took in the streets.

A toddler ran across the road, her slightly webbed feet pounding the earth furiously, and her face firmly set in a scowl. Even *she* looked hardened, which I supposed shouldn't be surprising. How would it feel to be a child amidst organized crime?

Before I could explore the question, a pair of young male fae flew out of an alley up ahead, their fists pummeling one another as they zipped through the air. The next second, a female started yelling at a male on the street for swindling her.

Had Zatus been like this last night? The tavern we'd gone to had been close to the inn. I didn't remember anyone threatening us or acting out when we'd walked there. And on the way back . . . well, I didn't remember that at all.

I shook my head. I'd been taking on so much lately that I was feeling scatterbrained. A quiet place to be alone suddenly sounded incredibly appealing, but there was little chance of experiencing serenity in this city. Or with another journey ahead of us.

"Lana!"

Maria's scream nearly made me fall off my horse. I whirled around to face her, only to see that she was pointing behind me.

I followed her finger to find a glint of silver coming straight for me. A massive, muscular fae with a red-tipped hat—a redcap—who looked beyond pissed, held his sword aloft, his arm unwavering.

I fumbled with my dagger in its sheath as he came closer and closer. High above, Naela screeched in warning, but my eyes were locked on the fae and his weapon.

"The spawn of Oberon must die!" he growled as he ran.

I'd just unsheathed my dagger when a horse rushed forth and plowed into my attacker, trampling over him. He fell to the ground. Crystal swung off her horse, whipped out her sword, and without hesitation, slit the man's throat.

I gasped and blinked rapidly. Crystal, the one person who caused me more grief than anyone else in the world, had just saved me.

Hands shaking, I sheathed my dagger.

Garrett rode up from the back of the train, his face strained. "Lana! Are you all right!? He came out of nowhere!"

Everyone else was gathering around us now, investigating the fae Crystal had killed.

"He's bare of any tribe emblems," Ryker said, as if that meant something.

"Which doesn't happen in Zatus." Crystal's voice was grim and sure. "He, or whoever hired him, didn't want to be discovered. A sword for hire to kill one of us . . ." she gestured to me, "or maybe just Lana."

My mouth opened and closed. I turned, feeling

overwhelmed and confused by what had just happened. But Crystal wasn't about to let me have a breather.

She marched around my horse, commanding my attention as she tilted her head up to meet my eyes. "You're welcome for saving your life. Perhaps now you'll be more alert and judgmental about what's around you." With that, she strode back to her steed.

I gaped, stunned. Like a slow boil, anger bubbled inside me, but instead of reacting, which was exactly what she wanted me to do, I kept my mouth shut. After all, she was right. I should have been more alert. But did she have to be so condescending about it? Couldn't I have a bloody moment first?

I rounded my horse and found Ebba, her eyes filled with understanding and dagger still drawn.

"If one person has been hired to attack our group, there will be more. We should get out of here fast, while the sun is still up." She gestured to the dwindling sun. "The city is rough, but the lands outside the city are even more dangerous at night. Lesser gangs patrol them and rob any group they can take advantage of. If we leave now, we'll be well away and can seek refuge in the Alatry Woods. We could be in the False Realm by tomorrow afternoon if we move with haste."

Ebba's eyes bore through mine, waiting. Although she certainly knew better, as the highest ranked among us, I had the final say.

Thank goodness for that, because I wanted nothing more than to get out of Zatus. To leave my shame behind and get out of this shite city.

"Let's move out," I said and urged my horse forward.

CHAPTER THIRTEEN

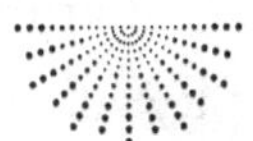

We made it to the base of the Cage Mountains right after sundown. For hours the mountains had been in our view, and I dreaded the long climb up those jagged peaks the next day. The mountains were cruelly and aptly named. Most areas were impassable and caged the giants within their realm. The Overbrim Sea on the western boundary completed their prison.

We constructed our tents, and deposited the fur blankets and pads around the fire, setting up camp. Every other night we'd journeyed, I'd enjoyed sitting around the flames with the others, joking and bonding. But tonight, I simply wanted to be alone.

Once the food was made, I fixed my plate, doing my best to ignore Finn, who kept trying to talk to me. I waited until everyone was situated and then chose a rock on the outskirts of the camp on which to take my meal.

The ball of light I conjured so that I could see my food flickered wildly, as silent tears fell hot and fast down my cheeks. I forced bites of food into my mouth so that no one suspected anything, making my dinner taste largely of salt. A pity, as we'd restocked our food supplies in Zatus. The sandwiches, cheeses, and fruits weren't battered or stale, as I'd grown used to over our week-long journey across Faerie.

"Are you all right?"

I sniffled loudly and looked up from my plate. I'd been so involved in my misery that I hadn't heard Garret approach.

"I'm fine."

He lowered to sit on the ground and set his plate of food on his knee. "I hear that's something people say a lot in the Old Land, and that it doesn't mean much. Or isn't very descriptive, at least. What do you mean by fine?"

For the first time since I'd stormed out of break-fast, I met Garret's eyes. His cheeks were flushed, as they had been all day. I wasn't sure if that was because he was embarrassed about last night, or because we'd just journeyed many miles, set up camp, and made food in record time. His eyes, however, were earnest.

A sigh escaped me. "Usually it means things aren't great. Or that they're boringly average."

Garret's eyebrows knitted together. "So . . . the opposite of what fine means here, which is that we are doing well enough. Not bad, nor splendid."

"It can mean that, too, but usually not."

"This changes my interpretation of the books I've read from your world. Especially the scenes between men and women."

Unexpectedly, a laugh burst from me, loosening the knot in my chest.

"Lana?" Garret spoke as my mirth died out. I tensed at his tone, knowing what was coming. "Can I talk to you about something?"

I didn't want to face what had happened the night before. Not now. But I didn't want to go through another day like this, so I nodded.

Garret inhaled a long breath. "Last night—when we were close . . . I liked it. I know I don't share my feelings or let loose often, but I'm attracted to you. I understand if you don't feel the same way, but I didn't want to go another day with you not looking at me or talking to me."

My heart crumpled. It was one of the most straightforward, the most *real* things a guy had ever said to me. Garret was right, he didn't wear his heart on his sleeve, but when he did . . . Wow.

"I'm so sorry, Garret. I acted like a fool today." My face dropped to my plate, and I gulped. "You should know I'm attracted to you too, but I don't think now is a great time for us to get involved.

Learning my new roles is more difficult than I imagined."

I worked up the courage to stare him straight in the eyes. They were misty. My breath stilled, and every cell in my body begged me to stop, but I couldn't. I was committed to this and had to push through.

"I think . . . I need this time for myself." I bit my lip, hating the words even though they were true.

Garret rubbed his hands on his pants, clearly processing. When he looked at me again, I could tell it was costing him a lot to put on a brave front. "Is it possible for us to stay friends?"

"I'd like to think so," I said, and patted him on the shoulder awkwardly.

"Good." Garret sighed, and his entire body loosened. "It was a fool's dream anyhow. Your father might have let me court one of your lower-ranked sisters, perhaps, but second heir to the throne? Never. My mother, of course, thought otherwise. She threatened to tell you how I felt the next time she saw you. Naturally, I thought I'd best reveal my feelings before she did."

A feeling like sunlight illuminating fields at dawn rushed over me as Alvina's sly smiles and vague remarks suddenly made sense. I chuckled. Alvina should have just gotten us drunk. Apparently, Garret and I let it all hang out after a couple of glasses.

I waved away his concerns. "Your mother was

charming. No need to apologize. Plus, I think you were the only one feeling awkward. I'm too dense and didn't catch on."

Garret laughed, and we fell into silence, both picking at our food.

"Now that we've established boundaries as friends, would you like to talk about today?" Garret asked a couple of minutes later.

I bit my lip and held back the tears I felt pricking my eyes. "I just . . . hate feeling like I have no idea what I'm doing. After all, I've learned and fought for, I truly *sucked* at being princess general today. Gory and all the other masters of swords could feel it. I wish I was more confident in my new roles."

"I thought so." Garret's mouth twisted in indecision. "May I speak plainly with you? As your friend?"

My eyes widened, and I nodded, hoping he was about to share a secret that would make me a better leader.

"Your inexperience wouldn't have stood out so much if Crystal hadn't been there."

I opened my mouth to agree, but Garret held his hand up, stopping me.

"I'm not saying that I wish she was absent. She gave us a chance at negotiating a larger army for Lyonesse, but her knowledge made you look ill-equipped by comparison."

Story of my life.

"I completely understand that if we get an army,

it will be all because of Crystal." I took a long inhale and turned to face Garret. "But honestly, it wasn't like I was asking for their men to follow me into a battle right *now*. I have time to get the details down."

"It's true that you have time, although not much." Garret gave me a tentative smile. A 'but,' was coming. "You've been through a lot, and what's expected of you is vastly different from your day-to-day life before, but . . . you're in charge of people's lives now, Lana. It's time you act like it." His voice was soft, despite the harshness of his words.

My mouth fell open. "Other than when my father gave me three days off, I've attended training every day!"

"Precisely. Did you *need* all three days off?" Garret challenged. "Perhaps one would have sufficed? What can we expect from our leader when a drunk lunging at them on the street puts them out of commission for days? What will happen when we're truly in trouble?"

"I . . ." I trailed off, unsure how to defend myself.

"I've never seen you reading one of the military strategy books in your room, or conversing over our tactics," Garret pressed on. "Yet you carry around the books brought in from the Old Land. To my knowledge, you haven't even approached a single soldier to ask questions." He pointed to himself. "I haven't been in a real battle yet, but some of the older guards are veterans of many. They'd surely help you."

"I didn't even think to ask," I murmured. Asking for help wasn't really like me.

Garret gave me a kind smile. "You were not born to this world, or this role, my friend, but you are part of it now. I'm confident that if you seek the counsel of those around you, you'll excel."

I gaped, unable to find words. My mind was reeling, trying to come up with a retort, something with which I could defend myself, but I was coming up blank.

I couldn't come up with anything because there was *no* excuse. Not really.

Garret had no motive or desire to be cruel. He'd only ever wanted what was best for me. Even now, after I'd just declined a romantic relationship with him. And in his usual levelheaded way, he'd hit the nail on the head.

I hadn't *needed* those three days off. I'd only wanted them, wanted to relax and to have my slow life back once more, even if just for a couple of days. But I'd left that life for something bigger—a chance to do something more for others.

It was time to start acting like it.

"You're right." I sighed, already exhausted by the idea of having to work even harder to prove myself. "I guess it's time to thicken my skin."

We were back on our horses by the light of dawn the next day. Though my thighs burned and felt like jello when I dismounted, I resolved to quit moaning and groaning. Today was the day that I started toughening up and taking my position as princess general to a new level.

The trek over the Cage Mountains was just as I expected. Miserable. Though the horses could scale the mountainside thanks to the roads that generations of fae had used to enter the False Realm, that didn't make the effort less taxing. Much of the time, we had been forced to walk alongside the horses, who tired after hours of climbing. Some even needed reassurance in spots where the road looked over a steep cliff face. Thankfully, my horse did not. I walked in front of her, rather than at her side along the cliff's edge.

By the time we reached the summit, the only beings among us who still seemed fresh were Naela and Kane. The hawks had alternated between flying and riding on the horses' rumps. The rest of us were covered to our knees in mud and dragging. Maria had even sustained a sizable scrape on her thigh, a result of her horse nudging her roughly from behind into the rocks.

"Bossy-ass horse," she complained as she took the final steps up the incline to stand on the peak.

Ryker, who had taken over guiding Maria's horse alongside his own after Maria told hers off, tried to hide a smile. "I'm no expert on horses, but I heard they take on the attitudes of their riders. She was calm for me."

Maria gave him a look that said, *"you did not just say that,"* and stormed over to Ebba, the most skilled of the guards at applying bandages.

"She'll be thankful for her horse when we ride back down. Even if it is bossy," I said to Ryker, who chuckled.

The road on the other side of the mountains plummeted, too steep for my liking. The trail disappeared about halfway down, when it merged with the trees. I allowed my gaze to wander past the foothills. There were no cities or towns in the False Realm, only a vast, lush wood that merged with the Overbrim Sea.

"Where do the giants live?" I asked.

Ryker opened his mouth to answer, but Crystal jumped in.

"They're nomadic and rarely stay in a camp for more than a week. A lot of them actually like to live in caves along the mountainside. We may even find them before we make it all the way down. Their way of life is why we had to bring all this extra stuff." Crystal gestured to a pitiable horse. All the horses were weighed down with lanterns, bolts of leather, rope, and other items that would be useful while camping. "They have no need for gold, but these are items they use daily. Or in the case of magically charmed lanterns, a luxury."

I recalled a snippet from one of the history books

I'd frantically devoured in the days leading up to the Successional.

"Why do they live like that?" I asked. "Didn't they build the castles in Sinkers Realm as payment into Faerie? Surely they could have built towns."

Though it annoyed me that, yet again, Crystal seemed to know everything, my curiosity won out over my pride. Giants weren't talked about much in the court of Lyonesse.

"It's not a giant's way." Crystal looked out into the distance. "They grew accustomed to being nomadic when they roamed the Old Land. Their tribes stayed on the move so humans couldn't hunt them. I understand why they still move around a lot. Most fae don't hold them in high regard."

That much was clear to me too. I'd heard the False Realm, a derogatory name in itself, also referred to as the Slave Realm by two masters of swords in Zatus.

"I don't know a lot about the Old Land," Ryker sidled up to Crystal's side. "Unlike Garret, I'm not much of a reader, but *I* understand where the giants are coming from. Many fae species are prejudiced against other races and those from different realms."

He gestured to his cousin. "Sai and I are prime examples. Our family has been in Sinkers Realm since its inception, but there are some in Lyonesse who would ship us off to the Free Realm because we're part hobgoblin. Never mind that our family line has mixed with nymph and elf."

His words reminded me of Tess, and once again I was faced with the truth. Though Faerie sounded whimsical, this land had problems similar to those in the Old Land—a discrepancy of wealth, a lack of food, and prejudice.

"Thanks for being real with us, Ryker," I said. "I want you to know I appreciate you and Sai."

His shoulders fell away from his ears. Only then did I realize how taut his skin and muscles had been. Though Ryker's tone was relaxed and conversational as always, what he'd just said mattered to him. A lot.

"Thank you," he replied. "You two should grab lunch. It's still a long way down the mountain. Take advantage of the rest while you can."

I nodded and went to find Sai, who was divvying up lunch. Crystal joined Ryker at the edge of the mountain, her arm wrapping through his.

We began our downhill trek a half hour later. I was thankful that we'd be able to descend all the way before dark. Especially now that I knew giants lived in the caves dotting the mountainside. The deeper we marched into their territory, the more my nerves grew. I was under no delusions that my time in Zatus had been anything other than a disaster. But I was determined to do better in the False Realm. To be stronger, more knowledgeable, more *Crystal-like*.

My sister had been spewing random trivia about

the giants to anyone who would listen during our ride down the mountainside, and I'd soaked up the information. I wasn't sure if it would be useful, but I knew I didn't want to be caught off guard again. Plus, her tidbits were a welcome distraction from the worry gnawing a hole in my gut.

When we reached what Ebba deemed a suitable place to stop, camp was set up quickly and dinner served. After almost two weeks of traveling, even Maria, the least outdoorsy among us, could now set up her own tent. I inhaled my food and fell asleep quickly, exhausted from the day's hike.

Tomorrow, we would search for giants and ask them to join our army.

CHAPTER FOURTEEN

The ground shook, jolting me awake from my deepest slumber in days. I blinked rapidly as an ear-piercing whistle broke through the camp.

"Get up! Everyone, up!" Sai yelled. "The giants are coming!"

What the hell!? So early? Shite! I rolled out of my bag and jostled Ebba awake. How she'd slept through the quake and the whistle was beyond me.

"Princess General?" Ebba rubbed her eyes and blinked as I pulled a pair of pants over the thick leggings I'd worn to bed.

"The giants are here!" I whispered, not knowing if they could hear me. Perhaps they had super sensitive ears like shifters or vampires?

"Thank the Sinkers," Ebba muttered. "Less tramping around the realm."

I'd have preferred a little tramping about, so I had

time to prepare. But that wasn't in the cards, so I simply pulled on my shoes and jacket, and ran out of the tent.

"How far away are they?" I asked, ignoring the butterflies whipping through my stomach as I approached Sai and Garret, our camp's early risers.

Sai shrugged. "Not far, judging by the ruckus." She whistled again, in case someone was deaf and hadn't heard the first one.

The others joined us minutes later, all looking as nervous as I felt.

Garret took the lead. "Remember not to use magic in front of them unless they ask. Giants have no magic of their own and find it very rude and intimi-dating when a fae uses it, *especially* in their lands. Princess General, do you recall the number of goods we're prepared to bargain with?"

I nodded. One hundred bolts of leather with a water-repelling charm placed on them, one hundred charmed lanterns, and three hundred meters of magi-cally enhanced rope were to be bartered for up to three tribes. As far as the goods were concerned, I was to negotiate as lean a deal as possible. Half of the goods were to be delivered now, the other half after the giants fought for my father.

However, the prize I suspected the giants would value most was not an item at all. My father had authorized each allied tribe five magical requests, which were to be used as a final bargaining chip.

"Good," Garret said. "If you'd like, one of the guards can assist you. Unlike the fae of Zatus, the giants do not look down upon a guard assisting in negotiations."

I shook my head. After my failures, I had something to prove.

"All right then," Garret cocked his head, and then his gaze searched the sky. "Where's Naela?"

My eyes widened, and I turned on the spot, searching for my familiar. Ryker had mentioned that giants inherently trusted fae who had familiars. It would be beneficial for Naela to be with me during negotiations. But it seemed like my hawk hadn't heard him, or didn't care, and had taken a morning fly instead.

The bloody independent beast was nowhere to be found when I needed her. Probably trying to get back at me for all the days I promised to fly her and didn't.

"Dios mío. Look!" Maria whisper-screeched.

I followed her finger through the thick forest to find a knobby, bald head floating above the trees. The giant's narrowed eyes were just visible above the canopy. Terrifyingly, he opened his mouth and released a heart-stopping roar that shook the ground beneath us.

I jumped. "Umm . . . should we be running?"

Ryker held up his hand. "I think he's telling his tribe that he's found us. Everyone except Lana and

Garret should kneel. Don't make eye contact unless the chief explicitly says so." Ryker took a knee.

"What?!" Maria shrieked. "And make my head that much easier to rip off?"

I sincerely hoped giants did not have good hearing.

"Only the leader and her guard should stand when they approach. That way, they understand our group is non threatening." Ebba wiped a trail of sweat from her face.

Garret shifted to stand behind me, and everyone else took a knee. Gio and Maria began fervently praying. Finn and Crystal were tense, but otherwise playing it cool. Dak, however, was barely holding it together. He was vibrating hard, his animal aspect trying to break out. I took a step closer to him and placed a hand on his shoulder.

"It'll be fine."

Although I barely believed my own words, Dak's back stilled beneath my touch. I breathed a sigh of relief. The last thing we needed was for Dak to shift into his lion. If the giants distrusted magic they didn't request to see, they would definitely consider a prowling lion a threat.

The lead giant's torso was now visible through the trees. From the shaking foliage on either side of him, I deduced others were nearby too. Why couldn't I see their heads?

My answer came when the bald giant bounded

through the woods and halted at the edge of our camp. Six other giants, all significantly shorter than the behemoth I'd spotted, followed a heartbeat later. Giant's breath wafted down on us, and the overpowering stench of unwashed bodies filled my nose.

I held back a gag and lifted a hand in welcome.

"Greetings. We come in peace. I'm Princess General Lana Fullfeather of Lyonesse. Winner of the recent Successional, second in line to the crown of Lyonesse, and messenger for my father, King Oberon. My personal guard, Garret, stands behind me. He means you no harm."

The bald giant's protruding eyebrows furrowed as he took me in. After the longest minute of my life, he finally nodded and stepped aside. A female giant at least three meters shorter than the male stood behind him. Her smaller size didn't really comfort me. She still looked strong enough to crush me and wore an expression similar to the one Naela wore when she spotted a rabbit.

The giantess approached with soft, careful steps. She was shockingly graceful for someone so big. When she was no more than five meters from me, she knelt on the ground and, to my great surprise, smiled. Her teeth were white and straight, though she appeared to be missing a couple of premolars. Her long, blonde hair was clean and brushed.

She laid a hand on the ground before her, and the refreshing scent of flowers wafted over us. Apparently, not all giants stunk, although a few in this group certainly reeked enough for all of them.

"I am Skade, Supreme Chieftainess of the western tribe of giants. Mirmir, my tracker," Skade gestured to the terrifying, bald giant, "scented your group early this morning. We've come to see why you're here."

My shoulders fell away from my ears. Crystal had mentioned that giants usually had long, unwieldy names, and they took great offense if someone got them wrong. A small slight could make a prideful giant less likely to do business with that person. Skade's simple name was a relief.

"Might we use only our given names? You may call me Lana, if you wish. 'Princess General' grows a little tiresome, as I'm sure 'Supreme Chieftainess' does."

Skade's eyes widened, and I knew I had played it right. They appreciated when a fae was down to earth.

"I would prefer that as well, Lana, daughter of Oberon Fullfeather."

I took in Skade's change in stance, how her breaths grew longer, more relaxed. My own breathing smoothed in response, and somehow, words bubbled up my throat on their own accord.

"You asked why we're here. We have come to humbly request your assistance—soldiers—for a battle to be fought in the coming weeks."

Skade sat back on her heels in a squat, a pleased

smile spreading over her lips. "Now I am quite glad that Mirmir scented you before the other tribes did. As for what you ask, we shall see if we can help. What will you give us for crossing our mountains and journeying across the Free Realm into Sinkers Realm? As I'm sure you know, we giants are not usually inclined to leave the safety of our home. It took us many years to earn a space for ourselves in this world."

I took a deep breath, preparing myself for the negotiations. "We're aware and would compensate you handsomely for your time and strength."

I gestured back to the horses. "King Oberon sends payment—bolts of leather that can repel rain, meters of magically strengthened rope, and enchanted lanterns that do not dim for years. My father is prepared to supply you with thirty bolts, the same number of lanterns, and fifty meters of rope to make your life here more pleasurable."

Skade pursed her lips, looking less than thrilled by my offer. "Surely we're not the first you have sought assistance from. You've entered our land from the road that leads to Zatus, not Lyonesse. One can infer that you have been elsewhere searching for soldiers. Did they deny or accept your proposal? Have you come to us for aid last?"

What the hell? Ryker and Garret had *both* assured me that giants would not be as cunning as fae. Was that their own prejudice shining through? Or was Skade different?

I took her in again. She was not as strong or large as the males in her group. Yet, she was their leader. Which meant she was probably of above average intelligence.

My suspicions were confirmed when the six giants behind Skade grumbled, their eyes narrowing as if I had already cheated them out of something. I would bet money that *they* wouldn't have thought twice about what road we came in on.

"Yes, we journeyed from Zatus, after meeting several masters of swords. We are still in negotiations with many of them." It was a white lie. The 'negotiations' were mostly one-sided, depending on if the master would accept or not. But Skade didn't need to know that bit.

"However, coming to your realm was always in our plans," I assured her. "No matter if we obtained every soldier in Zatus or none. The battle my father intends to fight is important, and he wants to take no chances."

Skade nodded slowly, as if taking it all in. "This wouldn't have something to do with the lost bonegate of Lyonesse and Queen Pari of Buyan, would it?"

"Does it matter?" I asked, doing my best to side-step the question. "The giants created towns, villages, entire cities, and enormous castles with their bare hands. You could surely destroy what you built too."

I arched an eyebrow. "Do your tribes truly care whose castle and walls we're asking you to demolish, when you constructed them all with your blood, sweat, and tears? Or are some castles and cities more precious?"

Laughter erupted from Skade. The tops of the trees shook, and the air from her mouth washed over me. It was enough to make my knees buckle, or at least make me cover my nose, but I stood my ground.

"You're right. We care not whom the battle is against. In fact, Oberon's ancestors were the first to free us from our agreements. We'd be more inclined to side with him, though not for so low a price as you're offering." She shook her head. The gesture both gave me hope and made me worry. What would she ask for?

"One giant's tent takes twenty-five bolts of leather to construct," Skade said. "What sort of leader would I be if I only bargained for my own waterproof dwelling? And you did not even mention magic . . . perhaps it slipped your mind?"

It had not. I'd only been trying to negotiate more adeptly. Too bad I got a genius giantess to bargain against. Still, coming back with one ally was better than none. And I *had* been allotted plenty more to offer.

We spent the next two hours in negotiations. Skade shocked me when she asked for five chests of gold—an item my father had not been prepared to pay the giants. I countered, stating Crystal's statistic of the effective chimera army costing not much more than that. In the end, I bargained a couple extra magical charms in place of gold. It would be a pain for whoever had to come perform the magic, but I was sure my father would be happy. I'd saved him— and by extension, his subjects—the coin.

Finally, we parted with assurances from Skade that her tribe would make the journey to Castle Phoenix in one month's time.

For the first time since we began our journey, my confidence soared.

AFTER MEETING SKADE'S TRIBE, WE DISCOVERED another band of giants, and received a tentative agreement that they'd show up in Lyonesse in a month as well. I wasn't holding my breath and planned to tell my father that only Skade's group would be coming. If the other tribe showed up too, it would be a pleasant surprise. Another win.

We left for home the next day. As before, the trek over the mountain was silent and when we made it down the other side of the Cage Mountain Range, we broke for lunch. Our plan was to hike inland for a few hours and make camp in the Alatry Woods bordering the cities of the Free Realm.

I sat with Finn, Maria, and Gio and dug into my stale sandwich. It tasted terrible, but we still had days of riding ahead of us. I would need the energy.

Maria arched her back, and her vertebrae popped one at a time. "I can't wait to sleep in my bed. This trip has been interesting and I'm glad I came, but I need some normalcy."

"Living in a castle in Faerie has become your new normal?" Gio teased. "Has seeing merpeople and selkies jump around in the sea become old news too? If so, you acclimate quickly. I still dream about working the fishing boats with my stepdad."

"I was born for a fancy life," Maria agreed good naturedly. "But to be fair, seeing those merpeople and selkies yesterday was so *not* normal. That was *awesome*."

My lips pulled up in a smile.

We'd found the Northern giant tribe near the Overbrim Sea. Their camp boasted an amazing view of merpeople sunbathing. As we'd watched the merpeople, a beached seal had slunk off her skin and transformed into a woman right before our eyes. It was my first selkie sighting, which was exciting, but the guys were on a different level. They'd gone crazy over the attractive, naked woman.

I chuckled, recalling how Maria had actually had to pull Gio away from the selkie so we could get down to business.

"It really was—*oomph!*" I jerked forward, as suddenly, someone's bony knee landed in the center of my back.

"So, Lana . . . Oh, excuse me, *Princess General.*

I've been wondering something." I turned to find Crystal standing there. "Do you want me to continue to feed you lines that you can repeat verbatim to close deals with later? Or do you think you have it from here?"

"Excuse me?" I blinked, totally confused by the interruption.

"You know what I'm talking about." Crystal placed her hands on her hips. "All the stuff you told the giants. How they built the cities and could easily destroy them. You even spouted off the bit of chimera trivia I mentioned at Gory's place. I mean, we closed the deal, which is why I stayed quiet. But a *little* credit would've been nice. Or at least a thank you in private."

"You want me to give you credit whenever you say something, and I repeat it?" My hands tensed as my frustration mounted. Crystal had been snippy since our encounter with Skade's tribe. I paid little notice, because as far as I was concerned, that was normal behavior from her.

"Proper accreditation is important." Crystal looked straight at Finn, who squirmed under her scrutiny. "You see people trying to take credit for the accomplishments of others all the time in academia. I guess they're just too lazy to put the effort in themselves. They probably also take days off when they don't really need them." Her brown eyes slid to meet mine, and she arched a ginger eyebrow.

Finn waved his hands to get attention. "Now, wait a min—"

I shot up from my seat. My arms and legs had begun to shake with anger. For the entire trip, I'd suffered Crystal's thinly veiled jabs on how a proper general should be able to ride a horse. Or negotiate. And how generals should know the *entire* history of the area. At the *very least,* a proper general should be able to hold their wine. In short, how a general should be Crystal Clawsin and not Lana Shea.

I wouldn't put up with it any longer. Even if she had saved my life in Zatus, that didn't mean she could walk all over me. Crystal didn't have to be my friend —that ship had sailed long ago—but she had to respect my position.

"From here on out, *Major,* you'll ride ahead." My gaze leveled her. "You'll set up camp for the group so we can make better time on our return journey. We're staying on this road the entire way through the woods, right, Captain Ebba?"

The blonde fae cleared her throat uncomfortably. "It's a straight shot until we reach the boundary of Lyonesse, which will be obvious by the barren landscape."

"And safe, since we'll be bypassing the rogue gangs of Zatus and traveling through uninhabited woods?" I pressed, using information Ebba had already told me to further my case. I didn't want to give Crystal an out.

Ebba gulped as her eyes ping-ponged back and forth between Crystal and me.

"Yes, General Lana."

"Good. Then straying off course should not be an issue. The rest of us will finish lunch here, but you might want to get moving, Crystal. You wouldn't want us catching up to you."

"Are you freaking serious?!" Red blotches stained my sister's cheeks.

"Dead serious," I retorted. I took pride that my tone was much more level than hers. "Stop in four hours, no sooner. And be sure to take an extra horse with you so you can start assembling camp. I expect to have the fire burning bright and at least four tents set up when we arrive."

Crystal pressed her lips together, and the pink flesh there turned ghastly white. I placed my hands on my hips, daring her to talk back. She opened her mouth, clearly about to argue, but then caught herself, straightened her spine, and stomped off to collect the horses.

A mix of adrenaline and relief washed through me as she disappeared into the woods with a scowl on her face. Maybe from now on, she'd recognize that, even if I wasn't who she thought a general should be, I *was* the one with power.

And I was no longer afraid to use it.

CHAPTER FIFTEEN

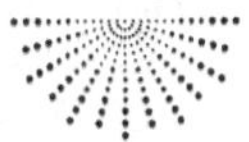

A breath gusted out of me as I stood before my father's chambers, trying to shake off the stubborn anxiety clinging to me. Nothing changed internally . . . I still felt jittery, so I resorted to simply begging the universe for my father's understanding.

My hand lifted to meet the door, and the resulting knock echoed ominously through the ever-empty hallway. Like usual, the door opened right away.

"Welcome back, Lana," my father said, and I jerked back.

He *never* answered the doors to his chambers. Normally, I had to wait a couple of minutes before he made his appearance.

"Lana? Are you all right?"

I nodded quickly and blinked, trying to settle into the moment and regain my tentative equilibrium.

My father smiled understandingly. "I missed you at the feast last night."

"I apologize, Father, but after the long journey, I decided I needed rest more than a full belly." Thankfully, the lie slipped through my lips just as I'd practiced it. I simply hadn't been ready to tell him about Zatus yet.

"Of course." He swept his arm wide, welcoming me inside. "I hope you find yourself rejuvenated."

I followed him to the cozy nook where the tapestry of my great-great-grandfather hung, and my father gestured for me to take a seat in one of the two chairs. I did so carefully, my legs still ached from riding.

I sighed. "It's good to be back."

"A soft featherbed is always preferable to a mat and a tent." He stroked the velvet upholstery of his chair thoughtfully. "But that is how soldiers sleep. Even kings and generals, when we travel to war. It was good practice, I'm sure. Now, tell me of your time in Zatus and the False Realm."

My temperature rose. I hoped that the dimness of his chambers would hide any pink in my cheeks. Sharing my failures was not something I relished.

Still, I filled him in dutifully, only leaving out the details about when Crystal made me look like an idiot. I already felt bad enough for not coming through. There was no need to add to my humiliation. When I moved on to my negotiations with the giants, I was able to elaborate a little more, using the knowledge Crystal had spouted in Zatus to my advantage.

"We have giants assisting us, then. That is excellent. In fact, I've heard of Chieftainess Skade's tribe—they're quite formidable. One of the largest tribes in the False Realm, I believe."

Abruptly, he rose and made his way to the table where we normally took our meetings. A scroll lay upon the smooth wood. He lifted it.

"In truth, I already knew the rest, but wanted to hear you tell it. This came from Gory yesterday, right before you returned. He was the last of the masters of swords to reply. One unfamiliar with his ways would assume this was because it took his men that long to come to a decision, but I know better." He extended the scroll to me. "Read it."

I joined him and took the page hesitantly. Whatever it said was sure to be unflattering.

After the first sentence, my stomach dropped. I was right.

Gory claimed he was appalled that King Oberon would send a general so green, so unknowledgeable. He said he could not find soldiers to bid their sword for King Oberon's cause at the low price. His offer of seven chests of gold, however, still stood.

I shook my head in disgust. After admitting to our delegation that his men were not nearly as good as the famed chimera army, he still had the gall to ask for comparable compensation? The nerve!

I set the paper down, my eyes following it, not wanting to meet Father's. No matter how frustrated I was with Gory, I was more ashamed that my father had to read Gory's poor opinion of me. It drove home my failure.

"Don't feel badly, Daughter. Spriggans are a cunning race of fae." Briefly, he laid a hand on my shoulder. "How do you think such a ridiculous-looking creature with no extraordinary magical powers could rise to such heights? They have brains and certainly know how to use them. I assigned you a very difficult task in approaching Gory. While I would have been delighted if you'd succeeded, I'm not surprised that you didn't."

"I have to admit, I'm embarrassed. He spoke so poorly of me."

He waved his hand dismissively. "I don't believe a word of it. And I shall send another delegation to Zatus soon. One led by Meegra. Some might call her methods harsh, but I like to think of her as persuasive."

With every word, my shame grew. Not only had I failed, but now we had to send another squad to clean up my mess and secure what I could not.

"I am, however, quite pleased with the tribe of giants you convinced. Skade is a notorious chieftainess. Her tribe will be a boon for our side."

My lips quirked up a touch. "Thank you, Father. You have no idea how much that means to me. Please know, I didn't want to leave Zatus without the army you requested—but after we spent hours imploring various masters, it was clear that no one would be willing to follow me."

He nodded understandingly. "I suspect that Gory sent messengers to the other masters of swords to make it more difficult for you to negotiate. He most likely counted on their refusal so that he could cinch a larger prize for his army later. It's a tactic allied fae gangs often use to drive a client's price skyward. As I said, spriggans are cunning."

My eyes widened. I hadn't considered the possibility that the other masters of swords had been *instructed* to deny me. While I wasn't sure that I believed that was what actually happened, it was kind of my father to give me the benefit of the doubt.

"Now," Father said, "let us discuss how to proceed. Now that the wheels are in motion, our troops and newest officers should be prepared to move out by the time the giants arrive to assist in pulling the cannons."

He sat at the table, and I joined him, relief sweeping through me. The worst was over. We could move on.

THE MEETING WITH MY FATHER HAD GONE MUCH better than expected. He'd understood that I'd failed, forgiven me for it, and moved on. I couldn't ask for better. So although I hadn't practiced magic in over two weeks, I strode toward the training room feeling positive about the day's conditioning sessions.

That was until I saw Casimir was present.

As soon as I stepped foot in the training space, the prince strode up to me, flanked by a half dozen Feathered Fae. It was the first time he'd willingly approached me since before the Successional. His oily smile did not give me hope that he was here to be besties.

Directly behind him, Ellette, the Feathered Fae who had given me the scroll that led me to Faerie, threw a little wave. The rest were stone cold.

"Hello, Casimir," I said when he was close enough.

"Princess General Lana." He nodded curtly. His use of my title did not go unnoticed. Normally, unless we were on a mission, my siblings and I didn't use those.

"Our father informed me of your return. I thought it great timing. I'd been hoping to expand my training regimen for some days. Our vila and shifter siblings—or even the weaver witch—didn't provide me with much of a challenge while your group was gone."

Casimir's eyes danced as Finn hurled fire like a

pro at the far end of the hall. "I see now that's because you had the strongest of our family traveling with you."

Casimir had been training with the others while I was away? My gaze sought Himari. A dozen weaver witch tornados swirled around her, lifting her black hair and revealing patches of severe burns on the back of her neck. Burns from lightworker magic.

Unease rattled my spine. What was Casimir playing at, inflicting that kind of injury? Had he used a higher energy spectrum that was difficult to heal? Or was Himari just too proud to seek a healer? That didn't sound like her . . .

"Did you hear me, Princess Lana?" Casimir's tone was hard, impatient.

"I'm sorry. What was that?"

He frowned, clearly disliking that my attention was not wholly on him. "How did you fare on your journey?"

My teeth bit the inside of my cheek subconsciously. "Well enough."

Casimir quirked an eyebrow, and slowly, one corner of his lips lifted. "Really? Then why am I hearing that another trip to Zatus will be necessary?" His tone dripped with false curiosity. He'd already known what had happened and simply wanted to rub it in.

I forced myself not to scowl. "That's true, although we had *great* luck in the False Realm. One tribe consented to fight for us, and another is strongly considering it. I believe we made a favorable impression."

The prince's eyes narrowed to dangerous slits. "No need to boast, Princess General."

Boast? I jerked back, surprised. What in the hell was he talking about?

"I understand you did not have such privileges before, but really—it's unseemly for royalty to brag of their travels." Casimir's lips twisted with disdain.

"That's not what I—"

"Don't worry, Prince Casimir," Meegra interjected. "Soon enough, King Oberon will allow you out of the kingdom. Once the bonegate is retaken, you may take all the princely quests you want."

Oh. So that's what this was about. Apparently our father was correct. Prince Casimir disliked that his new siblings got to do things he couldn't, and it was stoking his insecurity. That made me feel a little better. It wasn't all about me.

"I'm sorry, Casimir. I didn't mean to sound as if I were bragging. I—"

"Don't apologize," he snapped, red splotches dotting his moon-pale cheeks. "I'm well aware of your failure to communicate properly. You'll need to work on that, if you're to be taken seriously as a Fullfeather. Our father only gives so many chances, and as far as I'm concerned, you've exceeded yours."

He shook his head as if disgusted. "Now, I shall go

challenge Crystal. I've heard word that she's been excelling in *all* areas of royal duty."

I sucked in a breath as he stomped away. A second later, the Feathered Fae followed with haughty expressions on their faces. Only Ellette appeared neutral, perhaps even sorry for me. I wasn't sure that was any better. I hated pity.

Did the whole castle know about my blunders? Had someone been gossiping?

My eyes swept the room. Even if I hadn't formed a strong bond with some of the people there, I couldn't see them talking behind my back.

Except for Crystal.

Had she mentioned it when she turned up before the rest of the group to declare our impending arrival? Had she told my father too? From what Casimir said, it certainly seemed that way. And then I'd completely neglected to mention in our meeting how Crystal had smoothed over the mission.

My face burned with humiliation, but my blood boiled with anger. I'd lived this life before I came to Faerie. I'd been the girl people talked about behind her back. Even if my father had been gracious, it was still messed up. In the Old Land, I'd always brushed off this sort of behavior, but not here. Not anymore.

I went to confront Crystal, but thankfully came to my senses before I'd even taken ten steps.

What was I going to say? Even if I railed against her like I wanted to, Casimir was the one person in this hall who outranked me. And right now, Crystal seemed to be his favorite sibling. Did I really want to cause trouble in front of him? He'd definitely developed an abhorrence of me after the Successional. Did I want to deepen that dislike and make life harder?

I'd confront her later, when he wasn't around.

"You look like you're about to punch someone in the face." Himari came up to me, sweat glistening on her skin.

"Why didn't you mention Casimir had been here training with you guys?" I said, unable to keep the accusation from my voice. "At breakfast, I asked what was new, and everyone just shrugged."

"It didn't seem important," Himari said, her eyes widening slightly at my tone.

I pointed at her neck. "Right. And those are just from your curling iron? Where'd you manage to plug that in here?"

Himari's cheeks grew dusky rose.

I sighed. "From those marks and how he just spoke to me, I'd say it's pretty clear Casimir thinks he has something to prove. Why wouldn't that be important?"

Himari closed her eyes briefly and shook her head. She looked tired, defeated. "Do you really want to know why we didn't mention it?"

I nodded.

"To be honest, Lana, you didn't really seem to care."

My mouth fell open. "Excuse me?! I asked, didn't I?"

"Yeah, but you sounded so flat. Like it was a recording. Since you've been named princess general, you haven't seemed to care about anyone but our father."

I jerked back. I'd been more social than ever!

"That's not true," I defended myself. "I talk to everyone."

"You talk to us," Himari agreed. "Sometimes you even joke around, but most of the time, it's like you're not *really* present. Finn can get through to you, but you've known each other forever, so that's different."

She paused and chewed her lip. "I know you were getting close to Kate and Kumar before the Successional. They helped you through it, just like Maria and I clung to each other. I didn't know them as well, but I know they were kind and good and now they're gone. Maybe you're subconsciously protecting yourself from experiencing that hurt again."

My eyes closed briefly as an image of my friends sliced through my heart.

Himari continued, her cadence softer. "Before the Successional, I thought we could become tight once all the tournament crap had passed. I felt like you wanted to know me too, but now it's like we're back to strangers that see each other every day."

I wanted to deny it, but something stopped me.

I thought back to our journey to Zatus. Gio's and

Dak's excitement that I was going out. Finn's astonishment and teasing that I never went anywhere. Of course, he'd teased me about being a hermit many times before, but he had been bringing it up more often lately. Had I been closing myself off without even knowing it?

I locked eyes with my sister and realized that she was right. Outside of training and mealtimes, I hadn't spent a free minute with her—with most of them, really. It was time to rectify that mistake.

"I'm so sorry, Himari. I had no idea you felt that way." I rubbed the nape of my neck. "Would you like to join me in my apartment tonight for a glass of wine? We can catch up and hang out? I'll invite the other girls too."

"All of them?" Himari raised an eyebrow.

I nodded. Though it pained me to invite Crystal into my sanctuary, I wouldn't be the sister who included all her siblings save one. "All of them. It's time we did some family bonding."

CHAPTER SIXTEEN

"Would you like me to get that, Princess Lana?" Tess dropped the clothes she'd been folding as a knock sounded on my door. A burst of giggles erupted behind the portal, and her eyes narrowed protectively. "I can tell whoever it is that you're in for the evening and that they must leave."

Must leave? I cringed. Yikes. Even Tess had noticed I'd been secluding myself.

"No, it's alright. I forgot to tell you that my sisters are coming by to hang out. In fact, I seem to have forgotten how to host properly, too. I was going to go by the kitchens earlier for some wine, but got side-tracked."

I set my crime novel down and stood to stretch luxuriously. When I turned my attention back to my maid, her arms had begun to tremble. "Are you all right? You look ill."

Her pallor greened noticeably, and I shook my head. "I think maybe you should go to the healers' ward. I'll walk you down there on my way to the kitchens. My sisters can chill here for a few minutes. I need to stretch my legs any—"

"No! A princess must not go to the kitchens! It is beneath your standing!" Tess lurched forward, and I reared back.

"But . . . you clearly need to see a healer for a tonic or something. You're turning positively green!" I waved my hand dismissively. "Seriously, Tess, I don't mind getting my own wine. You wait on me hand and foot every day, but I can do stuff for myself. I've done it all my life."

"I refuse to let my lady demean herself in such a manner. I will go to the kitchen and bring back the wine."

I arched an eyebrow. "If you insist. Make sure you stop by the healers' ward too, so they can do a quick checkup. It'll make me feel better."

"I shall do so, princess." Tess bowed. "And after I return, you will hear no more of me—unless you desire."

A chuckle escaped me. "Tess! You know you don't have to be a silent shadow. You're more than welcome to stay and hang out too."

I might have been slacking on my sisterly relationships, but there was something about Tess—probably the fact that she reminded me of myself, before Faerie

—that hadn't allowed me to give up on befriending her.

Predictably, she shook her head emphatically. "I must decline my lady's offer. I . . . have a bit of wood-working to do tonight. If it pleases you, I shall be in my room. You only need to ring the bell for assistance. I will hear it."

I ignored the reminder that Tess probably sat on her tiny bed in the room next to mine at all hours, waiting for my beck and call, and grinned at her. "Sounds good. Do whatever you wish. Maybe even get out of the castle for a good time. Although, if you do, I want to hear those stories later," I said, hoping to pry a smile from my maid.

Instead, she lunged toward the door, yanked it open, and bolted past my giggling siblings down the hall.

My sisters fell silent.

"Who was that?" Maria asked, watching Tess run down the long corridor.

I sighed. "My maid, Tess. She's getting wine because I forgot. I told her she could join us, but she's really into being proper, so the invitation freaked her out."

"You have a maid?!" Victoria's voice was high with disbelief.

My brow furrowed. "Yeah, don't you guys?"

"Uh, no. But we're not Father's favorite." Maria stepped into the room and spun about. "And I definitely don't have this glamorous of a room. Mine's probably half this size. Still big . . . but nothing compared to this."

A flash of red at the back of the group caught my attention, and I stiffened. I'd asked Himari to invite Crystal, but I never believed that she would actually show up.

I was wracking my brain with ways to avoid confrontation and make this a pleasant experience for everyone, when Arlo stepped around Wikolia's tall frame.

The air that had been caught in my chest whooshed out. It had been *his* carrot-top I'd spotted, not Crystal's.

"I know this is a girls' night, but I hope you don't mind that I invited Arlo," Victoria said, after catching me staring at him. "He's basically one of the girls anyhow, aren't you, bae?"

I blinked. What?

Arlo batted his ginger eyelashes and blew Victoria a kiss, which she caught smugly.

The clouds parted. How did I not realize that my brother was gay?

Heat rose in my cheeks, and I turned to light the fire so that Arlo wouldn't think the wrong thing.

Himari had totally been right. I'd been too into myself and my own problems to get to know my siblings. I supposed it really shouldn't come as a surprise. Going solo had been my modus operandi in school. During university, too. But then again, these weren't random students, these were my *siblings*. People I was genetically related to . . . and I barely knew them at all.

Bloody hell, I really sucked.

"Sorry I'm late!" Himari burst into my apartment, her chest heaving and her hair a mess. "Holy crap! This is your room?"

"She even has a mini suite for her bird!" Maria called from the far side of the tower as she peered into Naela's mew.

"Wow. I knew Crystal's room was larger than mine, but she has nothing on Lana." Himari meandered about the space. "They really are serious about their ranks here, aren't they? I wonder what Casimir's quarters are like?"

"You know what I wonder?" Arlo's green eyes narrowed, and he grinned playfully. "Why's your hair a hot mess, Himari? Where were you?"

Himari blushed. "Oh, hush. You're just jealous that my little fling is on my team and not yours."

"Sure am! Hell, who wouldn't be? Those guard outfits are hot!"

The room erupted into chatter, which only got louder and more raucous when Tess arrived, her thin arms laden with baskets full of wine bottles. After assuring me she felt fine, I released her from her duties, and the group settled in by the fire.

Glass after glass of wine was poured, and slowly, I

learned more about my siblings. Like how Arlo, born and raised in Manhattan, had been about to embark on a conservation trip to Alaska when he was sucked into Faerie.

"How crazy would it have been if we met?!" Arlo exclaimed when Wikolia mentioned she knew exactly where he would have been stationed, as it was located only miles from her home. "I wonder what we would have said to each other?"

"I definitely wouldn't have called you brother. You're too damn white for that. But then again, look at our papa." Wikolia took a sip of wine and shrugged.

"What does everyone's families in the Old Land think about this?" I asked, curious.

"My mom was shocked—still is," Arlo admitted. "Although shifters are primal, she's never seen me as the warrior type. It's kind of awesome to be actively proving her wrong."

I laughed. "Defiance just for the sake of it?"

Arlo lifted his glass and toasted me. "You know it!"

"Well, my madre and stepfather *hate* me being away, but I told them that this was the chance of a lifetime." Maria flung her curly, dark hair over her shoulders.

"To be honest, the longer I'm here, the more I can see myself staying," Maria said. "I even broke up with my man—he was hot, but not the forever type. Plus, I couldn't let Himari be the only one getting all the guard action, now could I? It would be such a wasted opportunity." Maria shook her hips.

I giggled uncomfortably, recalling my night with Garret in Zatus.

"My mom asked to come. She wants to get away from my stepfather—fifth of his name." Victoria rolled her eyes. "I told her she'd had her chance enchanting all the rich men in Toronto, and now it's my turn." Her super-white teeth gleamed as she grinned wickedly.

I turned to Wikolia, who sighed. "My parents are on the fence. They're super religious, so me being in Faerie bugs them. It's too much of a reminder of the supernatural world that they like to pretend doesn't exist—despite Mom being a full shifter. They're delusional about that shit. Still, they think maybe I'll have better opportunities here than in Anchorage."

"Well, my mom says I'd better grab a crowned prince while I can because I sure as hell won't find one in Tokyo." Himari paused. "*Obviously*, I'm not telling her about Ronan. Or that I'd just as soon find a princess—if the right one were to come along!"

It went like that for hours, my siblings spilling bits of their lives. Inside jokes were explained, which made me feel like a loner at first, until I realized they only explained them because they *wanted* to let me in. Even Victoria and Wikolia shared a few more intimate tidbits, though less than the others. Perhaps they were thinking of Crystal, the leader of their trio, and how she would feel if we got along too well.

We emptied our last bottle in the small hours of the morning, and shortly afterward, everyone left to snag a few hours of sleep. As I shut the door to my room, I couldn't help but grin. Although Casimir had been cold enough to freeze over hell earlier, it didn't seem to matter much anymore.

I'd learned long ago that not everyone was going to like me, but I was pretty sure a few here did, and that was enough for me.

WHY WAS WINE SUCH A GREAT SOCIAL LUBRICANT?

I pressed the heels of my hands against my temples to stop my head from pounding.

"Hey! How was last night?" Finn's eyes shone as he joined me in the training hall.

I'd skipped breakfast in the great hall, opting instead for more sleep, so he hadn't been able to question me earlier.

"Too much fun. I'm paying for it now."

Finn smirked. "Bring my best friend to Faerie, and she becomes a party girl. Who knew you had it in you, Lan?"

I rolled my eyes. Clearly, I didn't have it in me. If I did, it wouldn't feel as if my head were about to pop off. The remedy that Tess had brought hadn't helped even a little.

Massaging my temples, I scanned the room. Almost everyone was present, warming up and stretching. Only Victoria and Wikolia were missing. I didn't have to guess why. If I'd had a lot of wine last night, that pair had put down triple what I consumed.

Should I have someone go wake them? Or be nice and let them rest? Should I be a general or a friend?

"Hey, girl, hey!"

Victoria strutted in, relieving me from making that choice. Wikolia was right behind her, looking green around the gills and like she wanted to throttle Victoria.

I shook my head as I took in Victoria's lively step and smile. *How* is she so chipper? What magic is this?

"We had a blast at your place last night!" Victoria exclaimed. "We should make this a weekly thing! I miss regular girls' nights."

My stomach heaved at the thought, but Victoria didn't seem to notice. Her grin only grew, and she flung her arm around Wikolia. "We can alternate rooms, too, if you want. But since you have a maid—oh shit! Wik!"

Wikolia had jerked to a stop and bent over. I whirled around, my hand covering my mouth, but unfortunately, I still heard the splat of sick on the floor.

Closing my eyes and taking deep breaths, I tried to ignore the trembling of my stomach and the quivering of my legs.

"Ewwww," Victoria sang, sounding half grossed out, half amused.

"I told you not to wear that damn perfume. It made me vom," Wikolia growled.

"Don't blame this on me," Victoria countered.

"Hey! Why don't we just work on cleaning this mess up and getting Wik to the healers?" Dak, ever the voice of reason, piped up.

There was a flurry of noise behind me, a calling of guards to fetch a servant, and then someone—Finn —took me by the elbow and led me away from the offensive smell.

"Don't worry, Lan. It'll be gone in a mo'," he chirped. I could tell he was trying to keep the laughter from his voice, but he was failing terribly.

By the time we made it to the other side of the room, my stomach had calmed enough to where I could stand on my own once more. I turned to face my siblings—all except Wikolia were still present. A guard must have shown her to the healers' ward. I highly doubted she would be back, which left nine of us training that day.

My spine straightened. *Nine.* An uneven number.

"Gather 'round, guys! Let's do a quick roundup and then we'll practice." I waved everyone over, pretending that I hadn't almost lost my breakfast, and luxuriated in the cool air my hand wafted around my clammy cheeks. "I'm thinking today we should do something different."

Eyes widened all around me.

"Not *too* different, mind you. We're still training. But I was thinking instead of one-on-one or two-on-one like we normally do, we'll split into groups and have a larger mock battle. From talking to Father, I get the feeling we're going to be sent on another mission soon—the *big* one—and we'll want to be prepared for multiple adversaries at once."

Nods came from all around. I rejoiced internally. An odd number of people meant one person should sit out. I was definitely volunteering myself. It would give me a brief reprieve.

"But the numbers are uneven." Crystal was smiling as she spoke, though her eyes were narrowed and shrewd. "I suppose that means someone will have to sit back and grade us, then? One guess who it will be . . . "

My stomach sank. Sinkers, why did I have such a bloody clever sister as a nemesis? I cursed Crystal mentally for calling me out.

"Of course not," I said, already regretting my pride. "I'm practicing. I'll call in a guard to even up the numbers."

"Ah. Garret will surely come running."

My face grew hotter than ever.

Crystal smirked, enjoying making me uncomfortable. "You know, after sparring with Casimir, I finally feel like I know exactly what lightworkers can do. It's been a while since it was just you and me, sister. I'm intrigued to see if illuminator witch magic is different from fae lightworker power."

What Crystal said was true and annoying. I'd watched her sparring with the crowned prince the day before. While he was more magically skilled than Crystal, she'd given him a run for his money.

Considering her elven powers hadn't materialized until she had arrived in Faerie, even I had to admit her abilities were impressive. What frustrated me was that Crystal knew darn well that Casimir was more powerful than me. She was just trying to rub it in— and intimidate me.

"Right," I said, hoping my voice sounded level, unworried. I turned to the guards who stood by the door. They were always there, watching us. "Someone get Sai."

One of the guards nodded and left the room. I didn't have long to compose myself. While we waited, I chugged water. Far too quickly for my liking, Sai arrived.

"I hear we're performing a mock battle?" she asked, grinning from ear to ear. Her long white hair whipped behind her and her violet eyes gleamed with excitement.

"You heard right. Finn and I are captains. Let's get started."

Finn and I chose teams. I considered putting Crystal in my group so she'd have no reason to fight me, but Finn beat me to her.

"Regular rules apply," I said, once the last person was chosen. "If you're disabled by teeth, talons, magic, or strength, you're out. Whoever is the last person standing represents the winning team. My team will take this side, Finn's will get the other." I swept my arm in one direction, and the groups broke apart.

The other team had the distinct advantage of having three element workers and a large shifter, whereas my squad had Sai and Gio as our elementals, a vila, a winged shifter, and me.

Victoria was a bit troublesome. Not that vila weren't useful as fighters; they were, especially against men who wouldn't see them coming, or if they'd already mastered their air magic. Unfortunately, everyone in the room knew Victoria's vila tricks, and she wasn't nearly strong enough yet to be a threat in the air department.

If we were going to win, we'd have to get creative.

"Huddle up," I said, gesturing for everyone to stop joking around.

It was unlikely we'd beat the other team, but I would try my best to lead us to victory. Despite being princess general for months now, I still felt like I had something to prove. Especially when it came to battling Finn and Crystal, each of whom could have easily beaten me in the Successional.

"They're probably thinking we'll use Gio, Sai, and me to disable the elementals," I began. "So . . . we'll do the opposite of what they're expecting." I turned to Arlo. "You should shift right away. Avoid Himari; her weaver capabilities are strong and might blow you off course. Probably Crystal, too, since her air magic has improved. Go for Maria. She won't affect your flying." I caught Sai's gaze next.

"Finn is the only logical opponent for me," she stated with surety.

I shook my head, and her eyebrows pulled together. "No. You're both gifted with fire, so they'd expect us to pit like against like. Go for Dak instead.

"Victoria, *you* go after Finn. Gio, you'll challenge Himari, but while you do that . . ." A grin grew on my face. "Cause a distraction. Make it crazy flamboyant, water all over the training room. We need obstacles we can use."

Gio's face split into a huge smile. My challenge was right up his alley.

"If anyone incapacitates their opponent, go find someone who needs help. I hope we'll disable a couple quickly, with our unexpected tactics."

"Well, one pairing is still pretty obvious," Victoria said, a perfectly shaped eyebrow raised. "You're going after Crystal, which is *totally* expected."

She was right. Despite my pounding head and

deep desire to be laying in bed, I'd kept Crystal for myself. She'd already said she was gunning for me. What was the point of putting it off?

I shrugged, feigning nonchalance and, I hoped, a confident air. "Sometimes, we just have to face what's coming to us."

CHAPTER SEVENTEEN

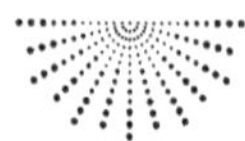

Our teams ran at each other like armies did in the movies—feet thundering and chests heaving, as growls and grunts of exertion slipped from our lips.

Arlo soared at the front of our group, outpacing even light-footed Sai, who was sprinting straight for Dak. The lion shifter was in the middle of transforming, unaware that Sai would be upon him in seconds.

Gio was on his game, too. Water was already spurting from the white marble floor, walls, and ceilings, creating obstacles, hiding spots, distractions, and possible weapons.

After weeks of training, I finally understood that nearly *everything* could be used as a weapon if you looked at it the right way.

I shot a glance to my left. Victoria brought up the rear, peeking around geysers every few feet, trying to find Finn and disable him before he caused real damage. Getting rid of anyone with elemental magic quickly was key.

As if on cue, a scream shot through the training room, and my attention followed the sound.

Arlo had hit his target, and a hank of Maria's dark, curly hair trailed from his talons as he zoomed away from a dozen thickets of trees popping out of the marble. At Maria's bidding, the tree branches moved like snakes, trying to rip Arlo out of the sky.

But Arlo had all but disappeared. The beams of wood that supported the training hall's ceiling served as an excellent camouflage for his feathered form. He was waiting it out, searching for another chance to disarm Maria.

An opportunity that, with Maria's focus on the ceiling, I could easily provide.

Not breaking step, a beam of visible light shot from my hands right into Maria's eyes. The rumbler cried out in pain, and Arlo made his move, swooping down from his hideout to clutch her neck lightly with his talons. He screeched in victory.

Maria swore in Spanish and held up her hands. Arlo released her, and, without another word, she stomped to the entrance of the training room to wait for the exercise to be over.

A grin bloomed on my face. Mere minutes into the exercise, and we were already up one. This crazy plan may just work.

Shooting a thumbs-up over my head for Arlo, I surged forward, searching for Crystal in the mayhem. Water shot up every ten feet, and what looked like miniature woods filled in most of the remaining space. Either our distractions were making it difficult for Crystal to find me, or she was waiting for the perfect moment.

My money was on the second option. Crystal was skilled and ferocious, but she was also cunning. Not one to expend needless energy. I'd just have to keep alert and help my teammates out in the meantime.

An opportunity to be of help presented itself immediately, as Gio and Himari stumbled through a thicket to fight a few dozen yards in front of me. Himari's dark eyes narrowed with pain as Gio lashed water against her torso. Not skipping a beat, she reciprocated with targeted ribbons of wind that acted like whips, and nearly hit Gio straight in the face.

I darted to the side and huddled behind a geyser, lying in wait. Gio was trying his hardest to advance, surging forward with every burst of water, but Himari's wind retaliated brilliantly, pushing him back just far enough to keep her out of his clutches. Yet, even as she increased the space between her and Gio, Himari was inevitably inching backward, closer to *me*.

I held my breath, determined not to give away our advantage by acting too soon. After what seemed like forever, they came within a meter of my hiding space, and I struck.

Gio's velvet brown eyes widened as I flew out from behind the geyser, my flaming hot blade shooting forth as I sprinted. Himari noticed her opponent's reaction and whipped around. Her hands shot in front of her, working frantically to conjure a gale that would send me reeling backward, but the element of surprise had worked in my favor. I aimed my blade carefully, halting the light from extending an inch away from the delicate skin of her neck.

"I surrender, you sneaky sneak," Himari panted. I grinned, and she stuck out her tongue before exiting the war arena.

Gio and I parted wordlessly. I continued moving through the training room, searching for Crystal. Though we'd been sparring in the same space for months, it'd never seemed so dangerous before, dotted with elemental obstacles and practiced opponents.

I was just debating my next best move, when a loud roar shot through me, raising the hairs on the nape of my neck.

Was Dak close by? Did he, with his keen animal senses, know I was around? And where the hell was Crystal? I had zero doubt she was coming for me. She probably just wanted to build my anticipation to heart-pounding levels before making a move.

Peering around a large geyser, I scanned for any hint of red hair or white mane. Instead, my eyes caught a motion and snapped upward to find Arlo dropping out of the sky, his tail feathers on fire.

My heart plummeted with the shifter eagle. I raced to where I judged he would land, wracking my brain for a way to cushion his fall. If he stayed an eagle, it would be easy, I could catch him. But if Arlo transformed . . .

Would he be that stupid?

I pushed harder, his eagle screech ringing in my ears. He frantically flapped his wings to maneuver himself into a geyser and put out the fire.

Fire. If there was fire, there would also be Finn.

My senses spiked, wondering if I was running into a trap, but I was too concerned for Arlo to truly care. Even in Faerie, a smashed-in brain was lethal.

My legs burned and my chest heaved as I pushed myself to run faster. I had nearly rounded a thicket when a screech and a *thunk* met my ears.

Arlo . . . No.

Surging around the final mess of trees, my senses were completely assaulted. The scent of smoke and burning hair filled my nostrils. Another scream, and the word "Surrender!" nearly shattered my eardrums. Then, to my great shock, water hit me straight in the face.

I sputtered and finally opened my eyes to make sense of what had just happened, and came face to face with Victoria.

"Oh my God! I'm sorry, Lana!"

Victoria was breathless, her hands patting her black hair, which was burnt off on one side. Behind her, Arlo, already transformed into a man, was going after Finn. His jaw was clenched as tight as his fists. Victoria lowered her hands and stared at them, her eyebrows knitted together.

"What happened?" I asked.

Victoria shook her head. "I'm not exactly sure . . . I caught Arlo, so he didn't crash. But as soon as I saved him, Finn set my hair on fire. I surrendered, but Arlo transformed really fast and went after Finn. I was about to run and find a geyser to stick my head in, when suddenly . . . water came out of my hands . . ." she trailed off and slowly her face split into a joyous grin.

I couldn't help but mirror her. "Holy shite, Victoria! You just discovered your elf power! That's amazing!" I hugged her, something we would have never done before last night.

"Too bad it came a second too late," Finn's voice cut through our joy, freezing my blood. I released Victoria to find that my best friend had Arlo in a headlock with a handful of fire next to his face. "What was that you were just saying, Arlo?"

Arlo's face was as red as his hair, his breath ragged as Finn tightened his grip.

"God dammit! I surrender," he croaked.

"Ah, good. I wasn't sure I heard you right the first time." Finn released Arlo, and the flame disappeared. "Looks like it's just you and me, Lan."

Oh, bloody fantastic.

Victoria and Arlo shot me apologetic looks and scurried away. Both were out, and neither wanted to be caught in a storm of fire and light magic.

I chanced a glance at the door. Dak had also joined those who had been defeated. That left Sai, Finn, Crystal, and me still in the mix. We were dead even.

I lashed out first, tossing a spray of visible light in Finn's eyes and calling my infrared sword in quick succession.

Finn seemed to anticipate my actions, because he closed his eyes and quickly brandished a sword of fire to match my infrared one. Then, just to show off a little, he tossed his sword in the air and caught it again one-handed.

I rolled my eyes. "You know Ebba isn't here, right?"

An easy grin crossed Finn's face. "I can't show off for my best friend?"

"As if that's not the story of your life," I teased, dodging his sword easily as he lunged.

I was about to run my mouth a bit more, when I noticed he'd spun back around and tossed two sizzling balls of fire. One zoomed past my left arm, while the other nearly took off my right ear. I froze for a second, giving Finn just enough time to advance. He brought his sword of flame down, and, thinking fast, I shot mine up. Our weapons met in a hiss of fire and light.

Changing tack, Finn twirled gracefully, and I scrambled to keep his weapon from searing into my shoulder. There was no doubt about it, he had superior strength, reflexes, and magic. Plus, he was a demon born, which meant that a terrifying, demon-gifted power could appear at any moment.

I shook the fear from me and took a wobbly step back. There was nothing I could do about his magical diversity. Finn's power would emerge when he was ready, and I would have to work with what I had. Fortunately, where Finn was concerned, I was a wealth of knowledge.

Especially relating to his weaknesses.

"Ebba! Help!" I screamed, waving my hands wildly.

He shot a glance behind him, and I darted to the outer edge of the clearing. In less than a second, I'd created an illusion, making myself invisible. I grinned as he whipped back around, his cheeks pink and eyes narrowed.

"Very funny, Lan."

I bit back a laugh because he was already on the prowl. Finn had seen me disappear before his eyes many times, and would know to strike at the tiniest sound or movement. I had to slow down.

Tiptoeing forward, I held my infrared sword inches from the illusion's boundary. One hasty move, and my weapon would poke through the fantasy of invisibility and give away my position.

Finn's pointed ears were alert as he eyed the small clearing and surrounding thickets and geysers warily. The water gushing from the ground muffled the noise I made, so I picked up the pace and, just seconds later, stood directly behind him. Barely daring to breathe, I lifted my sword, preparing to tear through my illusion and place the tip inches from his neck. Surrender was inevitable.

Then the world shifted.

I sucked in a breath as Sai leapt out from behind a geyser. Finn, reacting to the sound, spun, and fire ripped through my illusion, coming dangerously close to my face. I jumped back with a shriek and fell flat on my rear. My infrared sword disappeared into thin air, leaving me defenseless.

Finn advanced on me, but Sai came to my rescue, ripping a few branches off a nearby tree and sharpening their tips in an instant. The next thing I knew, Finn darted away to avoid being impaled on a particularly dagger-like branch.

"Get moving, Lana. There's someone lurking nearby, and she's looking for you," Sai yelled as Finn's sword met hers, and they began the dance of battle.

I pivoted away from the pair, my eyes darting from side to side, taking in the space and searching for Crystal. Carefully, I made my way through the trees.

A couple of minutes later, I could no longer hear Finn and Sai. Nor had I sensed another's presence. Needing a breather, I paused in an area free of geysers and trees, about four meters across. With nothing blocking my view, I felt a little safer, less on display. The throbbing in my head pulsed harder now that I'd stopped moving. My fingers gravitated toward my temples and rubbed the tender spot there, just as Mam had taught me to do. The sharp ache subsided slightly, and my eyes fluttered closed as I savored the brief relief. As soon as this training exercise was over, I was heading to the healers' ward and demanding another remedy.

A rustle of leaves sounded, and my fingers froze.

Ugh, already? I forced myself to open my eyes and confront my demons. Just as I knew I would, I found Crystal standing before me, smirking. I dropped my arms and called my sword to me, but Crystal reacted even faster. Wind nearly as strong as Sai's stole my breath and pressed my body back, keeping me from charging forward.

There was no way I could wield an infrared sword against her at this distance, and cunning Crystal was already squinting, prepared for me to attempt to blind her. I wasn't sure what her plan was, but knowing her, she was probably trying to work out how to steal the breath from my lungs and end the game without really engaging me.

My mind working rapidly, I scanned Crystal's form, and my gaze latched onto the gold necklace around her neck. An idea struck.

It was risky and likely wouldn't work. If it did, I

was going to have to get closer to have a real chance at fighting. But it might buy me time.

I took aim and sent a cascade of infrared flashes at my opponent. The first few missed as Crystal darted and wove around them, but one finally hit bang on.

Her bellows filled the training room as the necklace transmuted from a light gold to bright, burning red in an instant. The gales railing against me released as Crystal's attention broke. She ripped the hot necklace off and plunged her chest into a nearby geyser to dilute the pain.

I sprinted forward. I'd nearly halved the distance between us when Crystal yanked herself out of the geyser, glared at me, and charged.

The infrared sword bloomed in my hands instinctively as I braced for impact.

It never came.

Instead, my head snapped forward and legs flailed as I was tossed upward. My skull met a wooden beam with a *crack*, and the world blurred. A groan escaped me, and my stomach heaved as I floated—no, *whipped*—around the edges of a tornado. Water and bits of trees whirled madly in my wake. Vaguely, I realized that I'd lost control over my sword, but was too discombobulated to care.

How was I going to get out of this? Shooting flashes of light were out. I was moving so fast that I'd just as likely hit those huddled near the door. Or no one at all.

Illusions were useless too. Crystal already had me right where she wanted me. She probably planned on spinning me around until I passed out.

My mind was still struggling to come up with a solution when suddenly, the tornado let up. I plummeted, and a scream tore up my throat. But before I'd fallen even halfway to the ground, the winds buoyed me upward once more. My stomach heaved from the jerky motion. I dropped my chin, prepared to lose the contents of my stomach.

I caught sight of what was beneath me. My eyebrows knit together. I was sitting on a bed of compressed air mixed with swirling dirt that resembled an opaque bench.

Why had she stopped? No part of me believed Crystal wanted to give me a reprieve. Maybe she just didn't want to be puked on? But still . . . it was weird and didn't quite add up. My head was still spinning, but I needed answers so praying that I wouldn't topple off the bench of air, I leaned forward slowly.

From my high vantage, I spotted Finn among the ranks of the surrendered. My heartbeat kicked up. There were only three participants left: Crystal, Sai, and me. I searched for a bright shock of white hair and caught it directly below me. Tears of relief filled my eyes.

Sai had come to my rescue and was battling Crystal, who had probably only paused the tornado because she couldn't maintain it *and* fight off Sai simultaneously.

The pair danced and darted around each other. Sai, like most elves, wielded all four elements with grace and the speed for which she was well known. Orange and red flame flew from her.

Adeptly, Crystal blew the attacks away, but in the process, she never had a second to initiate her own strike. And then, as only an elemental master could, Sai changed her tactic mid-assault. A lasso of flame flew behind Crystal and shot back like a boomerang.

Abandoning distance, the only advantage Crystal had maintained, she launched herself at Sai, landed just before the white-haired fae, and sent a fist straight into the guard's gut.

I winced as Sai groaned. A hit like that would have taken me down. But not Sai. She collected herself with astonishing rapidity, spun, and slashed Crystal's thigh with her blade. A shriek pierced the air, and I watched in utter amazement as Crystal toppled to the ground.

A bit stupidly, considering how badly my head spun, I leaned far forward and peered under the bench to get a better look.

Sai placed a foot on Crystal's chest, and a waterfall of fire poured from her hands, just inches from landing on Crystal's face. The glint of fury was discernible in Crystal's eyes, even from a distance.

I grinned. This was it. We had her.

Unable to contain my excitement, I fist-pumped the air. The motion caught Crystal's attention, and her gaze shot up to me. Slowly, a chilling smile came over her face.

Then she dropped me.

When I came to, there were people, my father included, all around. A healer knelt close by, her smooth hand caressing my forehead as another checked my pulse. Heat rose in my face as my father's eyes bore through mine and then snapped away, as if he were embarrassed to see me in such a state.

"This was a highly impressive display of power." He stood to address the group. "Had I known this type of exercise was happening, I'd have sat up in the box to watch the whole thing. Extraordinary fighting, especially from you, Major Second Order."

At his side, Crystal puffed out her chest.

I wished I'd stayed unconscious a little longer.

"Meegra, remind me to have invitations sent out as soon as they're completed. Our mission is approaching faster than I could have dared to hope, and I want all of Lyonesse to see our soldiers off. The entire kingdom should be involved when we win back our bonegate."

Meegra frowned, but quickly caught herself and nodded. "Yes, Your Majesty."

"Now, Major Crystal, if you would join me in my chambers, I'd like to have a chat with you."

The circle around me wavered, and a glint of red stepped over me and followed the soft, regal footsteps of my father.

I closed my eyes as the throbbing in my head returned with a vengeance.

CHAPTER EIGHTEEN

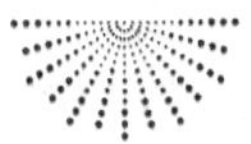

My spot at the top was slipping away, just like the hours I needed to keep it in my grasp.

The mere thought made me break into sweats.

It was for this reason that, instead of interacting more with my siblings, as I said I would, I became hypervigilant about training and studying. After all, I hadn't worked my arse off to have what I wanted most evaporate at the last minute. I was determined to catch up with Crystal—and to best her.

Socializing could wait until after the mission.

Soon, Skade and her tribe were slated to arrive to help pull cannons across the sandy wasteland between Lyonesse and Buyan. The hired swords Meegra persuaded to join our cause after my lousy performance in Zatus had agreed to camp out between the kingdoms. We would meet up with them in less than two weeks.

Time was short, and my siblings and I were on pins and needles. Those who hadn't left Lyonesse since arriving in Faerie, couldn't stop wondering about the giants and the journey ahead. The rest were ready to hit the road and take a break from the monotony of training. I, however, mourned each day that passed because I hadn't improved enough.

I supposed it served me right. What kind of person attempted to better an ex-Olympian and medical school prodigy? But even as doubts swirled in my mind, I opened the massive, velvet-bound book titled *Military Tactics of Faerie*, for what felt like the hundredth time.

I sighed as I stared at the first page. At least the writing was large and there were diagrams. Diagrams always helped me keep my eyes open. For a bit, anyhow.

I dove into the material, hoping to find this book fascinating and completely understandable, unlike before. My desires were fruitless, and when Tess opened my door two hours later with breakfast, I'd barely read ten pages.

Placing a ribbon in my spot, I slammed the tome shut with a frustrated huff.

Tess' lips squished to the side. "Are you sure you wouldn't like to join your siblings in the great hall for breakfast, Princess Lana? A bit of socializing might do you some good." Even as she suggested it, she set my tray on the table, already knowing the answer.

I'd taken most of my meals in my room for the last three weeks. As we drew closer to our mission, dinner was the only meal my father reliably turned up at, so it was the only one that I, too, attended.

"There's no time for relaxing, we're leaving in a few days. I have to be prepared," I replied before stuffing a monstrous bite of egg into my mouth. A screech emitted from Naela's mew. She'd probably scented the sausage.

Or she wants your attention, a tiny voice in the back of my head said. It was the same voice that I'd been silencing a lot lately. The one that reminded me there was more to life than just work.

It was a voice that clearly had never had anything to lose.

"Tess, would you mind asking the gamekeeper to fly Naela today? I don't have time before training, and even though she has free rein, she likes to be accompanied and tossed meat."

Tess nodded and bowed her way out of the room.

***

Hours later, I slammed my bedroom door shut behind me.

Tess, who'd been stoking the fire in anticipation of my arrival, let out a cry of surprise. Her watery blue eyes widened as she took in the bruise blooming on my jaw.

"Princess should see a healer before dinner. That bruise looks awful," she squeaked.

"I'm fine," I snapped, and then trying to modulate my tone better, added, "Please run me a bath and put lots of salt in it."

Tess' sentiments were in the right place, but I didn't have time for a healer. I needed to get in a few more pages of that military book. Every second counted, and I couldn't be wasting time at the healers' ward.

Tess leapt up from her crouch and ran into the bathroom. The sounds of running water met my ears a moment later.

I peeked into Naela's mew. My hawk was gone, hopefully out with the castle gamekeeper. I bit my lip as guilt pinged inside me. This was the longest span of time that I'd gone without flying Naela myself. Both of us felt the strain. Lately, when I said goodnight to my familiar, her feathers bristled. She was pissed at me, and rightfully so. I'd been a shite handler since returning from Zatus.

It can't be helped, I thought, shutting the door to her mew and shaking my head. I had more important things on my mind. We'd have plenty of time to fly when we left for the mission, anyway.

"The water is ready, princess." Tess appeared at my side, performed a little jerky bow, and sped out of the room before I could snap at her again.

I undressed and sank into the water. Daily baths

had become my single luxury. I inhaled deeply, bidding the scent of lavender to wash over me. My eyes closed, my body's way of savoring the fleeting calm. Unfortunately, my mind could not relax, and immediately, unwelcome images from the day resurfaced.

Behind my eyelids, I watched as Crystal bested me once more in one-on-one weapons-only combat. The match had been so obviously one-sided that after only a few minutes, I'd gotten frustrated and unsportingly attacked her with light magic. She'd retaliated with a gale so intense it nearly toppled me over, and a firm punch to my jaw.

My teeth gnashed together at the annoying memory.

No matter how hard I worked, she was always a step ahead of me. To make matters worse, now that our father had seen how wonderful Crystal was, he *always* asked about her in our meetings. My progress always seemed meager by comparison.

I was tired of watching his eyes dim when I told him I had yet to expand my range on the electromagnetic spectrum, or discover my elven powers. Besides being more in shape, which counted for practically nothing, as *all* my siblings were fit, I hadn't made a speck of progress. It was infuriating.

The dinner bell tolled outside. On autopilot, I pulled myself out of the water and wrapped a towel around my body. When I glanced in the mirror, the face of a stranger stared back at me. Black circles ringed my eyes. I looked paler than ever before, which was saying something, as I'd never had a tan a day in my life. My new muscles made me look impressive. Even so, I still resembled a buff corpse.

It's only temporary, I reminded myself. Life wouldn't always be like this. I just needed to work hard now for a massive payoff later—a life I could never have dreamed of back home. One where I actually made a difference. Once I proved myself, everything else would fall into place.

The slam of my *Military Tactics* book on the table didn't even make a dent in the cacophony in the dining hall. Still, people looked up from the tables surrounding me, their eyes cautious. Internally, I winced at their reaction. Tess wasn't the only one who'd learned to be wary around me in the past weeks. But some things, like changing the fate of Lyonesse and making sure my father knew I was reliable, were more important than being liked right now. Once Lyonesse was safe, and magic returned to it, then I could work on bonding with others. To make a real change, sacrifices had to be made.

Keeping that in mind, I sat and cracked open the tome.

"Was wondering if we'd see you here tonight. You're hit-or-miss nowadays, my friend." Finn materialized at my side and, despite my obvious 'keep away' vibes, joined me. "Can we talk?"

My fingers, which had already begun flicking through the pages of the book, fell to the table. "Sure. But make it fast, I have work to do."

Finn arched a single blond eyebrow. "So I see. Bringing a book to dinner, huh? It's like we traded places."

I rolled my eyes. "Finn, you've never brought a book to dinner a day in your life. You may have been more bookish than me, but your mealtimes were always strictly reserved for socializing and having a pint."

He laughed. It seemed like it had been a long time since I'd heard that laugh. When was the last time I'd really chatted with Finn, and not just bossed him around during training?

"You have me there," he said good-naturedly. "So what makes you think *you* need to carry a book to dinner? What's so important it needs to be studied during mealtimes? Why not take a load off and have a chat?"

"You know our mission is coming up. There's a lot to learn before then."

Finn examined the cover of my book. "Like military strategy in Faerie? Don't you think delegating some of that workload might be smart? And less stressful?"

"I'm a *general*, Finn. The top of Lyonesse's army.

Even if others study the same material, I have to know it too."

My words came out as if I were speaking to a child, and immediately, I regretted my tone. Still, I didn't take it back. It was almost game-time, and I needed everyone to stop questioning me. If that meant dishing out some sass, so be it.

He leaned forward. "You know that's ridiculous. The best generals in history were only the best because they knew how to manage others well and leverage their strengths. Giving others tasks won't make you any less respected. It's intelligent." Finn's blue eyes darted around my face, scrutinizing me. "Can't you see you're wearing yourself to the ground? There are massive bags beneath your eyes. Have you been sleeping at all?"

Heat rushed into my cheeks, and my fingers tightened around the book. "I don't see how that's any of your business. And perhaps generals in the Old Land were successful with delegation, but Faerie is different, in case you didn't notice. Not to mention, our mission is *unprecedented*. We're about to infiltrate a city with people who barely know anything about this land. I have to be the one to guide them."

Finn pressed his lips together, and silence seemed to expand between us, taking up the air and making my heart beat faster. Finally, the retaliation that I knew was coming presented itself as Finn leaned forward.

"Or," Finn allowed the word to trail out. "You could use Crystal as a resource. I know there's an intense rivalry going on between you two. But instead of killing yourself every day to best her, why don't you ask her for help?"

I opened my mouth to say my piece, but he held up his hand, cutting me off.

"Clearly, Crystal has developed a maniacal drive and ability to absorb knowledge and skills. But only a unique person can operate that way. It would be smarter to take advantage of that rather than fighting her every step of the way." He took a deep breath and shook his head.

"All I'm saying is that you could use your time better, Lan. Take proper care of yourself and focus on your magic. You're an illuminator witch. Your energy would be best spent solely on trying to harness your rare abilities. Not doing magic, running hundreds of laps, lifting weights, horseback riding like you're training to become a jockey, *and* staying up all night studying."

"I need to do those things to get better at them! How else can I lead a mission?" Why didn't he understand that?

"Looking at you now, I wonder if you can even make it to Buyan. You look dead on your feet."

That was the limit. I slammed my book shut just as the servant brought over my meal. It was hard to believe that in five minutes, I'd gone from a bit exhausted to positively fuming.

"Clearly, my appearance is offending you, so I'll just leave," I snapped.

Finn's eyes popped open, and he started to say something, but I whipped around, unwilling to hear it. A servant holding my tray stood before me, trembling.

I pointed at the food. "Have that taken up to my room."

With that, I stormed out of the dining hall without a second glance back.

In the training room the next day, Finn gave me a wide berth.

I *hated* when people acted like I was off my rocker for experiencing strong emotions. While I'd felt a little guilty over my outburst the night before, all that guilt evaporated at the sight of Finn walking on eggshells. I wasn't ready to let it go yet, so I didn't. I went about my morning, working out and training. I kept to myself as if nothing had ever happened.

When I left the training room at mid-morning for a meeting with my father, my eyes were bleary and exhausted. As usual, the door opened by itself after I knocked, and my father appeared from his secret hole in the floor a moment later.

His gold eyes widened as I joined him at the firlon, and I cringed. It had been three days since our last meeting and he hadn't looked at me like that then. Perhaps Finn was right, and I was wearing myself a wee bit too thin?

Then again, Finn had never experienced the pressure I was experiencing. The worst of his worries had consisted of pleasing his stepfather, who loved Finn deeply. He'd never seriously failed or been at the bottom of any test—unlike me. What did Finn know about falling from grace?

"Come, sit with me, Daughter."

I complied, practically collapsing into the chair my father pulled out for me.

"Is something wrong? I noticed you left the feast rather abruptly last night. And it looks as if you rested poorly. Did you quarrel with Finn?"

My heartbeat sped up. Had Finn said something to him? Despite my inner anxiety, I played it cool and shrugged. "You could say that. He was trying to help, and I was being stubborn."

My father nodded understandingly. "It's a Fullfeather trait if there ever was one. I hope you two can mend fences soon. I'm sure that whatever sour words were said came from a place of love."

"You're probably right," I admitted. Somehow, just telling my father the truth, or bits of it anyway, made everything better. "We'll work it out."

His lips quirked upward. "Good. For there is

much to accomplish. I was going to tell you last night, but after your quarrel, I decided it could wait until today. If you're anything like me, sometimes you just need a little time to cool off." My father tented his hands beneath his chin and his smile grew as I nodded. That was exactly what I needed. I was glad he understood.

"Skade's tribe has been spotted by one of the Feathered Fae on patrol," the king continued. "They should be here soon."

"Where will they stay?" I asked. It was something I'd thought of earlier, but still had not figured out. It wasn't like Lyonesse had giant-sized homes or anything.

"Good question. As we have little space in Lyonesse for beings of their size, it would be best if you set out quickly once they arrive. In fact, there is a ball being prepared for your send-off as we speak." Father's eyes glittered with excitement. "We have not had a celebration of this sort in years. The ball is an important morale-booster for the troops and subjects of the kingdom who attend. I expect each of you to be present and in excellent form."

My head spun. There was a ball already being prepared? Bloody hell, my father moved quickly.

"When is the ball?"

"Tomorrow night. The next day, you will set out on your mission. Meegra has already been informed, and supplies are currently being prepared. You should spend your remaining time becoming familiar with the landscape around Pari's castle, as well as the castle itself. I will, of course, send my best tracker with you, but he can only take you so far."

"Because of the wards?"

My father nodded. "Queen Pari has use of an outstandingly powerful and precise wardmaker. As it wouldn't be beneficial for wards to alert the queen to everything that crosses into Buyan's territory—animals, for instance—the wards on the outskirts of the kingdom are weaker than those closer to the city. Therefore, the tracker can cross into the kingdom but not into the capital."

"But we can?" That was the implication, but I didn't understand why.

"Precisely. The wards nearest the city are set off if a *full* fae crosses. As all of my children from the Old Land have at least a little non-magical blood in them from human ancestors, you are undetectable. My hope is that the diversion we create will draw guards toward the bonegate, making your entry over Buyan's wall and into Castle Dalir easier."

"I see. That's pretty cunning," I said, somewhat startled by the amount of planning that must have gone into this.

My father rubbed the nape of his neck in the anxious gesture that we shared. This probably should have made me even more nervous, but I actually found it endearing. He never let his nervous tics show in public.

"Perhaps," he said, his tone tentative. "But remember, I am a dimwitted fool when compared to Queen Pari. Even though a distraction will be underway, you must remain alert at all times, and know your way around."

He paused and swept his hand in the direction of the firlon. "These chambers and the firlon will be open for your use until you leave. Simply lay your hand on the door and use the password, 'bonegate'. The firlon is an excellent tool to help you familiarize yourself with Queen Pari's lands and castle—much better than any books you may have referenced, I daresay."

"Thank you. I'm excited to give it a spin." I was too. I'd seen the item many times but never used it myself. It would be an experience.

"It would be best if you brought your majors in here, too, for backup," Father replied. "More than one person will need to know the layout of Castle Dalir. Your maid may accompany you into my personal quarters, so you want for nothing while you prepare, but no one else. I treasure my chambers. They are my sanctuary, and I wish to keep them as private as possible."

Although he was giving me a compliment by letting me into his chambers without him, my mind didn't allow me to focus on that fact. It was his suggestion that I needed Crystal and Finn's help that struck me the most. Father was practically reciting Finn's words from last night. Perhaps Finn had even planted them there?

I hid my scowl and nodded. "Thank you for giving us the tools to succeed. I won't let you down, Father."

CHAPTER TWENTY

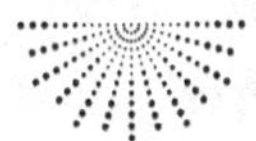

After completing afternoon training, I made my way back to my father's chambers with Tess in tow. I intended to send her to the dining hall for food once dinner began, so that I was not interrupted. It was the best plan I could come up with to maximize my time with the firlon. Plus, sending Tess meant avoiding Finn, which I was keen on. I was pretty sure that he'd gone straight to our father to insist that I needed help, which rubbed me the wrong way.

For once, I wanted to be right. That meant not needing Finn to come and save me.

We'll have a tracker guiding us most of the way there, I thought, as I neared Father's chambers. Besides, how complex can a castle be?

As soon as the thought materialized, I cringed. Only weeks ago, I'd been lost in Phoenix Castle.

That won't happen in Buyan, I told myself.

I had use of the firlon, and I'd make sure to draw meticulous maps for the others. This mission would be perfect. Even if I had to stay up all night to create maps and memorize routes, I'd make sure it went off without a hitch.

I placed my hand on the door to my father's chamber and whispered the password. The door swung open, and I entered with confidence, only to jump when Tess released an astonished gasp behind me. Her awe reminded me that most who lived in the castle had never been inside this space. And even though I was used to the king's hideaway, it was still an impressive sight.

Lit torches illuminated the dark room. This space was in stark contrast to the swaths of white marble that dominated the rest of the castle. Exquisite tapestries featuring historic Lyonesse hung from the stone walls.

I glanced at the one depicting my great-great-grandfather, a Sinker of Faerie. His piercing gold eyes seared through us, motivating me. In the center of the room, the firlon burned brightly, welcoming me inside. I walked toward the enchanted object, my palms shaking.

Although my father had shown me how to use the firlon many times, I'd never actually been the one in control of it. I wondered if it was like the internet. What would happen if I asked to see Beast Realm or

Water Realm, or even Mam's home back in Ireland? Could it even reach the Old Land?

My heart clenched at the thought of Mam and her soft, soothing ways. Her presence would be so welcome right now, when I felt exhausted and perpetually not good enough. I wished I could see her. That she could come to Faerie.

A clatter sounded behind me, making me jump. I whipped around to see Tess standing next to an old tapestry of Lyonesse, her expression guilty. On the floor next to her were the books I'd requested that she carry when my own hands became too full. Most were military and geographical reference books, although there was one, a sci-fi novel, for Tess. I didn't want my maid getting bored while I worked. Plus, I thought the story would knock her socks off.

"Apologies, Princess Lana!" Tess squeaked. She gathered the volumes off the floor and clutched them to her chest. "It's only . . . I recognize that building."

She pointed to the woven tower that stood just off Choral Bay so the fae could spot incoming ships. "I've never seen my home look so . . . green."

A lump formed in my throat. Tess was a young goblin, which meant she'd never seen her homeland in its full glory. Her only reality had been black, brittle, and barren lands. How depressing.

"It's okay," I reassured her. "The tapestries are astounding, aren't they? My father told me that the one you're looking at was created right before he was crowned."

I pointed to the one I'd been introduced to during my first meeting with my father. "And this one over here was made in the likeness of my great-great-grandfather."

Tess' eyes widened, and she inched closer. The instant she was close enough to take in the full tapestry, she dropped the books once more and fell to her knobby knees. The resounding *crack* that filled the room made me wince.

"Sinkers be praised!" Tess wailed, her hands on her heart as she prostrated herself before the imagery of my ancestor.

My eyebrows arched, but I refrained from sighing. It was a dramatic reaction, but I should have expected it. Tess, like most fae in Lyonesse, worshipped my family.

"Er, Tess . . . do you mind just sitting over there?" I pointed to the table where my father conducted meetings. "I need to get to work, and what you're doing might be distracting."

What an understatement. I wouldn't get *any* work done with Tess groveling around the weaving. Still, I didn't want to make her feel bad.

Tess leapt up from the cold ground, her entire body trembling as she picked up the books and scurried over to the table. Even as she sat, her watery eyes never left the tapestry of the Lyonesse Sinker. I had a feeling the sci-fi book I'd picked for her would go unread.

I turned my attention to the firlon and hovered my hand over the tall flames. The heat rose, warming my palm, a welcome sensation. I'd been so cold lately, although whether it was from lack of sleep or the weight loss brought on by intense exercise, I wasn't sure. Nor did I care. I'd simply piled on more layers. My current discomfort was temporary.

"Show me Castle Dalir." My hand swooshed through the flames.

Tess yelped, and fast steps approached as my maid came to check that I was unhurt. But my hand came out the other side of the firlon unscathed, just as Father's did every time.

"I'm fine, Tess." I grinned at her, more relieved than I was letting on that my use of the firlon had actually worked.

She blinked, and after a thorough assessment of my palms, sat once more.

When I looked down again, a castle had already materialized within the fire. I stared at Castle Dalir in awe. It was enormous—at least twice the size of Castle Phoenix—with immaculate grounds, more elaborate gardens, and, from what I could tell, a thriving little town just outside the castle gate. From my bird's-eye view, there were fae dressed like guards *everywhere*. They lined every entrance and exit, and were even stationed below castle windows.

A high proportion of guards seemed to gather in a specific garden, so I zoomed in, hovered my clenched fist above that specific patch of greenery, and opened it slowly, as one would do with a computer tablet.

The scene grew larger and the figures more clear. I sucked in a breath, sure that I was seeing Queen Pari in the flesh.

Despite being one of the most evil people I'd ever heard tales of, I had to admit that she was lovely. Even more so than the painting I'd seen.

Queen Pari sat, poring over a page filled with tiny symbols, as two guards dressed in imperial purple hovered over her. Raven-dark hair trailed down her back, except for the bit she twirled through her fingers. Pari's skin was impeccable, dark and creamy. Her brown eyes crinkled at their edges, and when she laughed, a mouth full of perfectly white teeth gleamed through the flame.

Clad in an all-white garment resembling a sari, she looked like a Bollywood movie star. Gold glinted on her hands and face, where she wore a small nose ring. It was the first facial jewelry I'd seen in Faerie, and she pulled it off well.

I shook my head. Why was I admiring the enemy? I was wasting valuable time.

My hand hovered over the firlon again. I moved to zoom in once more, intent on reading the sheet Pari studied. As she grew larger, I leaned in, squinting to see the figures on the page, and hoping they weren't written in an unreadable Faerie language.

I still couldn't quite make anything out, so I zoomed in again and leaned forward as far as I dared. The flames parted for my face so that I could hover my nose two inches above the dancing flames that made up Queen Pari and her guards.

I let out a sharp exhale as what the queen was looking at became clear. A map on which Buyan and Lyonesse were clearly labeled, with pins stuck in them.

"Ah ha," I breathed, sure I'd stumbled onto something important.

Suddenly, Pari's head jerked up, and her eyes searched the sky disconcertingly, before landing in my general direction.

My eyebrows furrowed. Could she see me?

As if in answer, Queen Pari scowled.

Shite! Fear hit me like a sledgehammer, and I zoomed out of the castle as fast as I could and stepped away from the enchanted object.

"Princess? Is everything okay?"

"She saw me," I whispered, my voice a ghost of what it normally sounded like.

"Who?" She tensed.

"The Queen of Buyan."

"Was she peering back at you in a firlon?"

I blinked. "What? No. She was in a garden, or something of the sort."

My maid's thin shoulder's loosened. "Then it is

impossible. I do not know much of firlons, but I know they are used for spying. You can only speak to another person, or see them, if they too look into the flames."

"Are you sure?" This had never happened to Father while I was in here, so I didn't know what to make of it.

It took many more reassurances from Tess that it was impossible for someone to see another person if they weren't peering into their own firlon, before I ventured close to the enchanted object once more. After that, I was especially careful, creeping tentatively around the city of Buyan, zoomed out farther as I documented streets.

To my great relief, after that first heart-stopping encounter, Pari was nowhere to be found. Even when I made my way inside the castle to explore two hours later, I couldn't find her.

And yet, the next day her dark, seeking eyes still haunted me as I struggled to stay awake and prepare for the ball.

"Princess, please stay still. Your short hair is difficult to pin, and I don't want to hurt you," Tess squeaked before plunging another pin into a low bun.

She'd been exceedingly careful with me all day, anticipating my every need. And for once, I let her baby me. I didn't have the energy to do everything myself after getting little sleep two nights in a row.

My siblings and I would leave the next morning.

As I had Tess to assist me, my packing had been easy, and I'd spent most of the day studying and *trying* to appease Naela.

Unfortunately, my attempt to bond with my familiar had been a total failure. After weeks of neglect, I'd pushed her too far. Naela wanted nothing to do with me, flying off my arm the second we were outside, not returning when I called, and worst of all, incessantly screeching insults from above while she flew.

My usual bribe to get her to land, meat dripping with blood, didn't even work. After an hour or so, I gave up and left her flying about the grounds. I'd barely arrived back in my room when I heard Naela swoop into her mew and continue screeching bloody murder.

After I shouted a few colorful insults at my familiar, Tess persuaded me I needed a nice bath to calm down. I had to admit, the soak had helped considerably. I soon let go of my squabble with Naela.

A pin poked me in the head, ripping me from memories of the day. "Ouch!"

"Apologies, Princess Lana, apologies. I'm simply not used to hair like yours. The fashion must be quite different in the Old Land. Why else would anyone chop their hair so short?" Tess mused for the tenth time.

"You have no idea," I said, thinking about my classmates with half-shaved heads and blue mohawks.

Tess worked a few minutes more before moving on to applying makeup. I told her I only wanted a little, to which the maid ordered me to close my eyes. After a half hour, I was deemed ready.

Striding into the bathroom—where we'd kept my red silk dress, hoping the steam from my bath would stave off any last-minute wrinkles—I glimpsed myself in the mirror. No wonder it had taken Tess so long to apply my makeup. I still looked sort of dead, but my face was a thousand times more attractive than before she'd worked her magic.

I slipped into the dress. "Tess? Can you button me up?"

She appeared in an instant, yawning sleepily, and climbed up on a chair to reach my top buttons.

I bit my lip. I hadn't even considered how exhausted Tess must be. She'd really gone above and beyond for me in the last few weeks.

"Hey," I said, my tone soft. "Thank you for helping me out so much, especially last night. I haven't been a ball of sunshine lately, but you've never complained. I appreciate that."

I closed my eyes briefly as yet another personal shortcoming came to mind. "*Also*, I know I haven't really been acting like a friend, as I said I would. Maybe when I return we can try again?"

I caught Tess' appalled expression in the mirror, but like any good maid, she simply nodded and continued fastening the buttons. I figured that was the best I could ask for. At least for now.

Finally, her calloused fingers brushed my lower back, and she stepped aside, gesturing for me to look in the mirror.

A woman transformed stood before me. Popping triceps had replaced my shapeless arms. My hourglass figure remained, but instead of being cushy, there was a hardness supplied by muscles I never knew I possessed. If someone looked at me from the neck down, they'd be impressed, jealous even. Although, once they got to my face, their opinion may change.

Lines brought on by my rapid weight loss were more prominent than they'd been just a week ago, and my gold eyes seemed to have dulled.

I sighed, the signs of stress weighing on me more than my impressive figure uplifted me.

"Thanks, Tess. I suppose this is as good as it's going to get, isn't it?"

"You look lovely, Princess Lana," Tess piped up.

I snorted and was about to tell her she didn't need to lie, when I caught her expression.

Tess, the maid who rarely even looked me in the eye, seemed sorry for me.

My words died in my throat. Unable to find an appropriate response, I left my rooms.

CHAPTER TWENTY-ONE

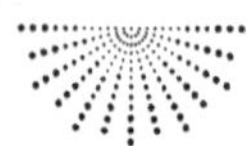

Notes of a soft guitar and a plucky flute met my ears as I descended upon the throne room. I'd passed a few of my siblings on the way to the ball, most notably Gio attempting to flirt with a duo of attractive females. Everyone tried to draw me into their conversations and merriment. I waved them off.

They might think the ball was all fun and games, but I knew tonight was important. I was here to be seen by the subjects of Lyonesse so that they'd understand that someone was fighting for their future.

Keeping this in mind, I took a deep breath as I crossed the threshold into the throne room. As soon as I entered, I halted, stunned.

The castle servants also understood the importance of tonight. They'd pulled out all the stops, and it showed in the glorious, small details.

Bright colors and precious metals flashed everywhere. The space, usually so white and austere, had been transformed into a riot of dreams.

Balls of light danced on currents of air, ensuring the room was perfectly illuminated. Shimmering streamers of fabric in red, black, and gold dropped from the ceiling and wafted in the faint breezes coming in through the partially open windows. Fountains of both water and wine flowed in each corner of the room. I watched in awe as fae strode up to the fountains and dipped their goblets into the liquid.

All classes of fae were in attendance and had dressed for the occasion. The females from the wealthier merchant class wore crimson, black, and gold gowns with skirts so large, they could swallow a man whole. Enormous headdresses, with feathers sticking up from the fabric, topped the heads of the merchant male fae, who wore velvet suits in Fullfeather colors.

While the poorer fae were less flashy, they were decorated too. Gold hairpins with petite rubies and stones of onyx were the most popular adornment among the working class.

At first glance, the ball was just as my father wanted: An event to see and be seen at, and a party to bolster the morale of Lyonesse.

I was just about to make my way into the crowds, when a guard extended an arm to stop me, and slammed his staff into the ground three times. A sound like cymbals reverberated through the room, startling me.

The music paused, and every fae in the place turned to face our way. When they saw who was being announced, their faces lit up. My cheeks warmed.

"Princess General Lana Fullfeather has arrived," the guard announced.

I performed an awkward curtsey, which the subjects of Lyonesse reciprocated. Once the formality was done, I dove into the sea of bodies. The fae parted, and hundreds of eyes followed me.

Despite the large crowd, the room remained so quiet that my footsteps echoed in the silent, large chamber. I was beyond uncomfortable, but forced myself to meet the gaze of anyone who sought mine with a gracious smile. Thankfully, when I was halfway across the room, the music started up once more. A few couples began to dance enthusiastically. Still, a discomforting number of fae continued staring— taking in my every move.

"Care to dance?" Finn appeared, his hand held out.

He looked dashing in his black suit trimmed at the edges with the slightest bit of gold. It was the same cut and style all my brothers wore. The Fullfeather ladies, on the other hand, all wore red. Red, gold, and black, our house colors.

Or the colors of assassins.

A group of females sighed as we clasped hands. I

snorted and forced myself not to roll my eyes. Even here, in a different world, Finn was a ladies man.

"Thanks," I mumbled as fae began going about their business, and my galloping heart rate slowed.

Although I was pretty sure this was a ploy to express his worries again, Finn had probably just saved me from dying of embarrassment.

"No problem."

We moved to the beat of a song I'd never heard before but imagined was like a waltz in the Old Land. As the tune ended, I made to break away.

Finn pulled me closer. "Lana, wait. Can we talk?"

I withheld a sigh, knowing what was coming and not wanting to hear it. But then again, dancing with him was definitely preferable to dancing with one of the merchants eyeing us, waiting for their chance to snag a princess or prince. So I nodded, and our bodies began to sway again. This time, the song was more upbeat. I was thankful that Finn had the rhythm to guide me.

"We're leaving on our mission tomorrow," he started softly. "None of us really know what to expect, and honestly, Lana, I'm concerned about you." He paused when I stiffened, but perhaps sensing I was about to bolt, plowed forth a second later.

"You look strong physically, but I can tell you're knackered. I can see it in the way you walk the corridors—even feel it in the way you're dancing now. I want to help you, take some of the burden. But you need to let me—or at least talk to me."

My jaw tightened, and I stared him straight in the eye.

"I'm fine," I growled, not trusting myself to say anything more.

"I *know* what fine is for you, Lan, and it's not this." Finn's finger hovered over the bags beneath my eyes. "I've never seen you look so exhausted."

My body was vibrating with anger now. I glared at Finn, who didn't shirk under my gaze. I was seconds away from exploding, when a soft hand landed on my shoulder.

"Might I cut in?" Garret asked.

"Absolutely," I said, dropping my arms from Finn's shoulders.

"*Lana*—" Finn started, but was cut off when a busty blonde fae inserted herself between us, allowing Garret to whisk me away.

My old guard guided me to the opposite side of the dance floor before releasing my arm. "We don't actually have to dance. I just saw how uncomfortable you looked and wanted to alleviate your unease."

His face reddened, and my heart clenched. Sinkers, he was kind—a real friend.

An obnoxiously loud giggle trounced a soft line of music. I turned to find a gaggle of girls about my age, each stunning with brightly colored hair and gem-toned eyes, staring at us. One of them not-so-subtly adjusted her cleavage and gave Garret a hungry glance.

Something inside me roared, and I grabbed Garret's hand. "No, let's dance. I want to."

"Oh, all right," Garret replied, his eyes widening with surprise, before pulling me close.

The aroma of metal and the outdoors—Garret's scent—enveloped me, and I relaxed.

He was an even better dancer than Finn. We floated together around the dance floor, our cheeks hovering inches from one another, and neither talking, simply enjoying the moment. We'd made a complete circle around the room, and the flirtatious fae from before scowled as we passed the group again. As Finn had been my best friend for years, it was a look with which I was massively familiar.

I chuckled, realizing that no matter how much had changed, I seemed destined to have exceedingly handsome guy friends and jealous female enemies.

"What's so funny?" Garret asked, pulling back to look me in the eye.

"Your admirers aren't pleased that we're dancing." I nodded toward the group of female fae.

Garret glanced over and rolled his eyes. "They're girls I lived near when I was young. They're not from my neighborhood exactly, but the next one over—the wealthier one. They never gave me the time of day before I became captain, because I was scrawny and awkward. But things change when you achieve a high post on the guard."

I stared at him. I couldn't imagine Garret as either of those things. He was one of the most gorgeous creatures I'd ever met.

Friends.

Right, friends . . .

"I can relate," I said. "Most people only ever interacted with me to get to Finn. When it became clear I was antisocial and wasn't going to help them, they dropped me. Especially the girls."

Garret raised a dark eyebrow. "You were antisocial? But you talk to people here. Or at least . . . you usually do."

I bit my lip, sensing his unsaid words. "Things are different here. I have responsibilities, and for once, I'm proud of my job and want to do it right. Even if it means isolating myself for a bit. That's just how I work best."

"You don't have to explain yourself. I only want you to be happy and healthy." Garret tucked a stray hair behind my ear.

My knees about gave out, but Garret caught me, his face coming closer as his grip tightened to keep me from falling. I stared into his mercurial gray eyes, thickly lashed, and a perfect contrast to his dark olive skin. The breath in my chest loosed, and I exhaled softly.

"Are you okay?" Garret hoisted me back up, so

that I stood on my feet again, but that smokey gaze never faltered.

"Fine," I breathed, fully aware of how *not* fine I was, and the whispers rising all around us.

"Are you sure? You don't have a fever, do you?" Garret's hand rose to brush my forehead, but he stopped himself before actually doing so. "If you do, we'll have to tell King Oberon right away so he can push our departure date back. We can't leave without you, you're too important."

My heart squeezed, and suddenly my face was inching toward his. Garret's eyes widened, but he did nothing to pull back. If anything, he softened and moved to meet me. Tingles flew up and down my spine, taking in the gorgeous man I was stupid enough to believe I could be 'just friends' with. My breath stilled as our lips hovered a disappointing hairsbreadth distance apart.

A resounding blast of brass shattered my trance. We jerked back, each swinging our head wildly to catch if anyone had noticed our near lip-lock. But everyone's eyes were trained on my father, who sat on his throne high above the dancing crowd. Casimir perched at his side. Behind the pair, Xerxes spewed a thin stream of fire from his beak.

"Ladies and gentlefae, thank you for coming tonight. This is a celebration I have wanted to throw for years."

The crowd screamed and whooped. Everyone's

eyes shone for their king, the man who would soon bring magic back into their city and lives.

"As you know, my children from the Old Land are in attendance tonight."

Many eyes turned and locked onto me. The heat in my cheeks flared and traveled down to my chest, where I was sure my skin was now blotchy.

"They've been training for weeks on end—conditions normally expected of our most elite soldiers and the Feathered Fae. Many have recently accessed powers of their fae ancestry in addition to their powers from the Old Land.

"You may ask why I've been training my children so hard. Why are they pushing their bodies to breaking?" Our father paused as his gaze swept the crowd.

Tension mounted, which he broke only after a few began to fidget. "I'll tell you why. They are doing it for *you*. Your new princes and princesses have been working day and night for one goal—to take back our rightful bonegate!"

The crowd erupted in cheers so loud that they made me jump.

The king waved his hand as if to say it was nothing at all. "And that is not all, my loyal subjects. My children are prepared to steal away into Buyan and put an end to Queen Pari's reign of terror by eliminating the evil one!"

Another deafening roar exploded through the cavernous room. I winced as a multitude of grateful hands brushed my skin, wishing me luck. Garret noticed my reaction and his jaw tightened, as if he was offended for me.

For everyone's sake, I did my best to relax. After all, a princess' job was to be accessible to her people, was it not?

"My children, please, join me on the steps," my father said, his voice magically amplified above the din of cheering.

Garret's strong hand guided me forward, through the overwhelming crowd of people who wanted to stop and thank me. He released me only when I'd reached the stairs and began the ascent with my siblings. After what felt like forever, we all reached the top of the steep stairs that led to the throne, and turned to face the crowd. Footsteps sounded behind me, and a second later, my father's hand landed on my shoulder. I looked up to see his moon-white face gazing out upon subjects with compassion.

"Let's hear another round of applause for my children, who will usher in a new, stronger Lyonesse!"

The crowd erupted in the loudest roar yet and began chanting our family name. My breath caught in my chest as I realized that this was just a fraction of the fae who depended on us. Although I'd been steady and sure of my desires before, their support bolstered me.

What we were doing would change lives in a way that I could have only imagined before. Although I did not relish the thought of killing again, I comforted myself with the fact that, overall, we were doing good. What my siblings and I were setting out to accomplish was right.

And I would stop at nothing to see the fae of Lyonesse happy, safe, and bursting with magic.

CHAPTER TWENTY-TWO

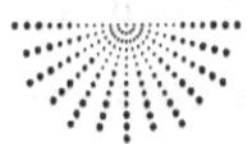

The next day, I found myself blinking into the bleak, early morning light, alongside my siblings and the army who would travel with us. Unavoidably, Meegra and most of the Feathered Fae were among them. However, as much as I did not look forward to suffering her company, I *was* pleased that my father had made clear who was in charge.

Me.

Meegra would take up the mantle only once my siblings and I split off from the main army. A fact that, judging by the purse of her lips, she did not appreciate, but accepted as a command from her king.

As it turned out, *Ryker* was the best tracker in Lyonesse. He would accompany us to the outskirts of the city of Buyan. As a full-blooded fae, Ryker wouldn't be able to cross the final wards around the city, much less get us into Castle Dalir. But he would be a great help in traversing the kilometers of thick jungle that surrounded the kingdom.

Horns blared, ripping me from the jumble of thoughts clouding my mind. Once the instruments stopped, the sound of Skade's clan shuffling and repositioning the cargo they carried became audible.

I tossed a glance back at them. A few giants wore harnesses that allowed them to pull canons without straining their backs or shoulders. The rest had bags tied to their hips. I felt a little bad about treating the giants like pack mules, but considering that the bags looked like fanny packs against their bodies, I figured it wasn't too much of a bother.

Just then, Skade emerged from the mass of giants to stand at the forefront of her tribe, and she caught my eye. A grin split her face, exposing her missing teeth as she waved.

I returned the gesture, pleased to see her too. I'd have to ride back and have a chat with her during the march.

"Citizens of Lyonesse!" My father's charismatic voice boomed from his spot on a makeshift dais, and the crowds quieted. "Thank you for dragging yourselves from your beds to witness the send-off of these gallant soldiers, princes, and princesses! Without them, there would be no hope for our kingdom. And because of them, in just a few days' time, our lives will change dramatically."

The crowd just outside the castle gates roared its pleasure. I stared out into the sea of fae. Unlike last night, most of those present seemed to be in the lower classes. As my gaze swept over their faces, I searched for one in particular. The green-skinned girl from the parade.

But despite being near the front of the line of troops and seated high on my horse, I couldn't find her. It wasn't too surprising, I guessed. She was a small girl, and the crowd before me was vast. Even if I couldn't see her, I hoped she could see me. I hoped she recognized that, while her vision of me sitting on the throne hadn't come true, and hopefully never would, I *was* doing something to better her life. I'd barely spoken with her, but the green-skinned girl had certainly made an impact on me.

"Thank you for that vote of confidence," my father continued once the cheering died down. "I'm sure the soldiers of Lyonesse and my blood—defenders of your homeland—will cherish your backing. Your passion will be the fuel they need to trudge north. Your support will be the anthem to which they sing. And dreams of your well-being will be the kindling that stokes the fire they shall ignite to change our world!" My father bowed his respect, and everyone in the army either returned his bend at the waist or, if seated on a horse, inclined their heads. "My subjects, please part and allow your saviors passage."

Suddenly the road appeared where only bodies had been before. Taking a deep inhale, I dipped my hand inside the pouch I wore at my hip. Just as when I'd left for Zatus, my satchel contained the bones of Kate and Kumar. And as the bones' hard, cold exterior brushed my skin, the familiar sensation of comfort that they'd provided then washed over me once more.

For Kate and Kumar, I couldn't fail. For the sake of all the fae before us, we *couldn't* fail.

With that firmly in mind, I kicked my horse forward.

"March!" I yelled.

The army moved as one. Showers of flower petals rained down, and fae wept tears of joy as we marched forth.

THE TREK BETWEEN LYONESSE AND BUYAN WAS AS bleak and ragged as I'd been led to believe. Black sands dominated the countryside. Sharp winds had made the dunes appear smooth as glass, and only the dead trunks of trees springing up at irregular intervals shattered that illusion. At one point, we spotted a flock of harpies. Ellette had rushed back, pointing them out. When I asked if we should be concerned, she'd laughed.

"Only if you're outnumbered. When we Feathered Fae fly over these lands, we always have to be on the lookout for flocks of harpies or serpopards. With an army this large, however, either creature would have to be incredibly stupid to attack. And scavengers are anything but stupid."

It was startling to realize that, at one point, this land had been a forest thriving with pleasant creatures and plant life, just like the Alatry Woods outside the False and Free realms. After four days of marching through such desolate scenery, I wondered when we would come across a green patch of grass.

"How long until the landscape changes?" I asked Ryker, who rode on my right.

"Not until we're much closer to the Buyan border, near where our bonegate is located."

I cocked my head, and he expounded.

"The Sinkers' descendants decided where to position their kingdom's bonegates, which were constructed from the bones of the ancestor who died to found Faerie. Most kept their ancestors' remains and powerful legacy far away from the largest villages and towns to avoid desecration. It was a precaution, should their line fall out of favor."

"Why would they put it so close to another kingdom, though?" I asked, not quite getting it.

"Buyan used to be a trusted ally of Lyonesse," Ebba piped up from behind.

Much about bonegates was still a mystery to me,

but there was one constant. The more I learned, the more I understood Faerie was an unnatural place.

Its forests and seas had been taken from the Old Land and moved to different planes by magic. While trees and animals from the Old Land could not move through the bonegates now, magic could and did. And its availability determined whether the creatures of Faerie thrived or not. If the magic was cut off, then the kingdom suffered. Bonegates were a clever way to complete an ecosystem in a world that needed to be fed power from the Old Land to survive.

"I still don't understand why, if they used to be allies, Queen Pari wants the entire kingdom of Lyonesse to suffer?"

Ebba pulled her horse alongside mine. "That's a mystery we'd all like to solve. My parents told me that when they were young, the royal lines got on well."

She leaned closer so that other soldiers, especially the less trustworthy swords for hire who had joined our army the day before, wouldn't hear what she had to say. "It's not talked about often, but King Oberon and Queen Pari were actually betrothed when they were teenagers. She was always visiting Lyonesse, and he often journeyed to Buyan too. That was before she turned dark and stole all the light from King Oberon's kingdom. His Majesty broke off the engagement without so much as a negotiation with either his grandfather—the sitting king—or Queen Pari."

A proud smile crossed her face. "To deny his

blood was bold, but he was just and strong even then. Can you imagine how it would've looked? Marrying a woman capable of stealing your birthright and source of power from your people? His Majesty was so ashamed that he hid in his castle for half a decade afterward."

A shiver tore up my spine. "I knew they were play-mates, but not betrothed. I wonder why Father didn't tell me?"

Garret, who'd been quiet for the duration of the march, shrugged. "It was a long time ago, wasn't it? Before any of us were born. Your father was younger than us when it happened. Heartache cuts deep, especially when you're a teenager. After he became king, he forbade mention of it within the kingdom. I can understand not wanting to feel that shame."

I'd never experienced heartache that devastating, but I could understand my father not wanting to hear about his ex-fiancée.

I turned back to Ryker. "So, how long until we arrive at the bonegate?"

Ryker shook his head. "*We* won't be going anywhere near the bonegate. We'll split off a few hours before the army arrives to fight. We don't want Queen Pari to know that the fight is a distraction, so we're slipping away much earlier than necessary. We should be at the fork this time tomorrow."

Goosebumps covered my arms as I realized that,

the very next day, I'd be stealing into a foreign kingdom, on my way to assassinate a queen.

***

THAT EVENING, WE MADE CAMP BENEATH A RIOT OF
stars. Just like the night before, soldiers erected my
tent while another soldier served me a slop of meat
and vegetables for dinner. It was far from the elaborate feasts I'd grown used to, but I wasn't about to
complain. The days of riding had been long, and the
watery stew smelled almost divine. Plus, once we
broke off, we wouldn't be carrying any extra equipment, and would be limited to sandwiches.

After the trip to Zatus, I'd had enough sandwiches
to last me a lifetime.

"Kind of surreal, isn't it?" Himari approached,
bowl in hand, and sat next to me. "Two months ago,
none of us knew our lineage, or that all this," she
waved at the wasteland around us, "even existed.
Tomorrow, we're going to fight for it. For people who
look up to us as rulers . . ."

"It is crazy." I gulped down a spoonful of stew,
savoring the moisture after the dryness of the desert.
"Back home, I could never have killed someone. But
every time I hear stories of Queen Pari, I'm reminded
of how evil she is. Thousands of lives were changed
because of her. All these guards, their families, and

how they live were altered so drastically. Even having children join the guard is bloody monumental."

I shook my head. I'd come to terms with the Harvest and now saw it as a positive thing for most families in Lyonesse. Even so, I couldn't imagine leaving Mam and Gran so young. "I know none of us grew up with our biological father, but imagine being just up the street from *both* your parents and not really knowing either."

Himari sighed. "I think about that a lot. Ronan swears he has a blessed life, but I just don't know. No one is perfect, and I believe Father did the best he could with a bad situation, but damn." She paused and her lips pursed in thought. "I've seen some shady dudes who deserved to get axed, but you're right—Pari's worse than any of them. She's got to go down."

I nodded. "And we have to be the ones to do it."

CHAPTER TWENTY-THREE

Despite the hard, cold ground and insistent chill pressing against the flaps of my tent, I slept better than I had in weeks. It was as if my body just gave up, finally allowing me to rest deeply. When I awoke, I crawled out of the tent and stretched wide, renewed.

We broke camp around noon, which was fairly early for most fae, and after marching for just over an hour, Meegra halted the line. I barely had time to wonder why we were stopped before the Master Feathered Fae rode toward the back of the column.

"Ellette just returned from a fly-ahead," she said, stopping next to me. "She tells me we're approximately four hours from the bonegate, and that there are half a dozen small camps of soldiers along the way—all wearing the imperial purple of Buyan."

"Is that normal?" Finn asked from where he rode slightly behind me.

"No. It's odd behavior . . . we Feathered Fae fly over these lands all the time. There have never been extra patrols before. Something must have made Queen Pari station her soldiers farther from the bonegate than usual."

My muscles tightened. How could this be happening? We'd been careful to tell no one the specifics of our mission while recruiting swords for hire. But someone in Zatus had gone ahead and informed Pari that something was up, anyway? Or was there a spy in Lyonesse who'd warned Queen Pari after my father spelled out our intent to the entire kingdom during the ball? If so, how had they gotten word to Pari so quickly? I'd never seen a single horse outside Castle Phoenix in Lyonesse.

A vision of Pari, in the firlon, surfaced. She'd searched the sky and her gaze landed right on me. But as soon as I had the thought that I might be the issue, I dismissed it.

Tess had assured me that there was no way Queen Pari could have known I was watching. Not only that, but had it been possible, my father surely would have mentioned it. No, it had to be someone from Zatus, or a well-connected spy.

Meegra cleared her throat. She was waiting for my response.

"Anything else?" I asked.

"I wanted to propose that your party split off now. It would be for the best if you were out of harm's way before we run into any camps of soldiers. But of course, it's your call . . . General," Meegra finished, her tone hard as steel.

She really hated being ranked below me.

"Are we close enough for you to find the way, Ryker?" I asked.

He nodded. "I've been noticing signs of plant life for the last hour. Which means some magic has leaked through the border. According to the maps I studied, the city of Buyan should be east, just over those mountains."

The mountains he spoke of were imposing, but they were nothing compared to the Cage Mountains we'd scaled to enter the False Realm.

"We'll go on our way, then." I nodded, my gaze locked with Meegra's sharp green eyes. "Best of luck. I hope to see everyone back in Lyonesse when the job is done."

Despite disliking the Master Feathered Fae, I meant what I said. I didn't want any of my father's people, *my people*, lost to this mission.

For a heartbeat, Meegra's eyes softened, but she seemed to catch herself, whipped about, and cupped her hands around her mouth. "Those coming with me, move forward!"

She rode to the front of the line without a glance back. The army followed her command, all except

Garret, Ebba, Sai, and Ronan, who approached us instead.

I sucked in a breath.

Although Garret and I had declared that we were just friends, I couldn't deny the attraction there, simmering beneath the surface. Being in his presence was . . . disorienting. And right now, the last thing I needed was a muddled mind. So when he rode straight up to me and dismounted, I remained on my horse instead of meeting him on the ground as I normally would.

If Garret was surprised, he didn't show it. He merely strode up to me, his gray eyes unwavering. When he reached me, he inclined his head. His scent filled my nostrils, and desire pulsed inside me. Hell, I was so confused.

"General Lana, I wish you and your siblings the best of luck on your mission. Please know I'll be thinking of your well-being the entire time. I wish I could join you."

I bit my lip and tried to focus on the other good-byes being said around us. Ronan and Himari were locking lips. Ebba and Sai were making the rounds, giving each of my siblings a last-minute hug and a word of advice.

My heart clenched. I wished Garret could come with us too—that they all could. Having him around would make me feel more secure. Plus, I wouldn't have to worry about him risking his life to attack the soldiers manning Lyonesse's bonegate.

But instead of saying that, I forced myself to put on a brave front.

Fighting down the lump rising in my throat, I nodded. "Best of luck to you too, Captain Garret. We'll see you when we return. You should probably catch up with the rest of the army."

It was a curt dismissal meant to make things easier for the both of us, but the damning waver in my voice betrayed my true feelings.

Garret wasn't having it either. For what was probably the first time in his life, he defied orders and extended his hand to pry one of mine from the reins.

My skin prickled and my breath grew tight. I could have said no. I could have reinforced our boundaries. I could have pulled my hand back. But I didn't. Instead, I watched, my emotions warring within me, and my mouth drying up, as Garret took my hand and brought it to his soft lips.

Tingles shot up my arm, and heat pooled in my hips. More than anything, I wanted to leap off the horse and embrace him. I wanted his mouth on mine, and to feel—truly feel—what it would be like to kiss him without a drunken haze over me.

But I didn't, because *just friends* didn't do that. I only sat there until he was done and slowly retracted my hand. Bloody hell, pulling away from him was torture.

"Sinkers be with you, Garret," I choked out, my voice thick.

With that, I bid my horse to turn, and trotted to the outskirts of the group. From a distance, I forced myself not to stare at my guard. I watched the awkward hug Ebba and Finn shared. I wondered what secrets Sai whispered into Ryker's ear. I felt the waves of passion rolling off Himari and Ronan, still making out like horny teenagers.

What felt like an eternity later, goodbyes ended, and the two halves of our army broke apart.

"Is everyone ready?" I asked, trying to keep my voice measured and calm.

My siblings' heads bobbed, and Ryker took his place beside me.

"Let's head out."

I urged my mare forward, determined not to look back. But with each smooth step she took, my need and the insistent pull of eyes behind me grew stronger. Every single cell in my body knew this was the worst possible time to entertain feelings of attraction, but in the end, I couldn't resist. I turned around.

A whoosh of air flew from me, leaving behind the sensation that I'd been punched in the gut. Despite my distance, emotional and physical, Garret still watched me, longing clear in his eyes.

My heart clenched, and, against my better judgment, I forced the corners of my lips up in a smile. He responded with a sad smile of his own, as if he'd been waiting for my recognition for forever.

Maybe he had.

Unfortunately, for both of us, a smile was all I could give. So I took a shuddering breath and tore my gaze from Garret.

Desperate for a distraction, I caught Arlo's attention. "You ready to fly? We need your eagle eyes to scout, now that the Feathered Fae are going west."

From her place on her specialized perch that had been mounted on my horse, Naela bristled.

"Eyes that are attached to a mouth that speaks English, Boss," I reassured her, twisting to run a hand over her silky feathers. Since we'd been traveling, she'd forgiven me—somewhat. At the very least, she deigned to land near me from time to time and not screech her beak off.

Arlo nodded and repositioned his sword on his hip. Somehow, his magic transformed the weapon into a part of him when he morphed into his animal aspect. It was a shifter talent that baffled me, but was certainly handy.

The next thing I knew, Arlo's horse was riderless, and a massive golden eagle swooped above us.

Naela screeched at the sudden transformation.

"Fly with him if you want," I laughed.

Naela launched into the air and soared after the eagle. A second later, Kane's brown body followed, joining in on the fun.

We rode at an angle from the rest of the army. Since the landscape was so bleak, the larger army was still visible. Particularly the giants lumbering at the rear. They remained within sight until we reached the mountains an hour later. After that, they disappeared behind a wall of rock, and a new world arose.

"Are we already in the greater kingdom of Buyan?" I asked, taking in a tiny green shrub hungrily.

I didn't miss much about the Old Land, but the emerald landscape of Ireland definitely made the short list. Along with Mam.

Ryker arched his eyebrows. "No, but I can feel the magic more strongly, so we're close. The old soldier I spoke to—the one who made this journey before—said we'll *know* when we actually see the Buyan border."

He was right. After a long climb dominated by rock, we crested the first mountain, and a chorus of gasps rose from the group. In the distance, a jungle, vibrant green and lush, rose in an abrupt line from relatively barren land. Sounds of life emanating from the jungle. All the stimuli assaulted our senses, which had grown accustomed to the bleak desert.

"Animals! It's like they came out of nowhere," I breathed.

Ryker nodded. "Few can thrive deep within Lyonesse, since the magic is restricted there. Cross the border into Buyan, however, and many live well."

As if to drive his point home, a gryphon burst out of the canopy. Its massive wings sent it into a corkscrew, while its lion's tail whipped through the air behind it. The next second, the beast had plunged back into the jungle, out of sight once more.

"Holy crap." Victoria's blue eyes lit up. "Is this what Lyonesse used to look like? And it had . . . those animals?"

"A wild gryphon." Ryker explained. "Lyonesse hasn't looked like this for a while, not in my lifetime. But I've been told that it once looked similar—green and overflowing with life." His lips pressed together, and a dozen emotions flashed across his strong features as he took in the jungle.

My mind drifted back to the tapestries in my father's chambers. Just the artwork of what Lyonesse used to look like had held Tess enthralled. Ryker was seeing an actual representation. No wonder he looked as if he were about to cry.

Naela screeched above me, her sentiment echoed by Kane and Arlo. She too was excited by the prospect of being surrounded by green again.

"Well, what are we waiting for? The faster we move, the faster we can leave this barren rock," I said, and everyone fell in step behind me.

We descended, and as we entered the dense jungle, fresh air flooded my nostrils. I released a heavy sigh. Sinkers, it felt good to be where nature lived and breathed again.

Naela swooped down, and I threw my arm out so she could land. The mixed leather and metal armor I wore was thicker than my usual gauntlet. I barely felt her talons digging into my flesh.

I smiled. It felt like old times.

We proceeded through the jungle as a close-knit group, everyone wary of what we might come across. Now and then, I'd overhear Victoria whispering about dragons.

I doubted a dragon could fit through the dense trees, as our horses barely squeezed through some spots. But this *was* Faerie, and as the only dragon I'd seen was chained up and ill at Castle Phoenix, I was definitely no expert. Perhaps there were smaller, thinner dragons too?

"We need to redirect east a bit," Ryker pointed to our right.

Our group adjusted our trajectory and kept moving through the thick brush as silently as possible, each still in awe of the lush vegetation and life all around.

Already, I'd seen flowers so vibrant and colorful, they would not be out of place in the Amazon, and trees with trunks at least three meters in diameter. The sounds of wildlife were rich, too, and after months of living in Lyonesse, they hit my ears strangely.

After about a forty-minute walk through the jungle, Wikolia claimed to see the golden rump of a unicorn running through the trees. I didn't catch sight of it, but the thought that a wild unicorn was out there somewhere was enough to excite me.

A couple hours later, Ryker came to a stop, closed his eyes, and tilted his chin to the sky. His dark curls slithered down his back as he assessed something I could not feel.

"I think we should stop to eat and let the horses rest," he said when he opened his eyes once more. "Nap if you can. You'll need the energy. We should be approaching the ward just as daylight fades. It will be perfect timing for you to cross it and enter the city at dark."

I dismounted from my horse and fed her. It was important to care for my mare, as once we broke through the inner wards of Buyan, we'd be pushing the horses hard to get us to the city wall quickly.

By the time I was done, Finn and Gio had already set out the meals. I veered toward Gio and took my portion of dry sandwich, one hunk of cheese, and a piece of fruit.

The rations were gone within minutes, and, following Ryker's suggestion, I laid on a soft bit of ground to rest.

RYKER HAD BEEN DEAD-ON IN HIS ESTIMATION. WE sighted the wards that protected the city and its surrounding areas right as the sun dipped low in the sky. Light would be completely lost soon.

"I can ride no further," Ryker said. He gestured to the faint shimmering wall at the edge of the jungle that indicated a ward capable of sensing his full fae blood.

My gaze followed the gentle decline of the hill we'd stopped on, and my eyebrows furrowed. Oddly, just beyond the jungle, a meadow sprang up. The open grassland seemed to encompass the entire city of Buyan, which we could see sprouting from the ground in the distance. I frowned. It would have been easier to sneak into the city through a jungle rather than an open meadow. Surely the manipulation of the land was yet another safety mechanism created by magic.

Ryker pointed. "Head straight that way, and you should bypass the central gate of Buyan. Don't forget to leave a trail to follow on your way back. Scorched land, large puddles—something your group can recognize, but won't look too out of place if scouts patrol the area. You'll want to enter the jungle at the correct spot and climb straight up the mountains. Use Arlo to catch sight of the fire I'll keep burning in the mountains."

Everyone nodded and someone gulped audibly.

Their nerves were relatable. Once we crossed through the shimmering barrier, we would be completely on our own. We'd have to get to the city undetected.

Those whose ears had become pointed, like Finn, Gio, and Dak, would have little issue passing as an elf. All the women either had pointed ears or hair long and thick enough to cover their lack of tips. Arlo worried me a bit, as his ears had never changed, but if worse came to worse, he could transform into his eagle aspect and act as someone's pet.

Although no one had said it out loud, I knew I was the most likely person to give us away. I'd have to be very careful about making eye contact as we made our way through Buyan. Either that, or I'd need to hone an illusion of light to cover up my golden eyes— a shade that the Fullfeathers were well known for, but was rare in Faerie.

"Thanks for your help, Ryker," I said, sheathing my blade. "We'll meet you here once the job is done. Sinkers be with you."

We mounted our horses and, not daring to hesitate, lest I lose my nerve, I made my way toward the ward.

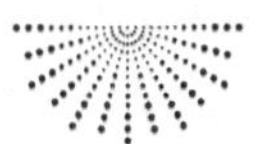

As Father had predicted, absolutely nothing happened when we broke through the ward of Buyan. No one came for us shortly after either. The bit of human blood we each possessed truly helped us fly under the radar.

I was surprised, but not as shocked as I was when we neared the city. Initially, I'd distrusted the intelligence that only the central gate of Buyan's wall was consistently guarded. But as I gazed upon it, I realized how many fae or chimera could simply fly over it, anyway.

It would be a waste to man a wall so easily breached unless an entire army was guarding it. So instead, Queen Pari placed her trust in the ward around her city to alert her that newcomers had arrived.

Unfortunately for her, the ward had meant

nothing to us. Between the encroaching night, the vast illusion I was projecting to hide us, and the scantily manned wall, it was almost a sure thing that no one would see us coming.

As we closed in on the backside of the fortification around the city, I heard the occasional small explosion of dirt and the bubbling of water behind me. Maria and Gio were creating divots in the ground and pools of water so that we could find our way back when the time came. Everything went as planned, and all nine of my siblings and two hawks were safe in the shadow of the towering wall a mere twenty minutes after walking through the ward.

An exhale escaped my lips as I dismounted. Although the ride to the wall had gone smoother than I'd anticipated, my heart was pounding hard. From the looks of it, I wasn't the only one.

Wikolia looked thankful to be in one piece as she dismounted and swayed on the spot. I bit back a chuckle as I watched my usually serious sister fumble. The memories of my troubles on a horse during our mission to Zatus were still fresh, and I could relate. Thank the Sinkers I'd worked hard on riding and progressed since then.

Maria was already in motion, creating deep holes in the ground so that Gio could fill them with water for the horses. Once that was done, she drove iron stakes into the rock wall with her magic, and tethered each horse as close to the fortification as they'd permit.

Finn pulled the horses' feed out and allotted each a portion. I was pleased that everyone gave the beasts priority. We'd need to run them hard again when we escaped. The planning meetings we'd had during the march clearly had been effective. We were running like a well-oiled machine.

Convinced that the wall hid us well, I called off my illusion, to conserve my energy for later, and pulled a rope from my saddlebag. Quickly, I sized up the wall and compared it to the length of rope we'd brought. "Arlo, fly to the top and scout for anything fishy. Screech if there's any reason we should not come up."

I turned to my rumbler sister. "Maria, once the coast is clear, you'll be next. When you get to the top, stay low so no one sees you, but begin searching for a rock you can pry from the wall." I handed Maria the rope.

"I'll come up third, but I'll want to descend first so I can have an illusion ready to cover everyone else. Who has the other rope?"

Finn pulled the other loop of cord from his saddlebag, and handed it to Maria, who slung it over her other shoulder.

"Himari and Crystal will float as many people to the top as they can," I added. People knew the plan, but saying it again couldn't hurt. We were all nervous, and sometimes nerves made us forget things. "This is a long way up, so be practical. Have your hand on the safety rope at all times, just in case. Airworkers, try not to exhaust yourselves . . . we may need your air magic later. Crystal, you scale the wall last."

Crystal could pull herself up Mount Everest, so I wasn't worried about her. But I *was* a little worried about my weaver witch sister. Himari may have been working with air her entire life, but this wall was huge. I knew she would push herself to get everyone up the climb quickly. What if she expended too much energy? If that happened, I wasn't sure she'd be able to climb the rope on strength alone.

I sucked in a breath, running over the directions again in my mind. Once I was sure I hadn't forgotten anything, I nodded. "Let's begin."

Arlo transformed and soared to the top of the wall to gaze down upon the city of Buyan. We waited with bated breath, but no screech escaped his beak.

It was safe.

I gave the signal, and Maria stepped forward to face the wall. She let out a yip as she shot up a second later, her arms flailing as she sought to steady herself.

"Maybe a little warning would be nice?" I shot an annoyed glance at Himari and Crystal. "We don't want anyone knocking their head on the rock and passing out on the way up. And she doesn't have a rope to hold onto if you falter."

"Sorry! We're trying our best," Himari replied,

her jaw clenched in concentration. "It's hard working together. Our magic is the same, but also different."

"Seriously!" Crystal added. "Thank goodness we didn't add Victoria to the mix." She shot a glance at our vila sister. "No offense, Vic, but you don't have great control yet."

Victoria's lips pressed together, but what Crystal said was true. We'd decided Victoria's air and water magic, both of which she still struggled to control, would only be used in an emergency. A mission like this was no place for rookie work.

Progress was excruciatingly slow, and nearly a full five minutes later, Maria crested the top of the wall and flattened out of sight.

I was next.

My legs shook. I thanked the Sinkers that my pants fit loosely so no one would see. Vaguely, I heard Crystal and Himari negotiating a new strategy. I was about to turn around and ask why they hadn't talked this over during the journey, when suddenly I rose two meters into the air. I tipped forward, and my hand instinctively hit a hard stone to steady myself.

"Easy, guys, there's no need to go fast. There's still no safety rope." My voice wavered, but I did the best I could to make it sound like a command. I had to be strong.

Air puffed gently below me, lifting me in a steady, even manner. I breathed a sigh of relief. If they could just get me to the top in one piece, everyone else's ascent would be easier . . . or at least safer.

Two unnerving minutes later, I was there, my hands gripping the side of the rock wall as I pulled myself over. All those pull-ups I'd done the past few weeks had finally paid off.

I crouched at the top, which was just over a meter wide, scanned the area, and then cast an illusion large enough to hide our infiltration scheme.

"Thank God," Maria breathed when I signaled that the illusion was in place. She rose from where she'd been lying flat on the top of the wall alongside Arlo, who had transformed back to his human aspect.

"No one will see this section of the wall for about two meters on each side and three in front of it," I assured her. "Did you find a stone?"

Maria nodded and extended her hands, which immediately shook. "Buyan's fortification needs repair, which suits us perfectly."

I watched in awe as she ripped a portion of a cracked block of stone the size of a small ottoman from the rampart.

"It's not as large as I'd like, or as heavy." Her lips pressed to the side as she assessed the block's sturdiness. "But if I keep an eye on it, we should be fine."

"Good enough," I muttered, laying the ends of two ropes down so that she could place the stone over them. She did so carefully, not even making a sound, and Arlo tossed one of the ropes to our siblings.

It snaked through the air, past Victoria, who was already halfway to us, and fell taut. I breathed a sigh of relief. It was barely long enough, its end falling to shoulder-height.

I turned to Maria and Arlo. "It looks like Himari and Crystal are getting faster. You guys stay here to make sure that rock doesn't budge. I'm going to start descending in case I need to tweak my illusion from the other side. Naela," I patted my shoulder, and Naela flew to perch there.

I didn't want her soaring down outside the boundary of the illusion and then suddenly disappearing. That would raise alarm bells if anyone was looking our way.

"Someone tell Finn to descend with Kane on his shoulder, okay? See you at the bottom." With that, I slipped off the ledge just as a shaken Victoria appeared at the top.

I gripped the rope tight and walked backward down the sheer stone. By the time I was halfway to the ground, my hands ached and my legs trembled. Still, I took each step methodically, not wanting to slip and plummet.

A few excruciating minutes later, my feet landed on dirt, and I exhaled. As soon as I released the rope, it tightened again. Victoria was already making her way down. Even from so far away, I could see the trembling of her shoulders and arms.

Hopefully she makes it here before they give out, I

thought, turning to assess my surroundings. No one had noticed my arrival within the city walls. Good.

When I was positive no one was looking, I stepped out of the confines of the illusion. After a perfunctory check that the magic had no holes or tells, I felt like I could finally breathe normally again. My lightwork had been thorough.

I returned to the safety of the illusion. Our only prerogative had been to break into Buyan far away from the main city gate, where the guards congregated. Otherwise, we hadn't known exactly where we'd enter. It seemed that we'd chosen to infiltrate the city on the edge of a market. The stalls faced toward the center of the shopping district, and no fae looked our way. It was a good spot for blending in.

So far, it had been too easy. I wasn't dumb enough to take that as a good sign.

"*Oof!*"

I turned just as Victoria landed on the ground. Apparently, she'd chosen to fall the last few meters rather than climb down. Sweat covered her skin, and her thin arms shook violently.

I held out my hand to help her up. "You all right?"

She nodded. "Yeah, I'm just tired. That wall is taller than it looks."

The rope tightened once more. Wikolia was descending, her form much more steady than Victoria's. She was already near the bottom when Dak appeared at the top, waiting his turn. Five minutes later, the crowd on my side of the wall was larger than that on the other side. Only Himari and Crystal needed to ascend now.

"It's going to take Himari a while to recover," Gio said as he joined the group. "She was already shaking from the exertion of lifting us all over. Crystal said she would help as much as she could, but her power is weaker than when we started."

I frowned. We needed our air workers strong for when Maria came down last. With no one manning the rock that helped keep the ropes in place, air would be our final safety mechanism.

A minute later, I breathed a sigh of relief as Himari's black hair appeared over the edge of the fortification. Even from far away, I could tell that her face was ashen, but as long as she gripped the rope tightly and kept moving, I had faith that she could make it.

She proved me right, making halting progress, but landing and then collapsing on the ground.

"I'm so exhausted," she wheezed as Gio helped her up.

"I bet," I said, fingering the Buyan coin Ebba had procured in Zatus. "We'll get you a snack or something in the market before moving on. It looks like you may need it."

"Sounds good," Himari sighed, her words thin.

Turning my attention back to the wall, I caught a

flash of white hurtling toward us at breakneck speed. A heartbeat later, a golden eagle landed on the ground next to me, and Arlo transformed.

Only Crystal and Maria were left.

Crystal shimmied down, her triceps popping as she moved like a spider releasing a string of silk, smoothly and naturally. I'd been right not to be concerned about her.

When she landed, her teeth flashed brilliantly. I imagined her smiling the same way when she stuck a landing in gymnastics.

"Stay alert. Watch Maria."

Crystal's lips flattened at my command, but she followed directions. We all watched as Maria inched over the edge of the wall, her curls swaying in the breeze. I suspected she was tired; moving that huge rock and keeping it anchored against the weight of the others couldn't have been easy. Yet, Maria surprised me by gaining her footing and descending almost as gracefully as Crystal.

She was a quarter of the way down when my shoulders relaxed and I dug into my leather side satchel for a map of Buyan. I'd nearly extracted it when a shriek filled the air.

My eyes shot up, and I gasped. The rope had slipped out from beneath the rock. Maria was free falling.

"Catch her!" I yelped.

Himari grunted, and Crystal grimaced. A weak

gale of wind burst by me, and a startled cry flew up from the market.

I bit my lip. The market-goers couldn't see us because of my illusion, but clearly we'd attracted some attention. Would they check out the sound?

We'll worry about that later, once Maria is safe, I thought, my heart pounding as my sister plummeted. Even with the help of winds buffeting her, slowing her momentum from life-stealing to only bone-crushing, she was still falling way too fast.

Himari collapsed, but miraculously, Finn caught her before she hit the ground. Another gale flew by slowly, Himari's last go at saving her sister. It was too weak—not enough to save Maria to avoid serious injury.

Shite, shite, shite. I wracked my brain for a solution.

Victoria rushed forward. Her beautiful face was screwed up in an expression I'd never seen as she lifted her arms high. A squall ripped from her, nearly knocking everyone around her to the dirt. My eyes followed the trajectory of her magic, and I exhaled sharply.

The air work, combined with a voluminous bush Maria had somehow grown as she flailed, caught her at the very last second. Maria landed in a bed of leaves with a soft *thump* instead of a horrible *splat*.

Dak rushed forward to ensure that Maria was uninjured, and Crystal gasped, as if she'd pulled the air she was working with from her very own lungs and not her surroundings.

"Fast thinking, Victoria," I said. "That was astounding, you guys."

Victoria looked unnerved by the circumstance, but otherwise fine. Himari, however, shook like a leaf, and while Crystal was stronger physically, tears still leaked from her eyes. We had to slow down and let them catch their breath.

I gulped. Resting was dangerous, but if we were to make it out of this city alive, it was also necessary.

We needed to alter our plan a bit.

"We can't venture into the castle with you two like this. You'll need to recharge. Maria will need a moment too. The rest of us will explore and find you food while you gather your strength."

CHAPTER TWENTY-FIVE

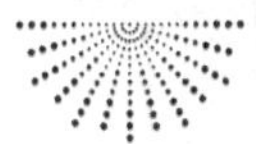

We found an inn not far from where we'd breached the wall. While the location was ideal, as the inn was partially hidden down an alley and totally devoid of other patrons, I hoped the girls would only need a couple hours' rest. I didn't think I'd be able to take the stink of cooked cabbage and unwashed bedding for very long.

On the positive side, what it lacked in amenities and cleanliness, it made up for by keeping its clientele's secrets. Or so the proprietor had assured Finn when we'd arrived looking disheveled, with Himari needing assistance to walk.

"Strange accents, I hear. Where are you young ones from?"

Based on his bark-like skin, and the many trees sprouting behind the front desk turning their branches in our direction, I guessed he was a dryad. A lecherous one, if how he studied Victoria like he wanted to eat her was any indication.

Finn stiffened at the question, but I quickly landed on the revelation that there was no point in lying. Neither of us had a hope of affecting a Buyan accent, which sounded similar to posh English, mixed in odd places with German.

"Ireland, by way of Ys. We're demi-fae who work for the crown there," I said, thankful that I remembered the name of the kingdom that bordered the western side of Buyan.

The dryad turned his full attention on me. I hoped that the illusion I'd placed in front of my eyes to dim the Fullfeather gold to brown was still working. It was a tricky bit of magic, as eyes were complex. But after landing just outside the market, I'd quickly decided that no matter how tricky it was, the disguise was also necessary. There were simply too many people who might see my golden eyes and raise the alarm.

"Ys?" he finally said, disbelief dripping from his tone. "I was unaware that the royal family there was allowing demi-fae from the Old Land to visit Faerie. Doesn't seem much like King Necho to me." His gaze shifted from me to Finn and back again.

"They are for the right price," Finn countered defensively.

The proprietor raised his eyebrows and chuckled as if he had meant nothing by his intrusive question.

"I can only hope you didn't deplete your coin paying your entrance fee. The Artemis Inn keeps its clients' secrets, but that's only if they're paying. Here's your key. The room is up the stairs, the third door on the right. Are you sure you won't be needing another room?"

I shook my head. "We'll only be here for a few hours."

"Ahhhh, of course. A young, attractive group like yourselves doesn't need much time to take care of business." He winked.

A wave of discomfort rolled through the room at his insinuation, but I shoved everyone up the stairs, anyway. It was better that he thought we were using the room for an orgy than to recoup energy so we could assassinate his queen.

"What a perv," Victoria said as soon as we'd all crammed into the rented room. "I'm definitely not staying in here. I want no part of whatever that sicko was picturing."

"There isn't space for many in here anyhow." As if to drive my point home, I turned and ran right into Dak. "Two should remain with Crystal, Himari, and Maria for their safety. The rest can explore the market and look for escape routes. Mark them on the maps I gave you, if you can. The better we know this area, the more likely we'll survive if we need to run."

"I'll stay," Arlo said. "I can always escape on wing,

so I don't need to know the streets or market as well as the rest of you."

"Me too," Wikolia added. "I can retrace our steps easily by smell. I should be able to leave just fine when needed."

Thank the Sinkers for shifters, I thought.

"If this place is anything like the Lyonesse market, it should close soon," I added. "We'll likely be back before then, as we'll capitalize on the exodus of fae from the market. Then we'll make our way to the castle."

The girls and Arlo waved us off, and everyone else left the room. Finn and I exited the Artemis Inn as fast as we could, trying not to make eye contact with the innkeeper. We called Kane and Naela down from where they'd perched on the roof of the inn to wait. Despite knowing she could take care of herself, I'd been nervous about leaving Naela alone. Only when she landed on the bit of leather jutting out from my shoulder armor did I breathe a sigh of relief.

The design was specific to Finn's and my armor, so our hawks could travel with us without tiring our arms. It looked a little ridiculous and made my neck kink slightly to one side, but it was better than holding my arm out for hours when we were away from Naela's custom-made perch.

"Nothing strange happened while we were inside, right, Boss?" I asked, smoothing her dappled gray and white feathers.

Naela quirked her head and let out a soft *kuk-kuk* sound to indicate she was fine.

"I saw others with birds, Lan. We should be okay," Finn offered, though he too looked a little worried.

And rightfully so. Those other birds had mostly been parrots and songbirds being sold in the market—not birds of prey from the Old Land.

I bit the inside of my cheek. There was no way around it; our hawks stood out. Especially to those who remembered that the Fullfeather family had an affinity for birds of prey. A fact we were hoping Buyan residents had forgotten.

"Ugh!" Victoria burst out of the inn's door and rubbed her hands together furiously. "Why am I not surprised the toilet was disgusting?"

"Just be happy they *had* toilets," Gio said. "In Zatus, that wasn't always a guarantee. It seems Sinkers Realm has updated its plumbing to be like the Old Land's."

Victoria pulled a face. "Whatever. I'd rather piss in a hole than *that* toilet."

"Anyway," I said, not really wanting to get into a debate over the various toilets of Faerie, "we should definitely split up to attract less attention. I think now would be a good time to stay with your group members—that way, you can rely on each other when we leave."

I moved to Dak's side, the only person in my group who wasn't recovering. "We'll go this way and meet you guys back here in an hour. Try to cover as much ground as you can. Don't forget to mark your maps for those who can't explore themselves. Pick up lots of food too. Everyone should eat a little to keep their energy up, and the girls will need a small feast after the magic they just performed. Questions?"

No one had any, so we split off and disappeared into the market.

TEN MINUTES LATER, OUR ARMS WERE HEAVY WITH food, and my head was full of notes to prepare for our escape. I needed to write them down before I forgot. I motioned for Dak to sit on a bench near a stall selling windchimes made of shells, sticks, and even rocks.

"Naela, up there," I said, pointing to the top of the stall. She'd gotten a few too many intrigued looks riding on my shoulder. While I wanted her close, I figured perching on the roof as I worked was better than her staying on me.

Quickly, I set down the food we'd purchased, brought out my map, and jotted down a few land-marks that could be helpful in navigating the twisted market. Once that was done, I put the map away and took a moment to puzzle over the chimes surrounding us, particularly a rock one.

I couldn't imagine how rocks would make an attractive sound when they knocked together, but I was proven wrong when suddenly, a fae child with purple wings darted in front of me and whacked the rock-laden chime with his hand. A symphony of music and otherworldly voices exploded from the decoration.

The stall owner shot out of his seat. "Damn kid! Come back here and pay for that!"

The tiny fae giggled and launched himself deep into the throng of market-goers.

I arched an eyebrow at Dak, who shrugged. My curiosity grew when the disgruntled stallkeep grumbled about the limited number of songs his rocks could produce.

Although my mind should have been on more serious matters, it took all I had not to turn around and ask him what the rock windchimes were called. Or if they did anything other than sing songs.

Unlike Lyonesse, where I'd only ever seen magical items in the castle, Buyan seemed rife with interesting objects. In the market, I'd already observed some that were used in everyday life, such as self-cleaning pots, or forks that floated to feed fae who were too old or too young to handle a fork with precision.

There were also knickknacks of the luxury sort: hats enchanted to make the wearer invisible, a ring with the ability to ward off all enchantments, a bottle of mermaid tears said to cure the most vicious ailments.

"This place is huge," I whispered and popped a

hunk of fresh bread in my mouth. After just a few minutes of exploring, the idea to scout the market had seemed more like a necessity than a way to kill time.

When I'd first drawn up the maps, I'd focused on the castle and larger streets. But it would be easy to get lost among the stalls and winding paths of the market. I wished we had longer to scout, but we'd have to make the best of the time we had.

"It is." Dak kept his voice low to avoid eavesdroppers. "I'm trying to do as Wikolia said and catch a scent. Her nose is better than mine, but between the map, your visual memory, and my sense of smell, we should be able to make it back." He gestured to the wall.

Before we'd sought the inn, Maria had insisted on carving an "X" the size of my palm into the stone wall so we'd know where the horses were tied up on the other side I could see it from where we sat, but hoped it wasn't as obvious to others.

"Good thinking." I grabbed a couple apples off the bench and extended one out to Dak. "Hurry and eat a little. We should really be scouting. You never know what path we'll have to enter the market from. *Ooh!*"

Something ran into my back, and I flew forward to land on my hands and knees.

Naela released a long, strangled screech.

"Lana! Are you okay?" Dak said.

"Sorry, girl!" The robust fae attending the stall

reached out a hand to lift me up. "I was trying to pull that stone chime down before another damn kid hit it, and I lost my balance." The stallkeep patted his rotund belly and then shot a glare at the rock wind-chime that had started the kerfuffle. "I swear the thing loses value every day. Soon, it won't sing at all."

"Uhh, it's okay," I replied, my face flaring red as I bent down to pick up the fruits that had flown out of my hands. As much as I didn't want to speak around him, it would probably attract more attention if I was rude or just ran off.

"Visitors, eh?" His face brightened. "Where you from? I've never heard yer accents."

"Traveled from the Old Land by way of Ys. We're on a long holiday, if you will," I said, praying that would be enough to placate the merchant.

"The Old Land!" the merchant roared. "Knew it was somewhere exotic. Don't see many of those birds around here." He gestured up to where Naela perched, her eyes staring daggers at him.

I winced and glanced around. The hubbub and noise of the market had worked in our favor. No one seemed to have noticed his loud tone.

"It's been ages since I met someone from the Old Land!" the merchant continued. "Most fae clans from there seem all too happy not to come visit their less fortunate kin. What brings you here? Pretty girl like you must be dying to see a mermaid, huh? No question about you, lad! Men are always willing to pay for that pleasure. They don't disappoint, I'll tell ya!" He winked at Dak, who looked away, his white cheeks turning pink.

"Uh . . . yeah, we would pay loads to see a mermaid," I agreed, thankful for the excuse, no matter how daft. Then my eyebrows knit together as I belatedly latched onto what he'd said.

"How do you mean less fortunate? It seems nice here." My tone soured as images of Lyonesse's poverty ran through my mind.

"Well, of course Buyan is nice enough. Could be better, though. More lax. I've heard that fae in the Old Land can go wherever they want! Just get on a flying metal gryphon thing, and they're there."

"A plane," I corrected. "Do you mean to say you're restricted here? They didn't mention that in —Ys."

The merchant shrugged, and his shirt came up over his stomach. "There isn't a realm that doesn't have restrictions of some sort. We're better off than most, certainly better off than False Realm or Water Realm, but still. What I wouldn't give to go anywhere any time I like."

My spine straightened. "Why can't you?"

He lifted a brow. "They didn't tell you at the gate? To be honest, I'm surprised they let you in. Said they'd be restricting visitors, but seeing as you're from the Old Land, I suppose . . ."

Shite, there was an alert out.

"Yes, they said we were fine because we were from there. But what's happening?" I arranged my features into what I hoped translated into fear and not curiosity.

"Should we be worried? I hope this doesn't derail our plans. I so wanted to see a mermaid." I stuck my lip out like a petulant child, and the merchant patted my shoulder.

"We all do, girl, we all do. It's just, I thought they'd be more careful about visitors. Usually this market is swarming with soldiers, but they were called to the castle yesterday and marched out this morning. Thousands of them. Just the ones you met at the gate and the queen's personal guard remain."

"That can't be many who stayed behind," Dak said, fishing.

"Even fewer than you'd think! My nephew went to the front, and he usually stays at the castle, close to the queen! It's a bad omen, if you ask me."

"How do you mean?" I asked.

"The common folk were only told so we can be on high alert for trouble. You probably don't know this, but we don't get along so well with one of our neighboring kingdoms. Her Majesty had to send who she could to protect what was hers."

Thousands of troops were heading to the bonegate. Toward Garret, Ebba, and Sai . . . My stomach hardened uncomfortably. Though we knew they'd have to fight, I don't think anyone expected a retaliation of this magnitude.

"That's terrible," I said, my voice wobbling at the thought of my friends fighting for their lives against an army of thousands.

"It is. Let's hope they make it back safe. You should probably talk to your innkeep if Buyan isn't your final destination. You may need to change routes for safety's sake."

This was it—a perfect exit. We still had about thirty minutes to sleuth before we had to return to the inn.

"Yes. We'll go do that now. Naela, follow!" I grabbed Dak's hand and pulled him up.

"Thanks for the tip!" I shouted over my shoulder as we dove into the crowds.

CHAPTER TWENTY-SIX

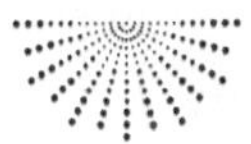

"Think your nose got enough info to lead us back?" I asked Dak as we approached Artemis Inn.

"I think so."

"Good," I said, not bothering to add that I hadn't retained much of the maze-like market—not after hearing what the merchant had said.

The entire time we'd explored the winding paths, I forced myself to focus on one fact: Queen Pari had sent thousands of soldiers to my father's ancestral bonegate, leaving Castle Dalir practically unguarded. Our mission might be easier than we thought.

If we moved fast enough. The downside was that our friends at the bonegate might be in great danger.

I pushed the inn door open, and the dryad behind the desk gave us an oily smile.

"Your turn now, is it? I like how your group is

making the most of the small space." His gaze shot to the loaves of bread and apples we carried. "Smart to bring sustenance, too. Such carnal adventures can really whet an appetite."

My eyes shot to the ground as I swallowed the vomit climbing up my throat. Behind me, I heard Dak's loud gulp and quickening footsteps as we rushed up the stairs. We couldn't get out of this place fast enough.

When we opened the room door, Crystal practically flung herself at me.

"Finally! We've been waiting forever. Give me that." She pulled the loaf of bread and three apples from my hands, broke the loaf into thirds, and tossed Maria and Himari their portions.

I watched them inhale the meager meal with disbelief. "Are we the only ones who brought back food?"

Arlo shook his head, and his green eyes widened as Himari consumed half an apple in one bite. "Finn's group came back, and then went back for more, just in case. The amount these three have eaten is astonishing. It's like they're ani—"

Crystal shot him a death glare, and Arlo's lips formed a perfect "O" before he continued.

"Really hungry," he finished lamely.

"Ravenous," she corrected. "The rest helped ease my sense of depletion, but I'm still *starving*. Dak, cough it up!"

Dak tossed her the second loaf.

"Well, eat as much as you like. We'll need you at full strength soon if we're going to infiltrate the castle." I sat on the edge of the bed, near Maria. "Speaking of which, I have good news."

I rattled off the information the merchant had divulged, stopping only when Crystal spit out a chunk of apple in shock.

"He actually told you the queen was unguarded? Don't you think that's a little suspicious?" Her brown eyes narrowed to slits.

Dak shrugged. "Not really. He clearly loved to talk. In Johannesburg, those are the merchants who make the most money. Especially where tourists are concerned—which he definitely thought we were."

"In my opinion," I started, wrangling everyone's attention back to me, "we couldn't have gotten any luckier."

Even as I said it, I felt a twinge of guilt for what Garret, Ebba, and Sai were probably going through, but I reminded myself that they'd trained for this their entire lives. They'd be fine—I hoped.

Soon after, the rest of our group arrived and handed over more food to the girls. As they ate, I gave a quick briefing, and then we trooped down the creaky inn stairs, talking loudly of a pub. The innkeeper, probably picturing more raunchy times, leered and winked as we exited.

Victoria faked retching as soon as we stepped outside.

"Daggers out," I said, all business now that we were heading toward the castle.

Naela fluttered down from the roof to land on my shoulder, and I patted her feathers, knowing that in just a few minutes, we'd have to part again. I wanted her flying high above until we breached the castle wall, ready to sound the alarm should we need it.

Metal flashed all around, appearing from where my siblings had hidden additional weapons in their boots or secret pockets in our custom armor. As tourists wandering the market, we would have garnered too much attention with three blades strapped to each of us. But now that it was full dark, and our mission was underway, I'd rather we be prepared than keep up a pretense.

Once everyone was ready, we left the alley that hid the Artemis Inn, and turned toward the main road.

"This leads straight from the city gate, and divides the city of Buyan," I stated, and then gestured to the right. "Just remember, our horses are tied on this side. That way, at the very least, you end up on the right side of the city when escaping. We should split here. Obviously, no one take this road."

The main road led straight up to the castle, which made anyone walking down it too obvious. Even from this distance, I could see two guards patrolling the entry to the castle.

"Dak, Himari, and I will take this side. The other two groups veer right off this street. Finn, you take the wide flank that I marked on your map."

As they knew less about the castle grounds than I did, I'd assigned the other two groups the same side so that they could protect each other. With seven going one way and my team of three going the other, they should be relatively safe—especially now that we knew that most of the city guards were at the bonegate.

"You know the signal if any one group finishes the mission." I patted Naela, our sounder. "Remember, Boss, if you need my attention, use only soft sounds. Unless it's an emergency, or we've completed our mission, of course."

Naela made a gentle *chwirk*, kind of a whistle rather than a screech.

I nodded, pleased.

Each team had a similar arrangement. Kane was the herald for Finn's team, and Arlo was the crier for Crystal's team. As long as our birds and shifter brother screamed their heads off after we accomplished our mission, we would know when to retreat.

Everyone nodded.

"I guess this is it, then. Good luck."

Briefly, my eyes swept across the circle, landing painfully on Finn. I'd never actually apologized for being so short with him when he suggested I delegate more. And while it was nothing compared to our first fight, our relationship *had* been strained lately. What if this didn't go as planned, and one of us died without clearing the air?

I rubbed the nape of my neck as indecision gripped me. The last thing I wanted to do was show weakness during a key moment of leadership. Plus, wouldn't making amends now indicate that I believed we could fail?

Recognizing that I couldn't allow that, I landed on one side of the fence.

"See you all when the deed is done," I said firmly, before turning and leading my team toward the castle.

Dak, Himari, and I wove in and out of the streets of Buyan, while Naela soared above us. Occasionally, we'd backtrack a block or two to make sure we weren't being followed. Still, no matter where we went in the city, the castle was always in sight, its gray stone face glowing in the multitude of torch lights.

Although the outside was less grand than Castle Phoenix, the royal seat in Buyan was definitely far larger. I was thankful I'd studied it in such detail and knew the exact location of Pari's quarters.

"Hey, beauties! Ditch the ghost and come with us!" A leader of a gang of young drunk fae, mostly elves judging by their pointed ears, called out to Himari and me. His eyebrows wagged suggestively as he made raunchy motions with his hips.

It took all I had not to blind him right there. But

exhibiting my power, which was rare in Faerie, would make us stick out too much. Instead, I opened my mouth to respond with who-knew-what, when suddenly, the gang leader was struck by a violent fit of coughing. I watched as his face darkened from pink to red to purple. His friends gathered around, grabbing his shoulders and shaking him to make sure he was okay.

"Quick, let's move. I have to let go soon." Himari pushed me in the back, and we kept walking.

"Bloody hell," I whispered as I realized what was happening. "I didn't know you could pull air from people's lungs!"

"I've been practicing in secret—with Ronan." I arched an eyebrow, and Himari bit her lip before adding, "It's messed up, I know, but he kinda likes it as long as I don't do it too hard."

"You little freak!" I couldn't hold back my chuckle.

"Oh, stop your judgy-judgment!" Himari shot back. "You're not the only one who's competitive around here—especially where similar powers are concerned. I had to have one up on Crystal. I bet she could pull air from people if she tried, but no one has given her the opportunity."

"I'm not complaining, or judging," I said, turning down another street.

I was actually amazed at what I'd just learned. Siphoning air from people's lungs was only an option among the strongest weavers in the Old Land. That Himari could perform such a feat spoke volumes of her progress. I felt even more thankful that we'd stopped so she could gather her strength.

The castle came into view again, as the side street led straight for its northern border. I guessed we were only a few minutes away. Then all we had to do was scale a three-meter wall unnoticed, and we were in.

Piece of cake.

Time for an illusion, I thought, glancing around to make sure no one was watching, before I gathered light and secured my team in a bubble of altered reality.

"We're invisible. I'm going to keep the mirage up until we get over the wall, since it's manned. Dak, you should transform. Himari and I will jump on your back and hop over the wall. Then you jump over. It's tall, so if you need a little help, Himari will give you a boost of air. Sound good?"

Two pairs of eyes widened, clearly astonished that I'd come up with such a thorough plan on the fly—or so they thought.

"Yeah . . . sounds perfect," Dak said finally, his tone impressed.

"Then let's move." I took off toward the castle.

Dak landed inside Castle Dalir's grounds, hardly making a sound as his massive paws touched down on lush grass. I motioned for Himari and Dak to follow, and they fell in line wordlessly.

Outside, in the wide open spaces, my illusion was a major advantage. We had entered the castle grounds on the northern side. I recalled from my hours of studying the firlon, there was a servant's entrance at the far east end of the castle. That was where we'd sneak in, safe beneath the protection of my illusion.

I gulped. Although I'd largely pushed it from my mind by keeping busy, the idea of assassinating a person still wasn't sitting totally well with me. The only other experience I had in this department was when I killed my sadistic brother, the murderer Nigel. Even after the fact, it had taken days to convince myself what I'd done was out of self-defense, and that I wasn't a murderer too.

Secretly, I hoped Dak would carry out the act in his lion aspect. One swift swipe of his paw could easily be fatal. And surely, being in lion form would help him put distance between his conscience and the act of eliminating a life?

Skirting the edge of the castle, I shook my head, desperate to clear the sudden unease from my mind. If anyone deserved to be executed for the good of others, it was Queen Pari, the fae who'd stolen my father's legacy and forced his people into half-lives and poverty by stealing their magic.

My hands clenched, and the illusion flickered in response to the surge of anger. Adrenaline rushed through me, and I put on speed as we surged around a sharp corner of the castle.

Wham!

I slammed into something hard.

"What the Sinkers?" a man growled.

I gasped and jumped back, unsure what to do as I took in the castle guard before me. My fingers itched to conjure my infrared sword, but at this point overt violence would be unwise. We hadn't even entered the castle yet. What if someone stumbled across this soldier with a gruesome injury and sounded the alarm too early? Above, Naela keened a warning. She was preparing to dive-bomb the soldier should he make a move against me.

The guard drew his sword, prompting fear. My illusion flickered, and the guard's eyes widened.

"Intruders . . . " The word left his lips in a soft hiss, as if someone was threading it out of him, and then, perplexingly, the guard dropped his sword.

What the hell?

His hands flew to his throat, rubbing the flesh there as his eyes widened. It was only when his face turned violet that I understood.

Himari was pulling the air from him. And although the thought was morbid and horrific, I couldn't help but watch as the fae's eyelids lowered, and he finally collapsed.

"Is he gone?" I asked, sheathing his sword back in his scabbard and yanking his body flush against the castle wall, so it would be hidden from anyone walking the grounds.

"Yeah," she responded a few seconds later. Her voice was thick, and belatedly, I realized that this was probably the first time Himari had actually taken a life.

To my knowledge, only Nigel and I had killed during the Successional—not that I'd asked around much.

I placed a hand on her shoulder. "It was self-defense."

Himari nodded and wiped her eyes.

As much as I'd have liked to give her a second more to recuperate, I couldn't. So instead, I gripped her hand and led her toward the door. We had to get inside.

While Himari had bought us some time, someone was bound to find the soldier.

And when they did, they'd sound the alarm.

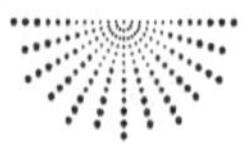

CHAPTER TWENTY-SEVEN

The castle door swung open, still radiating heat from where my infrared sword had torched the lock. We crept in, and Naela landed on my shoulder. I repositioned my illusion, securing us in a bubble of safety. After the fiasco on the grounds, we desperately needed to get our bearings.

"Looks like we're in the kitchens," I said, taking in the stoves and pots and pans lining the ceiling.

It was exactly where I'd hoped we would enter, which meant I hadn't chosen the wrong door. From my night of studying the castle in the firlon, I knew we needed to head straight down the hallway leading out of the vast kitchens until we hit a massive staircase. From there, we'd ascend three flights and find ourselves outside Queen Pari's bedchambers.

"Thank God," Himari said, grabbing a half-eaten hunk of bread off a table littered with scraps, and shoving it in her mouth. A fruit I couldn't identify followed, along with an unpeeled carrot.

Naela followed my sister's lead and flew over to a bucket with bones poking out of the top. She pecked at the carcass, stripping the leftover meat.

Let her eat for a bit, I thought, recognizing that Himari was probably still feeling depleted. We needed her at full strength to succeed.

Turning on my heel, I took in the kitchen more thoroughly. I'd never been in the kitchens of Castle Phoenix, but I knew they were on the lower levels. I imagined them to be similar to the one I stood inside.

The equipment and serving ware I had seen come in and out of the kitchens were pretty universal across Faerie and the Old Land. I often wondered if the many commonalities between the two planes were due to the fact that fae still crossed over, occasionally bringing in new technologies, or if Faerie had simply evolved alongside humans.

A glint of gold, obvious against the dominant tones of purple and gray that decorated the kitchen, caught my eye. I tilted my head. My feet moved, taking me into a dark corner, far from my siblings. As I crept closer and comprehended what I was seeing, my lips flattened.

It was a shrine the likes of which I'd only seen in *National Geographic* photos of Tibet. A table laden with candles set in gold votives, and a sea of white flowers spread out before me. Occasionally a purple bloom dotted the white, adding color to the altar. My hand trembled as I picked up a particularly pretty flower, purple with a strange, curly blue stamen protruding from the center. It reminded me vaguely of a lily, but with peony-like petals.

My gaze drifted up to the focus of the shrine. A photo of the queen I despised hung on the wall framed in gold.

Pari stared back at me, white teeth gleaming. Her dark brown eyes crinkled at the corners when she smiled. The queen wore her gold nose ring in the photo, its dainty chain linking from her nostril to her earlobe. Pari had the most impeccably shaped eyebrows and full lips I'd ever seen.

Even though I hated her, I couldn't deny that she was gorgeous and regal.

My eyebrows furrowed as I moved on, taking in what she wore. Was this a bridal photo? Or maybe she always wore intricate white garb? I thought back to the day when I'd seen the Queen of Buyan in the firlon. She'd been wearing white then, too. Perhaps it was what royalty wore in Faerie? Father did, although Casimir didn't . . .

I shook my head and moved on.

Next to the central photo of the queen were smaller frames, filled with pictures of her and those who I presumed were her subjects. Old men and women, babies, teenagers . . . fae from all walks of life smiled back at me, their hands clasped with Pari's, some pulled tight in her embrace.

Would they love her if they knew what she'd done to Lyonesse? *Did* they know what she'd done? My fingers tightened around the soft petals in my hand. I couldn't bring myself to believe that was true. There was no way that every single person in a kingdom could be so corrupt and cruel.

I dropped the strange flower back onto the altar and turned to find Himari and Dak, now in human aspect, watching me. The pile of fruit rinds and cores on the table indicated that Himari ate at least six different types of fruit in the short time that I'd been occupied with the shrine. Naela was cleaning her feathers. A few bones lay next to her talons, stripped clean of meat. Dak, always the thoughtful one, watched me with questioning eyes.

I didn't have any answers for them, so I swept my hand toward the door. "If you're done, we should be on our way."

The hallways were very dark, lit only with sconces bearing torches at occasional intervals.

Dak led the way in lion aspect. His large, padded paws made no sound on the stone floor. His white nose twitched and his ears, perked high, listened for guards.

I held no illusion before us. If we came across a soldier, I wanted to be able to use all my power to fight. Plus, illusions were always trickier in the dark.

Where there was a shortage of light, they required a more subtle touch. I could do it in the case of an emergency, but I also knew when to ration my energy. That time was now.

The long corridor was a straight shot through the center of the castle. Distance was difficult to judge in the firlon, but I hoped we would soon come across the staircase that led up to Queen Pari's private rooms. With any luck, only then would we meet more guards.

So far, the castle seemed empty. I was inclined to believe that what the merchant had claimed about the castle guards being sent to the bonegate was true.

With each step, my muscles loosened and my breath eased. Could this be as simple as sneaking into the queen's room and slitting her throat? Would we be able to walk out of here without a single unplanned incident?

No sooner had I dared to wonder than an avian screech, followed by a blood-curdling scream, shot down the hallway.

I froze. On my shoulder, Naela ruffled her feathers. I knew that scream.

Dak stilled in front of me, his snow white mane standing on end. Himari grabbed my arm.

"Was that . . . ?"

I nodded. "Victoria."

We sprang into action. Naela launched off my shoulder and took up position above us. We dashed down the hall, and Dak flew up the staircase, his powerful haunches propelling him up three steps at a time. Himari and I sprinted after him side-by-side. My heart pounded with each step.

The moment we reached the next floor, we were assaulted by five soldiers wearing imperial purple. Dak spun off first, his claws slashing into a fae before he charged another. Himari followed, and great gales of air whipped up particles of dirt and pushed another opponent back.

My head twisted wildly in search of Victoria, but there was nothing. No flash of white wolf fur, no fire or flying metal that told me that any of my other siblings were here. They were probably fighting another group of guards, somewhere close by.

My worries ground to a halt as an elf nearly as fair as Prince Casimir leapt at me, his sword drawn. A heartbeat later, my infrared sword blazed in my hand and met him halfway, slicing through the air.

Violet eyes widened, and he leapt back, curses spilling from his lips.

"Illuminator witch! Call for backup!"

My blood froze. Backup? And how did he know I was a witch, and not a light elf like Casimir?

Unease rolled through me as I lunged forward again, my sword positioned to slice him in the gut.

Again the elf leapt back with the grace of a cat, and I ended up hitting his upper thigh. Purple pants sizzled and split. Crimson blood sprayed across my face with such force that I knew I had hit his femoral artery. The elf fell to the floor with a grunt of pain, dropping his sword and clutching his leg.

I pointed my sword at his face. "How did you know I'm a witch?"

The fae's eyes narrowed, and his lips pressed firmly together.

"If you don't tell me in two seconds, I'll slice your throat open," I growled.

Fear surged through my veins. Had they been *looking* for an illuminator witch? Had someone tipped them off? Someone in Lyonesse? Or Zatus?

An image of Gory rose in my mind. Gory would certainly give us up for the right price.

The fae merely shook his head, his gem-like eyes glinting up at me defiantly.

"Tell me!" I hissed.

He spat in my face.

Fury flashed through me, and reflexively, the deadly light of my sword shot forth until it was a hairsbreadth from the soft skin on his neck.

"Tell me or I'll do it," I threatened even as my arm began to tremble.

The fae barked out a laugh. "Can't even do this, eh? What makes you think you're any match for Her Majesty? My queen is *powerful* and *bold*. She shall crush every intruder in this castle."

Emotions warred within me. This would be my first kill that was not in self-defense. While I'd come prepared to do away with Queen Pari, I'd hoped not to take more lives. I didn't want to become a *murderer* —only a liberator.

Despite his precarious predicament, the fae sneered. "Just as I thought. You don't have it in you."

A gust of wind from another fight nearly blew me over. It knocked my sword to the side, and the fae shoved himself up, ready to fight once again.

But he didn't see the blur of gray soaring toward him as Naela swooped down from where she'd been circling. Her talons extended, she ripped open the fae's neck. The soldier collapsed to the floor, and the taunting violet of his eyes dimmed.

My hand flew to my mouth and a strange whine choked out of me, like a dog caught beneath a fence. Vomit surged up my throat, and blood pounded in my ears. My breath came in a thin stream as my vision tunneled to the line across the fae's neck from which blood poured.

CHAPTER TWENTY-EIGHT

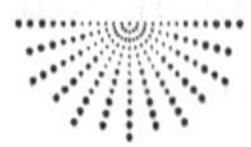

Realizing quickly that this was the worst possible moment to lose my composure, I pulled myself together and took in my surroundings. The hallway was long and straight on both sides. Had anyone living remained on this floor, I'd have seen them, but that wasn't the case.

My body tightened. Where had Dak and Himari gone?

Another scream sliced through the air, chilling my blood. It came from above. Without hesitation, I charged up the stairs to the next floor, hoping to find Dak and Himari still alive and kicking butt.

When I reached the top of the landing, I saw I had been right about their whereabouts. But to my horror, they were losing. Himari was fighting off two soldiers simultaneously, and Dak had been captured. A net of fire magic enclosed him, burning through his perfect white fur and digging into the underlying pale flesh.

"Naela! Help Himari!" I screamed, and my hawk soared toward my sister while I raced in the opposite direction.

The three guards who were manipulating the net around Dak didn't even see me coming. My sword blazed in my hand as I sliced the backs of their knees. Two fell to the ground, and the cage of magic disappeared. Dak let out a monstrous roar before leaping forward and swiping at one of the downed guards with his claws. The only guard still standing turned to hobble away, but the light of my sword extended without thought or directive. I gasped as it ran him through.

My throat closed up. I clenched my infrared sword tighter, my emotions warring as I tried to convince myself that I was still under control.

What had just happened? How had my magic acted without my bidding? Or had I wanted it to happen and not realized? But he'd been retreating . . .

My heart dropped as the uncomfortable truth rained down around me.

It didn't matter. I couldn't claim that I'd acted in self-defense this time. I'd killed him, and there was no going back. I was now officially a murderer.

Dread spiraled through me, threatening to pull me

under. My breath grew tight, and my limbs began to shake.

"Lana! Help me! Lana!"

Himari's terrified voice yanked me up, away from the mess of hysterics in which I'd nearly drowned. I turned to find my sister inside a wind tunnel of her own making, fighting off three soldiers. Naela was nowhere in sight. Instinctively, I searched for her. It took only a second to find her lying lifeless along the side of the hallway.

More than anything, I wanted to go to my familiar, to see if she was alive or not, but Himari's danger was more imminent. I just needed to figure out how best to help.

One of the Buyan soldiers seemed to be weaving a rope of water through Himari's wind tunnel. At first, I couldn't see why, but when the ends of his water-rope met, it clicked. At any second, he'd tighten the rope, and use it as a lasso to capture my sister.

Not if I can help it, I thought. Still not having a plan, but needing to do *something*, I dashed forward.

The fae saw me coming, but instead of fighting, like I expected, he dropped the rope. "Illuminator witch!" he yelped as he ran the other way.

I stopped in my tracks, dumbfounded. How did they know what I was?

Thankfully, Dak was less inclined to lose his head. He took the opening, disabling the other two soldiers one after the other with swipes of his paws.

Himari released her gales the moment the second guard fell.

"Lana! I'm so sorry! Naela—!"

Naela . . . My stomach twisted, and I rushed to my hawk.

As soon as I reached her, I breathed a sigh of relief. She wasn't dead, or even bleeding. Just unconscious. A fae had probably hurled her across the hall with air, and she'd hit her head.

I stroked Naela's feathers, hoping she'd wake up, but there was no response. Carefully, I cradled her, wondering what to do. Himari and Dak approached.

"Is she okay?" Himari asked tentatively.

I nodded. "Just unconscious."

My sister exhaled loudly. "Thank goodness. I'd feel so terrible if she died after you sent her to help me. One of those fae shot her into the wall like a torpedo. I was trying to get to her, but then the third fae arrived, and I panicked." She trembled violently as she spoke.

I shook my head and slowly set Naela down before pulling Himari in for a hug, hoping to calm her down quickly.

"It's okay. We're all still here," I said, rubbing her back the way Mam used to rub mine when I freaked out. "But we should act fast. They sounded the alarm. After I hide Naela from sight, we need to get to the third floor as fast as possible. Pari's room is up there. If we can just—"

Himari suddenly stopped quivering and pulled away from me. "How do you know that? It wasn't on the map. Nothing inside the castle was." Her eyes narrowed.

I bit my lip, conflicted. I hadn't wanted my siblings to know what I'd done and think me selfish—or glory-seeking. Even if it was the truth.

But as I met Himari's hardened gaze, I knew I didn't have a choice. She'd nearly died. I couldn't lie to her. Plus, standing around was dangerous. We had to move.

"Father let me use his firlon to examine this castle. I memorized how to get to Pari's chambers."

Himari shook her head. "Only you? Wouldn't it have been smarter if someone else . . . actually, *all* of us, knew what the castle looked like inside?"

More screaming met our ears, coming from the floor above. There was no way I could deny that Himari spoke the truth, but this was not the time.

"Can we talk about this later? I'm going to hide Naela with an illusion. Then we should get upstairs, do what we came to do, and make sure everyone else is safe."

Her lips pressed together, but she didn't argue.

Quickly, I set Naela on the windowsill. A perfect spot, where she wouldn't be trampled. When she came to, she'd be able to fly to safety. I wasn't worried about her ability to seek me out. Naela had always found me in the past.

Once my familiar was safely hidden behind a display of light, my team made our way back to the stairs. We met no more obstructions as we climbed, although the sound of screaming, metal clashing, and winds whipping somewhere in the castle told me our ease of movement may not last long. But we were almost there, to the third floor.

We will make it, I told myself, and pushed harder. A half dozen strides later, I flew out of the stairwell—Dak close on my heels, and Himari directly behind him—and my heart stopped.

I wasn't sure where the stallkeep had gotten his information, but he was clearly misinformed. A line of at least fifty guards stood before me, filling a massive, open foyer meant to funnel into the queen's quarters. Their weapons were drawn, and various magics were brimming their hands.

My arms flung out, keeping Dak and Himari safely behind me. There was no way we could complete our mission at these odds.

I twisted my neck. "There's too many," I whispered, my eyes darting from Dak to Himari. "Run. That's a command."

Himari did as she was told, turning on her heel and bolting down the stairs without a glance back. I turned my attention back to the soldiers. Dak growled, low and menacing.

"Move, Dak!" I backed up to assure him that I was coming too—that he wasn't leaving me.

Catching my gesture, Dak turned tail and vanished down the dark stairwell. I was just pivoting on my heel to follow when someone spoke.

"That's her, Your Majesty. The illuminator witch." The fae who had conjured the water lasso to capture Himari stared through me with turquoise blue eyes.

I quirked my head. Goddammit, I had to ask.

"How do you know what I am?"

A faint tinkle of laughter arose behind the wall of armed soldiers. A laugh belonging to a person who was not at all threatened by what was happening in the castle.

"I told them," the smooth female voice rang out, strong and powerful. "I felt you. Your presence was undeniable, so different from your father's—yet similar. I knew you would come, and when you did, we would need to talk."

Queen Pari stepped forward, dressed in a nightgown of white silk edged with gold.

My breath stilled in my chest as I took in the queen, exposed.

This was it. My only chance. For the fae of Lyonesse and my father, to avenge Kate and Kumar, I had to try. Even if it meant my death.

I lifted my hands, and many of the guards shifted, preparing to fight.

"I surrender," I said, trying to sound as if I meant the words, all the while calling particles of light to me.

Queen Pari made a gesture for her soldiers to

drop their weapons. They did so one by one, two striking female soldiers nearest her being the last to drop their swords.

"I'll tell you what you want to know," I supplicated, buying time.

The queen nodded and stepped forward again. "I'd like that." She was nearly halfway to me now, breaking through her imposing line of defense. "I must say, I'm stunned that you—"

White light, more than I'd ever controlled at once, flashed from my hands, and every single Buyan soldier flung their arms over their faces and dropped to their knees in pain. The queen alone remained standing, but even she shielded her eyes, the gesture leaving her defenseless.

This was it, my moment to make a difference.

I brandished my sword and sprinted toward the queen.

CHAPTER TWENTY-NINE

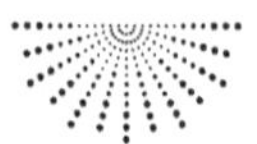

Adrenaline tore through my veins as I closed the distance between me and the queen. Knowing these could easily be my last seconds, I pulled out all the stops, calling an illusion around my body. Fear ensured that it was a relatively shoddy one, riddled with holes that left me flashing in and out of sight, but the overall effect was good enough.

Curses flew up from the guards as they uncovered their eyes and searched for the disappeared illuminator witch. Three seemed to latch onto my flickering form and positioned themselves before their queen.

And then Queen Pari did the unexpected. She stepped forward and pushed her soldiers *behind* her.

I stumbled and released my illusion completely. Had I seen that right?

As if in answer, the queen glided closer, her dark eyes penetrating as she opened her arms wide.

Was she asking for mercy? If so, she was asking the wrong witch. I wanted nothing more than to end this mission, to free my father's people from tyranny. The thought of survival didn't occur to me—not anymore.

I nearly laughed out loud at the irony of it all. I'd never known what I wanted to be until I came to Faerie, but seconds before I was surely set to die, it seemed so obvious.

I was born to help the fae of Lyonesse.

The soldiers' eyes were wide for their queen, though no one defied her order to stay back. Surely, once I cut her down, they'd be on me in a second. We'd die together, Queen Pari and me, in a heap of royal blood.

Time seemed to slow. I felt every breath, every blink, until finally, I was a mere meter from the queen. Pari blinked, baleful as a doe as she tilted her head, taking me in.

Disregarding her calm, I struck, sending my infrared sword forward in a powerful thrust.

A clap rang through the foyer as Pari's hands met inches from my sword tip, and flames surged forth from them. No, not flames—an *inferno*. Hot air hurtled around me, followed by a force that threw me high into the air and backward at breakneck speed.

A scream ripped up my throat. Tears pricked in my eyes as failure crashed down on me. I'd had one shot, and I'd blown it. The moment my head hit the stone floor, I'd be dead, or at the very least knocked out. But death would undoubtedly come.

I closed my eyes, waiting for the end—for blackness.

Instead, a blast of wind rose up from the ground to meet my body, buffering me from hitting hard stone. The wind whistled as loud as a woman's scream as it groped and wove around me and finally positioned me so that I was upright. I gasped as my feet hit the ground so hard that my knees buckled.

A hand, strong and sure, reached out to steady me. Not expecting the contact, I sucked in a breath and opened my eyes.

Crystal stood at my side, her mouth set in hard lines, her eyes drilling through Queen Pari.

"Impressive." The queen's melodic voice echoed through the expansive antechamber to her rooms. "I can see that you're one of his, too. How many more are there?"

I opened my mouth, but no words came out. Only gasping breath from trembling lips. But it didn't matter. Crystal was here now, and she had enough words for the both of us.

"Many more, and we've come to avenge our father, the King of Lyonesse."

Without warning, she hurled a dagger at the queen.

A guard with long, blonde hair leapt in front of Queen Pari, her shield extended. Crystal's dagger hit the shield and rang against it like a mallet to a gong.

Unperturbed, Queen Pari motioned for the guard to step back, exposing herself once again.

"As I said before, impressive. I can see why Oberon would want you both. I wonder, though . . . why have I sensed only the illuminator witch if there are many?"

Sensed? I stiffened as a memory came rushing back. Me staring into the firlon. The queen looking up at me, and me falling to the ground and scurrying away. My stomach sank.

"What do you mean you sensed Lana?" Crystal demanded, her head cocked.

"Just days ago, someone was watching me. I know the feeling of Oberon's firlon well by now. He's observed me for years, and after all, I was the one to help him learn how to use it. It must grow tiresome really, lying in wait for a moment of weakness that will never come." She smoothed her black hair thoughtfully.

"That's impossible," I whispered. "My maid told me those being watched could never know."

"Your maid is ill informed," Pari waved her hand. "All one needs to do is cast a drop of their blood into the firlon and they will be linked. It's dark magic and not many people approve of that, but considering our war, I do not much care what others approve of. I always know when Oberon watches me, but this time was different. The gaze, the *intent* of the watcher, was not Oberon's—whoever it belonged to wasn't even full fae. It took me a while to sort out what I'd felt, having only interacted with one illuminator before."

Crystal's eyes slid to me. "You were watching her in Father's firlon? What does that mean?"

My mouth opened and shut and opened and shut, like a fish gulping for water.

Shite.

The supportive pressure of Crystal's hand left my shoulder, leaving me to stand on my own.

"Did he let you use it to spy on her?" Crystal gestured to Queen Pari. "And you didn't tell us because . . . ?" Her eyes narrowed suspiciously.

"I got to use it the night before the ball. But I thought you and Finn wouldn't want to—"

Crystal cut me off. "You thought we'd rather do what? Play cards? Read? Traipse around the castle, rather than . . . "

Red creeped up her neck now, and her fists clenched tightly.

"I m-m-made you maps," I stuttered. "I didn't think—"

"Stop lying," Crystal snapped. "I know *exactly* what you thought! You thought you'd be the hero. Do you know what happened down there?" She thrust her finger in the direction of the stairs. "Victoria was knocked out, and Gio is slashed wide open. If they die, their blood is on your hands."

"Victoria? Gio?" The names squeaked out of me, and my limbs began to tremble. "No . . . that can't be true. You're just saying that—"

"*I'm* lying?" Crystal roared, flinging her arms out wide.

The next thing I knew, hurricane-force winds hurled me toward the wall of imperial purple.

Queen Pari's voice rang out, demanding yet barely audible over the wind that encapsulated me. "Seize them!"

I collided with metal, and someone grunted as my body weight threw us both to the hard ground, where my skull hit stone, and my world went black.

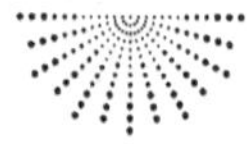

CHAPTER THIRTY

The blackness receded slowly as I blinked my eyes open. The neon spots that swam in my vision dimmed. And yet darkness prevailed. I shifted to find that I was lying on a pad filled with feathers. One much too thin to keep out the cold stone below it. The sound of rain out a window met my ears.

Rain? Was I in Ireland? Maybe I'd passed out in the shed behind my Mam's house? Had Faerie all been a dream? Where was Naela?

"Finally, you're awake. Get up. We need to talk."

The cold voice shot through me, shattering the daydream that would make everything right. Make everything I'd seen and all the shitty things I'd done the past few months disappear like a bad dream.

Shifting my hands beneath me, I pushed myself up. Unsurprisingly, my head spun and pounded as though someone was hitting my skull with a hammer.

A groan slipped through my lips, and I pressed my hand to my head. It was wet.

I yanked my hand back to stare at it. Even in the dim light, I could identify the substance that covered my trembling hand.

Blood.

"What happened . . . ?" I trailed off and took my first look around.

I was in a cage—not a cage, a dungeon of sorts. Crystal sat with her knees pressed against her chest in a cage across from me, her narrowed eyes boring through me.

"Where are we?" I asked instead. This time, I dared to meet Crystal's gaze.

"Queen Pari's dungeon. They caught us—well, caught *me*, you were knocked out. They threw us down here yesterday. You've been out ever since."

I raised my hand to call my magic.

"They warded the place. We can't use our powers here."

My hand dropped to my lap. "What about the others?"

Crystal shook her head. "I haven't seen them. But I heard a guard talking when he thought I was asleep. He mentioned search parties roaming the jungle, so I'm assuming they all got away."

A sigh flew from me. Tears spilled onto my cheeks. "Thank the Sinkers."

Even while relief flooded me, nagging guilt was

there too. My eyes dropped to the ground. "How can you stand to talk to me—even look at me, after what I did?"

Crystal snorted. "It's not easy. But if I ignored you, how would I demand an explanation?"

I shifted so that my back was against stone and arched my neck, so my head rested on the wall. It was wet and cold, but it felt better than trying to support the weight of my throbbing head. I closed my eyes once more, willing the pain away.

"You already know why I did it. You said it yourself."

"Oh, I know. I just want to hear *you* say it. I need confirmation, so I can be justifiably pissed off at you for the rest of my life."

My eyes opened and locked on Crystal. Why couldn't it be Himari or Victoria here with me?

I bit my lip, already regretting the thought. How could I wish that on them for my own comfort? My weaver and vila sister were strong, but not as strong as Crystal. No one was. I should be *glad* it was her here with me. She, at least, had a chance of surviving whatever Queen Pari would throw at us.

"Like you said, I wanted to be the hero . . . to remain our father's favorite." The image of the imperial guard I'd killed flashed before my eyes. My stomach clenched. "As it turns out, I can take things *way* too bloody far."

Crystal snorted, and she began rubbing her hands

against her legs and arms in an effort to warm them up. It was then that I noticed the bandage near her exposed ankle.

"What happened?" I pointed to her leg.

She unfurled herself so that the blood soaking the wrap was more apparent. "One of the fae lassoed me from behind when I was trying to get away. I fell on a freaking dagger someone had dropped." She shook her head and resumed rubbing her extremities.

It dawned on me that after spending months together, this was the most that Crystal and I had ever spoken to each other in one sitting. It took putting us in a dungeon together to get us talking. How pathetic.

"I'm sorry," I whispered. "You wouldn't be in here if it wasn't for me. I should have aborted the mission way earlier. I should have let you join me at the firlon. But of course, I wanted to have the glory. Shite . . . I never thought I'd say that."

Crystal frowned and then released a sigh that sounded as if she'd been holding all the air in the world in her lungs. "No. I would probably still be here. You weren't the only one who wanted to be the hero and impress our father. I'll admit, I was jealous that you got to talk to him every day. That you got to learn about him and discover what little bits of your-self came from him. I was more jealous than I'd *ever* been, which is saying a hell of a lot. Worst of all, I was willing to take extreme action during the Succes-sional to get his attention."

My mouth fell open at her thorough admission.

Crystal shrugged at my reaction. "If that surprises you, then you'd be shocked to hear some of the other things I've done. You don't become an Olympian at fourteen and get accepted into one of the best medical schools in the world at barely twenty-one without doing some stuff you wish you hadn't. Or at least, I didn't."

My eyes narrowed. I didn't fully trust her. "Yeah, right. Like what? Studied your face off for four years? Worked out every day since you were three? That's basically all you do now. It's not really all that hard to believe."

She squirmed. "There was a lot of that, yes. And one instance of slipping my fiercest competitor a food I knew disagreed with her on the day of Olympic trials. She still competed *and* almost beat me. But I think my sabotage tipped the scales."

My lips parted in disbelief. Well, that was unexpected.

"Yeah, pretty shitty, huh? Well, it gets better. I slept with a professor on track for tenure at my college. He probably never would have done it, but I'd learned a thing or two from my mom. She's a piece of work, I tell you. I suspect she's still secretly mad that our father loved her and left her. I think she takes it out on every man she meets by manipulating them."

"Oh, wow." I didn't know what to say. Mam was the opposite of that.

"Anyhow, I was earning a B in his class, and knew it wasn't enough to get me into my top medical school. So I came on strong. He would have lost his job if anyone found out about us, so I blackmailed him into giving me an 'A'."

She shook her head. "There were other misdeeds along the way, but those were the worst. It seems I can be overzealous too. So really, I understand why you didn't tell us about the firlon."

My spine straightened, and Crystal waved her finger in the air. "Don't get me wrong. I still think what you did sucks. That knowledge could have helped Finn and me guide our teams and get through the castle, but . . . well, it's not a huge stretch for me to see myself doing the same thing." She fell silent.

Weren't we a fine pair? How did I not see how similar we were before?

"Well," I started when the silence became too much to bear. "All I can say is I hope the rest of our siblings got back safely. The fae at the bonegate too. Maybe they even took it?"

A phantom sensation of Garret's hand brushing my back came over me. I shivered.

"Maybe . . . we won't know for sure until someone comes to save us or kill us." Crystal shrugged again. "To be honest, I don't see any other options."

Neither did I.

A DAY AND A NIGHT LATER, JUDGING BY THE MEALS that had been provided, and the light coming in from the window at the far end of the room, the prison door opened with a creak. Soft steps echoed off the walls, filling the void.

I sat up straight. These weren't guard boots.

Crystal's brown eyes shot across the hallway to latch onto mine. She arched an eyebrow, and I shook my head in response. I didn't know who it was, although I had a suspicion.

One that was confirmed when Queen Pari appeared before us.

Her dark hair, flatter than before, gleamed in the early morning sunlight streaming in through the slit of a window, and her eyes had evidence of bags beneath them that had not been there days prior. The queen had been busy since I'd seen her last.

"Good morning, ladies. I trust that I find you well cared for?"

There was no denying it. We'd been fed every meal, escorted to a decent toilet down the hall, been checked up on by the castle healers, and even offered reading material, which we'd both taken gladly to stave off the boredom.

We nodded, but kept our lips shut.

"Good. Now," Pari motioned for a guard, who brought in a chair and placed it directly between our cells. She sat down gracefully and looked from Crystal to me. "I have some idea of who you two may be from the pins on your armor, but since you're here, there's no need to jump to conclusions. Why don't you tell me about yourselves?"

Crystal pressed her lips together tightly. I mimicked her. Though Pari's demeanor was nonthreatening, there was no way I was cooperating with my father's enemy.

Queen Pari arched an eyebrow. "No? All right then, let me tell you what I already know."

Her dark, probing eyes turned to Crystal. "We tested your blood when we brought you down here. Your fae blood is strong, not quite full, but still strong. Your mother had dwarf mixed in with her human blood. I'd bet my kingdom that you're the intelligent dwarf my sources warned me about."

Sources? But she couldn't have known about Crystal from my time spying in the firlon. Or could she? Sinkers, did the firlon allow her to read my mind too?!

Crystal did not respond, though the widening of her eyes likely told Pari more than my sister wanted.

The queen turned to appraise me next. "And you are unmistakable. You're an illuminator witch. I never thought I'd meet one again, but here you are, and clearly of Oberon's line." Her dark eyes drilled into me, as if she was trying to see the depths of my soul. "You have his eyes . . . his power, too. The hawk we've spotted circling the castle must be yours?"

Naela! My heart dropped to my knees.

"Don't you dare hurt her!" I lurched forward and grabbed the bars.

"That majestic creature? I wouldn't dare. She's safe, though I will admit she does not think so. She's . . . rather distressed."

I gulped at the thought of Naela soaring through the skies outside, screaming out her anger at not being able to find me.

"Though of course I would expect nothing less from a Fullfeather familiar. Your father must be proud you inherited the family propensity for winged creatures. I've heard his heir did not. Is it true?"

Queen Pari's tone was conversational, but I knew better to divulge anything. From the look on her face, Crystal did too.

My lips pressed together. I was unwilling to share any information—now or ever. Countless lives depended on my silence. And while I may never leave this cell, I'd die before I failed the fae of Lyonesse again.

CHAPTER THIRTY-ONE

The dungeon door groaned open the next morning. Heavy footsteps yanked me from my never-ending loop of worry, and I glanced up to find a guard standing before my cell, keys in hand.

"Her Majesty requests your presence, *Witch.*" He spat out the word as though it was a dirty one.

"Why?"

The fae sneered, though it did little to mask his attractiveness. Like in Lyonesse, all the castle guards seemed to be too attractive for their own good.

An image of Garret filtered through my mind, but I pushed it away. Thinking of him right now only served to upset or confuse me. I needed to be clear-headed.

"That is an excellent question. One, you may ask her yourself, as I do not question My Queen, no matter how much I disagree with her choices on how to keep captives. Likely, she did not want to venture down here again and smell your filth."

He opened the cell door and gestured for me to exit.

"Fine." I stood, brushed the crust of dirt and blood off myself, and strode out the door of my cell.

The guard shut the gate with force, then turned and walked toward the door leading into the more livable areas of the castle.

I froze.

"What about her?" I gestured to Crystal, still behind bars.

"My Queen requests the company of the Princess General of Lyonesse."

"Go ahead, Lana. See what she wants," Crystal urged.

But there was no way I was leaving her alone. Crystal may not be my favorite person, but we'd made progress in our days down here. I wasn't letting her out of my sight.

"If the queen wishes to speak to me, my sister must join."

A loud sigh rang from the doorway, and heavy footsteps came closer once more.

"My Queen is always right," the soldier said, rolling his eyes as he unlocked Crystal's cell.

We followed the disgruntled guard to a part of the palace that I hadn't seen in real life, but vaguely remembered studying in the firlon. It was far from

Pari's bedchambers and the throne room, but the dozens of soldiers lining the walls told me that wherever we were being led must still be important.

I kept my mouth shut as we walked, taking in everything around me. If we ever managed to break out of our cells, I would need to have my bearings straight.

After some time, our escort stopped before a door, fitted a key in the lock, pushed the door open, and gestured that we enter.

I blinked in confusion, taking in what appeared to be a bedroom. There were massive windows that let in crazy amounts of light, a large bed, thick furs, and plush chairs before an unlit fireplace.

Was this the queen's rooms? It didn't seem nearly grand enough, but then again, what did I know about the queen, other than that she was evil to the core? The location seemed off too, though. I didn't recognize this part of the castle.

"This is your new chamber." He herded us inside. "The dwarf's room will be next door. There is a door adjoining the rooms, usually used by handmaidens, but you may use it to speak to one another. Like the dungeon, these rooms are warded against your magic. Guards will be posted in the hallway at all times, and the windows are warded, as well. You may open them, but unless you wish to perish slowly, I recommend not attempting to escape. Queen Pari requests you bathe, change, and seek her audience in the throne room. Any guard will show you the way. Questions?"

Crystal and I glanced at each other. It was clear that neither of us had any clue what was happening, so we simply shook our heads.

"Good," the guard said, and slammed the door to my new cell closed on his way out.

EPILOGUE

FINN

Moonlight glinted off golden feathers.

I held my breath as Arlo soared over the vast meadow surrounding Buyan, heading toward the jungle where we were hidden.

It was a reflex to extend my arm for birds of prey to perch, but Arlo, of course, didn't need my help. He landed on the ground and shifted right away, his bird body transforming into a man who looked nothing like an eagle, except for his beaky nose.

"They have Lana and Crystal," he said, confirming my worst fear and opening the floodgates for my anxiety to rush through.

I gulped and tried to quell my shaking hands. "Did we succeed?" I asked, not really caring, when Lana was in the hands of an evil queen, but needing the information so I could decide how to proceed.

Arlo's lips pressed together, and he shook his head.

Bloody fecking hell.

My eyes shot to the city walls. From where I stood on a small hill ensconced in a thick jungle, I could see three dozen men patrolling the gate and the meadow that surrounded the city. There was no way we'd be getting back inside Buyan tonight—especially without Lana's light magic to hide us. And once Queen Pari realized what Lana and Crystal were, *who* they were, she'd likely have her wardmaker tweak the protections to detect fae with human blood.

We'd lost the advantage of surprise.

"We have to go back to save them." Himari, who was pressing a bit of ripped shirt against her temple to staunch the blood, wobbled where she stood.

I scanned the rest of the group. Only myself and Arlo, who had been in eagle aspect the entire time, seemed unscathed. Gio's leg, in particular, looked scary bad. If only Ryker were here, I'd have had the pair of them ride together so that the fae captain could hold Gio up, but he was waiting for us some-where deeper in the jungle, behind the wards.

"No," I said.

Wikolia placed her hands on her hips. Quickly, I explained myself.

"Some of us can barely stand. We'd surely be captured—or worse. We have to return to Lyonesse and tell Father what happened. Two of his daughters are in there. He'll come up with a plan to save them. It will be loads better than what we could devise on the fly."

"But what if Pari kills them before we return?" Victoria, the last person who I expected to want to enter Buyan again, stepped forward. "Maybe just a couple of us go? I could, probably . . ." She trailed off and blinked rapidly, the effect of the vicious whack on the head she'd sustained most likely making her lose her train of thought.

"No. You can't. I can't. We can't even go together right now. How would we get past all those guards without Lana making us invisible?" I lifted myself onto my horse. "We need to get far, far away from here. When they don't find us inside the city wall, they'll expand their search. We should head out."

No one moved. Ten seconds passed, then a minute. Sounds from the soldiers near the wall grew louder as more of Buyan's finest joined the search.

A growl emanated from Dak, his protective lion-shifter nature kicking in. Fear trickled through me. What if they didn't listen? What if I was forced to go back right now? What if I had to use my power again to get them all out? Could I even do it? I wasn't even sure what the dark magic that had flowed from me was.

Visions of eerie black ribbons twisting and turning as they strangled the life from the Buyan guards filled my mind. I didn't know how I'd done it, but I knew one thing—my demon gift had reared its ugly head tonight.

I shuddered at the memory of the shadow babies that had gone forth and done my bidding. It had been terrifying to behold, and I wasn't sure I could control them again. Plus, even though my new power had helped us all escape, none of my siblings had actually seen it in action. I was keen on keeping it that way.

Finally, thankfully, Wikolia nodded and saddled her horse. It was as if her acceptance broke the idea of revolt. One by one, my other siblings hauled themselves up on their animals—Gio with the help of Dak and Arlo.

When everyone was stable in their saddles, I nodded. "We'll go slowly. Leave no one behind."

I made eye contact with each and every one of them before continuing. I wanted to make sure they knew I was serious. "I promise we'll come back with help. There's no way in hell I'm leaving Lana or Crystal here for good. We *will* get them back, no matter what."

Every head nodded, the same determination that I felt burning through me, glinted in their eyes. With that, we moved, our horses trudging slowly through the jungle, and my vow repeating through my head with each step.

<u>Spellcasters Spy Academy Series (Magic of Arcana Universe)</u>

A Legacy Witch: Year One

A Rebel Witch: Year Two

A Crucible Witch: Year Three

An Academy Witch: Prequel

The Complete Spellcasters Spy Academy Boxset

<u>The Wonderland Court Series (Magic of Arcana Universe)</u>

Alice the Dagger

Alice the Torch

<u>Standalone Novel</u>

Stealing Maid Marian's Heart (Magic of Arcana Universe)

<u>Fanged Fae Series - A Bonegates sister series</u>

Blood Moon Magic

Faerie Blood

<u>The Bonegates Series - A Fanged Fae sister series</u>

Hawk Witch

Assassin Witch

Traitor Witch

Illuminator Witch

<u>**The Royal Quest Series**</u>

Dragon Prince

Dragon Magic

Dragon Mate

Dragon Betrayal

Dragon Crown

Dragon War

<u>**The Starseed Universe - An Irish Witch Urban Fantasy**</u>

Prophecy of Three

Souls of Three

Rising of Three

The Starseed Universe (five-book boxset)

ABOUT THE AUTHOR

Ashley lives in Portland with her husband, Kurt, their dog, Flicka, and the house ghost that sometimes makes appearances in her charming, old home.

When she's not writing urban fantasy and portal fantasy novels she enjoys traveling the world, reading, kicking butt at board games (she recommends Splendor and Dominion), and frequenting taquerias.

For all the latest releases and updates, subscribe to Ashley's newsletter, The Coven, today!

As a Coven member you will receive a weekly update from Ashley and exclusive teasers, information about giveaways, and sneak peeks into her author life. You can also find her Facebook group, Ashley's Reader Coven and join in on the fun there!

facebook.com/Ashley%20McLeo%20Author

instagram.com/a.mcleo

bookbub.com/profile/ashley-mcleo

ACKNOWLEDGMENTS

As always, thank you to my husband, Kurt. You are my rock, my love. The person who is always there to pick me up when I'm down and make me smile when I stubbornly do not want to (it's a Taurus thing). Without your support none of this would be possible.

A great deal of thanks goes to my author pal and writing partner Kelly N. Jane. I'm so glad we met and have grown as writers together.

To my cover designer extraordinaire and friend, Kim Cunningham. I remember getting the cover for *Assassin Witch* from you and simply dying from happiness. I still love it just as much as the first day I laid eyes on it.

To my editor Jennifer Roop, thank you so much for all your help and willingness to go with the flow. I appreciate it always.

To my proofreader Jen McDonnell, your eyes are

so keen! I'm really happy to be beginning this partnership with you.

To my devoted reader group and ARC team, you guys rock so hard. I love getting my books to you first and hearing everything you have to say!

And to everyone who has ever bought one of my books, left a review, asked their library to stock my books, followed and friended me or simply given me a word of encouragement as I set out on this path of blended artistry and entrepreneurship, thank you SO much for being there. I appreciate you more than you could ever know.

All the magic,
Ashley McLeo